I0596225

Cover Art by
Stefan Prodanovic

First Edition

Printed in the United States of America

Published by XYMYTH
New Jersey, USA

Library of Congress Cataloging-in-Publication Data
[2025909975]

ISBN [979-8-9988952-0-3]

CONTENTS

CHAPTER ONE — 1

CHAPTER TWO — 13

CHAPTER THREE — 23

CHAPTER FOUR — 33

CHAPTER FIVE — 41

CHAPTER SIX — 51

CHAPTER SEVEN — 61

CHAPTER EIGHT — 73

CHAPTER NINE — 83

CHAPTER TEN — 93

CHAPTER ELEVEN — 107

CHAPTER TWELVE — 117

CHAPTER THIRTEEN — 129

CHAPTER FOURTEEN — 139

CHAPTER FIFTEEN — 149

CHAPTER SIXTEEN — 159

CHAPTER SEVENTEEN — 171

CHAPTER EIGHTEEN — 181

CHAPTER NINETEEN — 191

CHAPTER TWENTY — 201

CHAPTER TWENTY-ONE — 211

CHAPTER TWENTY-TWO — 223

CHAPTER TWENTY-THREE — 235

CHAPTER TWENTY-FOUR — 245

JACOB R. COLON

MANHATTAN 24

CHAPTER ONE:

12:00 AM: MANHATTAN: NEW YORK CITY:

October gales threatening a premature winter swept over the Hudson. Towers like glittering black spires scraped the low-forming clouds. The streets were still alive, people and cars filling the air with a strangely comforting raucous. Even on the Lower East Side, where a short brick building four windows wide and squeezed between a block of apartments stood, unsuccessfully hoping to embrace the quiet for one night.

John's yellowing apartment was small but not cramped. It was minimalist. A still-new nylon couch in the center, across from it a wooden table where a TV might stand but instead housed several rows of books with dull titles and colorless bindings so that his mantel looked like a chessboard. The fireplace was decorative, dust gathered around the mesh curtain suggesting it had never been touched. A few shelves lined the walls, holding some more books and picture frames. One was of John, a rare smile sparkling in the flash. He stood, arm around the shoulders of his brother, Henry. The Spears brothers shared many features— ivory skin, dark brown hair and eyes, a strong, shaven chin, squared face and thin nose, eyes not far spread— though it was all but obvious that John was the eldest. John was tall, broad-shouldered and muscular, even through his long sleeve thermal. He wore his hair short around the sides, but a thin, choppy patch of it lay on top, sticking up over his forehead. Henry, on the other hand, had his hair combed over and wet-looking, much longer on the sides and more efforted. He was shorter. Not by much, but skinny enough to be considered half John's size. Henry's eyes were less baggy and rather filled with a youthful joy. It did not seem he was forcing his smile as much as John had been. Another photograph atop the shelf was of John and an army squad, each of the ten soldiers covered in camouflage and drenched in sweat under a desert sun that flared the image.

John sat at the edge of the bed in his room, now with a short scruff on his face, hair thick on the sides and back of his head. He was fully clothed in a black thermal shirt and blue jeans, as though he either just got out of bed, or never intended on resting. The sounds of passersby were feint but enough to deny him a substantial sleep. He stared at his phone, swiping between a set of pictures of him and a beautiful woman with a warm tan complexion. Stephanie was the center of every photo, her smile like a set of glistening diamonds, her long, almond hair like curling, cascading waterfalls. They were the only pictures where John's smile hadn't seemed forced, but welcome.

Buzz... buzz.... The reminiscing was cut short by Henry's caller ID greying out the screen. John lifted the phone to his ear. "Hey, Henry," he said, his voice authoritative and unwavering.

"You're not gonna believe this, John." Henry rarely minced words with a greeting. It was straight to business. "Jeanne Leroux, her right-hand man, Alec was spotted *here*. In New York."

John got to his feet not wasting a moment. "You sure it's him?"

"Facial recognition caught him crossing a red light ten minutes ago. Someone's been a little careless."

CHAPTER ONE

"That's not like them. Must be in a rush somewhere," said John, wrapping a black digital watch around his wrist and pulling open his bedside drawer. "You following him?" John pulled out a cold black pistol, forty caliber, from the drawer, and stuffed it in the holster at his hip.

"Way ahead of you," Henry replied resolutely. "That's why I waited to inform you. I knew you'd probably want to come all the way here to headquarters, but he was spotted closer to you."

"Smart. Don't want him to slip away," complimented John. He stepped into the apartment, grabbing a set of car keys next to a red hex-shaped bowl of fruit atop his granite counter. "Where is he now?"

"Cameras got him parking in Tribeca. Trying to narrow down the exact building he entered. In the meantime, I sent you the location."

John made for his front door. "Thanks, Henry," he said, unhooking a black chore jacket next to the door and departing.

The National Intelligence Bureau headquarters was situated in the Upper East Side, down the street from the Guggenheim Museum and across from Central Park. The main communications hub was a large atrium with rings of cool blue lights overhead. The rings were reflected below where circles of desks descended several levels into the ground like an amphitheater. At the center there was an unoccupied glass table that projected a hologram of Manhattan. Outside the pit were even more desks and walkways, where analysts and agents went about their business. Henry was sat at one of these desks. He could not turn his head without a glowing set of images filling his view and straining his eyes. The walls were flanked with screens, not including the monitors his desk. Henry rubbed his eyes as they were feeling hot, not because he was tired, but because of the time he spent not blinking. He had a cup of cool, spilled coffee creating a ring at the edge of his black wooden desk to keep him awake, but like John, he was used to being up at this hour. NIB was a nocturnal business.

Henry got out of his seat and stretched. Whilst tucking back in his undersized white button-down into his beige khakis, he glanced up at a glass office on the silver-grated catwalk, agents passing and up and down the stairs next to it. Henry made for the steps, letting a few analysts down first with a polite head nod. After ascending he tapped twice on the glass door reading ASSISTANT DIRECTOR JAMES MICHAELS: HEAD OF COUNTER ACT DIVISION.

"Come in," ordered a thick, welcoming voice. Henry entered the office, flipping his backwards red tie. Michaels was a surly man, though an aspect of him seemed tender enough (perhaps his voice, which was low and grumbly and warming). The assistant director had a lack of hair, his dark cheeks pockmarked and blanketed with experiences. "Spears. What is it I can help you with?"

"Just wanted to check in with you before I moved forward—"

"How considerate, given your last unsanctioned forays with Bison," Michaels scrutinized with a slight grin.

"John hates that alias." Yet Henry looked like he was about to laugh. "Anyway, Sir, I've found Alec. With your permission, I'll send John and a back-up unit to his location to arrest him. And I'll need help reverse tracking where he came from."

"I'll grant approval for the reverse satellite tracking. But spare the back-up unit."

"Sir?" Henry beckoned.

"We don't need to be making a lot of noise right now, Spears." Michaels unbuttoned his navy blue suit and sat in his chair, a grand leather seat too large for him to even scoot his legs under his glass desk. "Instruct Bison. Reconnaissance only. If he could help it, that is."

Henry took this to be a backhanded critique of John's methods, though everyone at NIB had always known John for his caution. It was Henry who tended to jump the gun and start impulsively an operation without higher-up approval (quite like now, not having mentioned anything about sending John before informing Michaels). Perhaps the assistant director was projecting his disapproval of Henry onto his brother, lest he somehow knew what he had done. Michaels did not look up but lifted his chin as to send Henry back out the door.

Henry reached the pit where it was loud with ringing phones and clacking keyboards. In the second ring down was a woman in her late twenties, clad in pink, with auburn hair, sunken, freckled cheeks, and a pair of oversized square glasses that heavily magnified her eyes. Henry approached, playfully knocked on the dividing wall of her cubicle, and said, "Hey, Jen."

"H-Hi, Henry," she muttered with a slightly nervous wince.

"Are you working on anything important?"

Jen looked as if she was going to say "Yes," but realized Henry was not her boss. "Not really. Just looking over this report sent down from CSD." (Cyber Security Division).

Henry walked from in front of the desk to her side, getting closer and keeping a low voice. "I was wondering if you could help John and I with a small operation."

"Let me guess, reverse satellite tracking?"

Henry grinned. "How did you—"

"Because I'm the quickest and best at that satellite analysis, remember?" Jen ticked the middle of her glasses to press against her nose, looking up at Henry with a smile.

"I think I recall mentioning that," Henry remarked, tapping Jen on the shoulder. "I'll send you the info?"

"Sure." Jen bit her lip and cranked her head to watch Henry mosey back to his desk.

12:33 AM: TRIBECA: MANHATTAN:

John drove his black government-issue SUV over narrow, cobblestone streets rife with traffic. One hand ungripped the leather wheel to answer the buzzing on his dash. "Henry, I'm pulling up now."

"Look for the haberdashery in the center of the street. That's where I got Alec entering. There's a textile mill around back but I haven't been able to get a good look at its entrance. He might not be alone," explained Henry.

"Copy that." John put the car in park. He clicked back the slide of his pistol, inspected the bullet entering the chamber, then placed it back in his holster.

"And John... I checked in with Michaels."

"Good. Maybe he'll get off our backs this time," said John, opening his car door to step out.

"He said recon only. 'If you can help it.'"

"'If I can help it?'" John mimicked.

"I know. Just humor him this time, will ya? Don't need him breathing down my neck the rest of the week," Henry implored.

"Alright."

"Oh, wait! This might be a good time to test out the glasses!" Henry seemed very excited at the premise, John less so.

John reached into the armrest storage box and pulled out a sleek black case. He flipped open the case to reveal basic black sunglasses. "Fashionable," he derided.

"Now, they're only prototypes sent in by R&D. But they'll help get a read on how many are inside."

CHAPTER ONE

"How do these work again?" John left the car, looking both ways on the stone road before crossing and placing the glasses over his eyes. His head darted around, the golden streetlight barely shining through the dark tint.

"TXPS. It stands for *Thermal X-Ray Projection Specs,*" said Henry. "Courtesy of our friends in Washington. Each lens has a glowing light. They can work independently or paired with one another. Green is night vision. Red is thermal imaging, to detect hot and cold signatures, and blue is X-ray, designed to detect injuries in the field." John clicked one of the various buttons on the either side and dim green, red, and blue lights appeared. "When you hold the corresponding button, the specs project that vision in your line of sight. For stealth, the lenses are tinted to avoid glowing in the front. For recon, I suggest using the night vision at first. But when you get closer, thermal, since it can only capture hot and cold signatures through thin walls or within direct view."

John pressed the green buttons on either side of the glasses and quickly— almost jarringly— his view was no longer pitch-dark. Everything around him, from the metallic scaffolding to the terra cotta façades, was cast in an emerald glow. "Right," he said. "I'm going in. Call you soon."

John pushed open an unlocked glass door. The shop was lined with rolled fabrics and drapes, atop of shelves and pinned to the walls like tapestries. There was a counter in the back and another door beside it, metal and gated. John twisted the doorknob and entered, instantly hearing indistinct chatter. He knelt behind a giant metal box, a bleaching machine where a thin sheet of wool was suspended and rolled onto a spindle. In the textile mill were rows of such machines for dyeing, spinning, and scutching hemp, cotton, and other material. The mill seemed to be operational, though most of the lights were dimmed, the machines running automatically without any employees.

John removed the glasses, knowing with all the metal in the room he would not be able to accurately discern thermal signatures. Instead, he followed the voices, remaining crouched between the machines. His footsteps were small patters; the only sound was of his jacket's bottom button lightly tapping the machines as he slid past. To circumvent that he buttoned up his coat. As he neared the voices, they became clearer. They were speaking French, a man and a woman. John peered around a carding machine where clean fibers were being split by wires like a comb through silky hair. He spotted Alec, the freakishly tall, pale-skinned right hand to... John's eyes widened. It was *her*, the head of the ACT terror group. Jeanne Leroux stood beside him just as pale, but instead of Alec's short, spiky black hair, hers was a long and flowing silver. She had a beauty to her, with thin green eyes, high cheekbones, and rosy lips, but her appearance was contorted by a devilish frown streaking down her brow line.

"Are things set at the port?" she asked. John was certain he heard the French word for "port" correctly, though the murmurs were quiet and discreet.

"Oui, Madame," Alec responded, bowing his head formally.

"Hopefully our friends *feel accommodated."* John recognized a derisive emphasis on "friends." There were four other men behind them, carrying heavy wooden crates outside through a garage door with a squeaking chain, illuminated by the scarlet light of the backside of a truck. What were they transporting? John doubted it was textiles.

Suddenly John felt a cool metal barrel press against the back of his head. *"Slowly,"* he heard behind him in a thick French accent. John slowly rose, hands by his temples. He snappily spun, hand first, shoving the enemy's pistol away from his head. Fist wound back, he hammered it into the man's nose, following with a jab to his throat with the other hand, then an elbow with the right. Each attack flowed into the next, the right arm wrapping around the terrorist's neck as he was driven back into the carding machine with a loud, echoing *bang*.

Leroux was spooked, gathering two of her men to carry what they had to the car and escaping through the open garage door. Alec whistled for the two remaining men to tread towards the sound.

John had choked out the terrorist, hoping he hadn't made too much noise. When he focused to a lack of voices and slow-moving, approaching footsteps, he realized he had. John glanced under the carding machine and saw legs on either side. It was only a matter of seconds before he was circled, so John made the preemptive advance. From a crouched position he launched his body around the carding machine, kicking one of the terrorist's legs from under him. He quickly turned to face the other two, kicking forward and knocking the first man into Alec. Whilst they stumbled, John stomped and knocked unconscious the first terrorist, then flitted forward to deal with the remainders. He expertly ducked one punch then dodged one from the other side, his reflexes remarkable. Alec landed a hook to John's ribs but it was weak. John clenched the other man around the neck and whipped him around. He kicked Alec away then shoved the other's head into the carding machine, knocking him out. All that was left was one, Leroux's right-hand man, squirming on the ground and trying to get air back in his lungs.

John knelt forward and dragged Alec to his feet by the collar. "Where did she go?"

"Like I would ever tell you, Spears!"

John headbutted Alec so that his nose was now unable to draw air, gushing with blood. "You thought we wouldn't find you? Huh? I can't go to your country without trouble. You think you can come into mine?" He took no pleasure in beating on the almost sickly-looking man. Despite Alec towering over John in height, he lacked intimidation over him. To anyone else, he might have looked intimidating. "What were you two talking about? Where did Leroux escape to?"

"You think she would tell me? The plan was to meet again later to-day—"

"Meet where?" John growled.

"That won't help you now. She will have changed the plan now that you clumsily made your presence known!" Alec started to laugh, blood trickling into his mouth.

John brought the point of his elbow to Alec's chin, knocking him out cold, then let his body drop to the floor. As he approached the garage door and the place where a few crates had been left behind, his first thought was to apprise Henry.

"John? What did you find?"

"You're not gonna like it," replied John, poking into an emptied crate. "I was found out. Handled it quietly but she got away."

"Who?"

"Jeanne Leroux."

There was a silence on the other end. John could tell that was Henry coughing up his cold coffee. *"Leroux?* She's in New York?"

"She left a couple of weapons crates behind. The rest she escaped with, an excess amount. She's moving to arm someone. Any luck reverse tracking Alec's car?"

"Yes, actually. He came from a seaplane base in Chelsea."

"I overheard them talking about a port. Sounded like they were expecting others to show up," John explained.

"Only thing is, it's hard to say whether they arrived by ship or plane."

"What do you mean?" John prodded.

"The camera feeds at the port don't actually show Alec or any other ACT terrorists arriving. It looks like they've been hacked into and made to loop on themselves. I called and there was no response."

CHAPTER ONE

"Alright, I've got Alec and a few others knocked out here. Get a team over here to scoop them up and send me that location." Henry had already done it. John left through the garage door onto the street and turned, fast stepping towards his car. "Inform the Coast Guard. Call Air Traffic Control. Find out how they got in. I'm on my way."

12:57 AM: SEAPLANE BASE: MANHATTAN:

John parked in a driveway behind an unmanned boom gate, where security should have been waiting in an empty booth. He got out and walked around the white and orange bar. The base was like a long parking lot with boats on either side, the strip leading down to where a couple of seaplanes had been docked. John crept up to a small, dark hangar where he heard chatter. Just outside the bay doors were two security guards, lying in pools of their own blood. John pressed his back to the cold, ribbed hangar wall, peeking around to get a glimpse.

Inside there were heavily armed men, speaking a language John did not recognize this time. They wore all black, picked assault rifles out of crates similar to those in the textile mill. They were standing between rusted planes and mounds of gears and parts like a hobbled-together scrapyard. John looked down at his feet. There were drops of blood trailing into the hangar. When he followed the trail closer, crouched behind large engines and scrap heaps, he saw another security guard, knelt between two terrorists. They were about to kill him. John leapt up out of cover, aiming his pistol. *"Get away from him!"* he called, perhaps foolishly.

He had drawn their attention away from the guard, but immediately seven or more rifles were aimed his way. They unloaded with a barrage, bullets panging against the metal cover. John sprinted out and deeper into the hangar, letting fly a couple of shots the terrorists' way but not hitting anyone.

Recalibrating behind a column of tires wrapped around steel beam, John inspected his magazine. He pulled out his phone and started dialing.

"J—? What— on? A— se— gun—ots?" The phone was breaking up. There must have been something jamming his signal.

"Henry!" yelled John, a seemingly unlimited hail of gunfire pelleting behind him. "Listen to me! There's six or seven men here at the port! Heavily armed! Two security guards are down, we need an ambulance and tac team ASAP!"

"Can't— ear— be— ful— ohn!"

Though John could hardly understand him, he knew there was worry in his brother's voice. He only hoped Henry got the message. John hung up the phone and put it in his side pocket. The gunfire stopped again. The pillar of tires was exploded, leaving a thin beam as cover. John jetted out from behind the beam towards a glass corner office, shooting over his shoulder and taking one of the terrorists down as he did so. Now there were six. *Who are these guys?* John wondered. *They can't be the ACT.* John smashed through the office door being chased by sparks and flying metal. He released his emptied pistol clip and clicked in a new one.

The office was tiny, but as he hoped, there was an exit in the back. John pressed against the bullet-ridden wall, held his gun by his chest and took in a sharp, determined breath.

CHAPTER TWO:

John fled the hangar through the backway. He remained crouched, back sliding against the cold metal fence that surrounded the base, pistol aimed at the doorway. When two of the six terrorists popped in, he let loose a burst of shots, killing one and leaving the rest bottlenecked to catch the body. John seized the moment to cross the base, risking himself in the open running between the boats and plane parts on either side.

The enemies fanned out on the other side of the base slowly, with close to the same care as John of being spotted, splitting between the rows of cars and boats. He heedfully continued down the left side of the base, away from the approaching armed unit. He knew if he crossed again, the risk would be greater than before, but his eyes fell upon the terrified security guard, tied by the feet and hands and knelt in the hangar.

John recognized what his shoulder blades rested against as a large, deflated tire with a rusty wheel inside. He holstered his pistol, bent in a deadlift position, and, legs tightening, hoisted the tire up on its side. He rubbed his aching lower back, his heart pounding. John peered around the tire, aiming his pistol at a light post nearby. He heard footsteps and chatter closing in. A few sharp breaths and he was ready. John shot at the light— missed— shot again and the golden bulb exploded. The terrorists' weapons shifted instantly towards the water, where John had pushed the tire and was running alongside it. Bullets began pelting the tire and the ground next to John's feet, sparks flying like fireworks inside the peeling wheel.

When he made it to the hangar, the heavy rubber fell flatly to the side, shredded to ribbons. John made a full sprint towards the center of the hangar, bullets chasing him. He slid to where the guard had been placed on his knees, zip ties around his wrists and ankles. John reached in his pocket and flipped out a small tactical blade, then with ease cut through the bindings. "Thank you! Thank you, Sir!" cried the guard. "They were gonna kill me!"

"Don't thank me yet," John insisted, pushing the man's shoulders down so that they kept low.

"Who are they?" The guard was drenched in sweat and shaking fast enough to shed his thick stomach in no time. He wiped his forehead with the back of his wrist and brushed away the few hairs on his head with his fingers.

"I have no idea." John checked his magazine again; only four bullets. He patted the back of his jeans to double check there were two more clips. *Five tangos,* he thought. *Just can't get cornered.* John pointed at the obliterated back entrance and said, "They'll be waiting for us over there. As of right now we've got no exit. The next one I take down, you'll have to take their gun and help be out. You okay with that?"

"Not like I have a choice," the guard grumbled.

John nodded, aimed his arm towards the left of the hangar so that the guard could head in that direction while he watched their six. His surroundings were replete with waves of stirring smoke, the scent of gunpowder and hot steel like pennies being shoved up his nostrils.

John had the guard kneel behind a cart holding gears and parts, whilst he climbed into the middle section of a plane's fuselage. It was suspended high enough to get a view of the entire hangar, where he mapped out the five terrorists like black ants weaving through a maze of metal scrap. As two came nearer, John inched towards the edge, the large round opening of the fuselage, aiming his pistol. He took a shot, killing a third enemy. The one beside him backed behind something to shield from John's other bullets, returning with a spray of machine gun fire.

Behind John, another terrorist had surrounded, climbing into the plane's body. The security guard grabbed the terrorist's leg and yanked. The black-clad enemy landed on top of the guard, pinning him down by the neck with his assault rifle. John leapt from the fuselage and wrapped an arm around he terrorist's neck and wrenched while the guard took hold of the gun.

John spun around, tightening his grip around the throat as the remaining three terrorists advanced around the hollow plane. *"Back up!"* yelled John, holding his pistol behind the man's back. Two of the terrorists held their aims steady; the third had the look of one in command. Their captain wore no coverings on his face, no tactical pocket vest, though still in all black. He had a tan complexion with scattered sunspots and curly, wet-looking black hair. He was built slightly smaller than John, but he was taller, and ever more intimidating walking slowly with a machine gun in his hands. "Who do you work for?"

None of the men replied. As they slowly advanced, John stepped backwards, nearing the wall of the hangar. "You're not ACT… so what then?" Still, they remained quiet, the captain of the group smirking wickedly. John pressed his gun harder into the small of the hostage's back, tightening his arm around his neck. "I'll ask one more time. *Who are you?*"

"Men you cannot touch," their leader said in a deep accent. This time it was the terrorist under John's arm that was smirking. John's eyes widened.

He shoved the man away as a storm of bullets dispersed without warning. The terrorist fell by his own allies' hands, the smile remaining on his face.

John and the security guard made for the rear exit again, but John cut back. "What are you doing?" whispered the guard. John did not respond. He reached into his pocket and dialed Henry's phone again. This time, nothing went through but static.

John waited for one of the terrorists to come close, ducking low to watch the pairs of legs inching slowly. When he crossed into John's view, he popped out of cover and grappled, knocking the gun out of the terrorist's hands. John swept the man to the ground, kicking his leg out from under him. He knelt over the terrorist, hoisting him by the collar. "The hacker, where is he?" John muttered through pursed lips. The terrorist did not respond. "Who is overriding the signal here? *Where is he?*"

The terrorist called out to the others in some foreign language at the top of his lungs. John took the back of his pistol and knocked him over the head with it. He vigilantly took out his phone and aimed the camera at the unconscious terrorist's face. "Let's get out of here!" pled the security guard. John snapped a picture of the man, stuffed his phone back in his pocket, and ran towards the exit with the guard.

They made a sprint outside the hangar before gunshots followed them to the entrance of the seaplane base. John whirled around, returning fire, missing his shots but sending the two terrorists into cover. "Get in! Quickly!" He and the guard kept their heads low, bullets piercing the doors and windshield of his SUV as he twisted the key to fire the engine.

"Drive! Drive!" The guard churned in his seat. John flicked the gear into reverse and sped out of the driveway, colliding into a parked bumper. Their necks whipped forward. John pressed the gas and drove away from the gunfire with haste.

Around the corner, not two blocks down, John parked. His head swiveled one eighty. "Keep a lookout," he told the security guard. John reached in his glovebox and pulled out a small laptop. He opened it and logged into the NIB landing, a blue screen with repeated presidential seals as watermarks. He opened a screen filled with white code over a black backdrop. The guard eyed his screen, bewildered.

John was slow to type, but within a few moments, he had found what he was looking for. The screen lit up with a GPS display, with two white circles being joined by a dotted line. John closed the laptop and set the car into gear again.

John raced down a street that was winding down with traffic. His eyes were darting back and forth between the road and his cellphone. Finally, when he received a signal, he was quick to dial Henry.

"John?" his brother answered worriedly. "Are you okay?"

"I'm alright, Henry."

"Thank God. I've been trying to find the source of whatever was jamming your signal over there but—"

"No need. I was able to trace the source on my computer," said John.

"*Really?*" Henry sounded impressed. The guard's face read similarly.

"Learned from the best." John parked across a police precinct, an old, greying, concrete building with a row of squad cars out front. "One second, Henry." He turned towards the guard and said, "You'll be safe here. Tell them what happened."

"How can I thank you, Agent Spears?" the guard replied, his thin few hairs still dripping sweat.

"Don't worry about it." The guard left the car. As soon as the door shut behind him, John was off again. "Henry?"

"Who was that?" his brother asked.

"A security guard. There were two others at the port but they're dead."

"There's a lot to fill me in on," said Henry.

"Indeed. The men who arrived there weren't ACT either," John scratched his head.

"What do you mean?"

"They weren't French, they sounded South American. I might've heard them speaking Portuguese," explained John.

"Maybe the ACT are working through some Brazilian proxy group?" posited Henry. "But then why risk showing their own faces in New York?"

"Can't say," said John. "I took a picture of one of their faces. Maybe run it to see if that leads us anywhere."

"In the meantime?"

"I'm on my way to Mason Tower. That's where the signal jammer has to be." John placed his phone in a holder next to the steering wheel.

"Good luck." Henry hung up. John pressed harder on the pedal, the engine growling.

1:47 AM: MASON TOWER: MANHATTAN:

John halted his car directly in front of the building. A security guard in all black approached, hand raised. "You can't park there, sir." John reached into his jacket pocket and flashed his credentials. "NIB?" said the guard. "Man, that's gotta be fake."

"If only," said John. "I need to speak with the head of security."

The guard led John inside through the gilded revolving doors. The lobby was covered in gold, the concierge counter glistening with strips of white light, fixtures like torches lining the walls, black carpet under their feet. There was a group of guests crowding around the lounge area, where a TV displayed coverage from ALN, the prominent news network. The press had already reached the seaplane port, footage showing police roping the entrance off with yellow tape.

At the gilt art deco elevators stood two more guards with hands cupped together. The head of security who the guard introduced John to had short blond hair and wore a silky black suit. He scowled at John, who was covered in dirt and smelled of burned metal, not the type of guest he was used to seeing. "What do you want?" he asked.

"My name's John Spears. National Intelligence Bureau. I have reason to believe a guest in this tower is using a signal jammer interfere in NIB operations." John pointed at the feed on the television screen.

"What do you need from us?"

"The people this hacker works for are dangerous. Once I find where he's operating, it'll be prudent to quietly evacuate," said John, pulling out his phone.

"There are fifty-eight floors in this building. It'll take hours to search every room," the head of security protested.

"Henry," John spoke into his phone.

"Still working on finding that facial match. Are you at Mason Tower?"

"Yeah. Any chance you narrowed down the signal?"

"No," Henry replied, "but there is a radio interference still coming from the building."

"The hacker must've relayed the signal somewhere else. You try finding out where the jammer's being bounced to, while I start the search."

John was about to hang up when Henry interjected, "You might not have to do that, John. You still have the glasses on you?"

John reached into his jacket and pulled out the TXPS case. "Yeah."

"There's a setting still being tested that can read radio waves. Look on your phone. There's an app I downloaded that can reconfigure the glasses."

"Don't appreciate you downloading apps without my permission," John quipped. He opened an application with a flat black logo.

"Sorry. Once you've paired and found the large signal, the phone will pinpoint the location exactly," clarified Henry.

John put on the glasses. Instead of a thermal or green night vision filling the lens, it was a dim, grainy black and white. Strange ripples filled the air, some emanating from the walkie talkies on the security guards' belts, some from the cellphones in guests' pockets, but when John looked up, there was something far more pronounced. It was like an orb with waves protruding outwards and warping. "I think I found it." John took off the glasses and looked at the phone, mimicking the wave ripples on a blueprint-like display of the building, with numbers ascending each floor. "Fifty-fifth floor. Almost at the top, no surprise. Three rooms west of the elevators."

"Careful, John. Who knows how many you'll find up there." Henry's voice wavered at first but toughened as his faith in his brother fortified.

"It's the only lead we've got." John entered an elevator with the three security behind him and pushed the button numbered fifty-five. He ended the call and placed his phone in his side pocket, along with his prototype glasses.

Above the golden doors was a display that where the numbers of the floors glowed red as they ascended. He unholstered the handgun at his hip. The guards shared a look with one another, then did the same.

The elevator doors swung open. John turned to the left, dim, flowery blue and gold wallpaper on either side. Two hands gripped his pistol, iron sights fixed at shoulder height. They reached the door, three rooms down. John took one side, the head of security the other. One of the security guards made to kick the door down, but thundering *explosion* filled the hall in front of the door with flames, shards of wood sending the guard into the wall. John and the others tumbled, ears ringing.

John stumbled to his feet, swiping away the smoke. Without fear he lurched into the hotel room and opened fire first on a man with an aimed gun, standing beside a waist-high, boxy metal tower: the signal jammer. "Clear!" John called out. He turned. The guards were knelt over the body of their own, fallen, face red with bits of wood sticking out of it, wheezing weakly.

John scanned around the premises. He took out his phone, nearing the body. He did not recognize him, but there was a device beside him that John picked up. It was a very cheap, old cellphone with a sliding keyboard and a sloped plastic screen.

"John? Did you find him?"

"I did. But it was a setup. The hacker is down, and so is one of the security guards. Have an ambulance sent quickly," John elucidated calmly. "The signal jammer was here, too. Looks makeshift. Like he built it in this room. He also had a phone on him. An old one. Obsolete."

"Copy that, Bison," he heard the voice of Assistant Director Michaels on the other line.

"Director?" said John.

"I'm sending a forensic team to sweep the room. You come into headquarters for a debrief," Michaels commanded.

"Yes, sir," sighed John. He stepped out of the exploded doorframe and made for the elevator, avoiding eye contact with the guests who peered into the hallway, shielding their faces from the smoke. After a moment, John called for Henry again, "He still there?"

"He's headed back to his office," replied Henry.

"I assume he knew I was headed to Mason Tower? Was he the only one?" asked John.

"Come on, John. I know you and Michaels don't really get along but, you really think he would've *warned* the hacker?"

"I don't know," said John as the elevator doors opened at the lobby, eyes of guests immediately on him. "But we can't rule it out."

When John got in his car, he set his phone aside and went for the computer in his glove compartment. "Stay on the line. I'm gonna have a peek at this phone before forensics gets their hands on it." John snapped off the plastic back of the phone and pulled out its memory chip. He slipped the drive into a reader and fitted it into the side of his laptop. John typed into the control window, a bunch of files and coded documents sprouting from the center. "Sending this to you, maybe you can make sense out of it. There're encryptions I won't be able to get past."

John typed under the file send section at the top of the screen and sent it to the NIB IP address. "Got it," said Henry. "Let's see... I'm in."

"You're gonna have to teach me that one sometime." John's screen and Henry's were connected. He could see the documents unlocking and duplicating into even more, some of them paragraphs of code, some of them pictures. "What are those images?"

"Oh my God," Henry muttered.

John clicked through a few blueprints filling the screen. "Schematics?"

"John..." Henry whispered, mortified. "These are plans for a nuclear bomb."

CHAPTER THREE:

2:10 AM: NIB HEADQUARTERS: MANHATTAN:

John took a right into a green fluorescent-lit parking garage across from Central Park. At a gate he pulled over to show the posted guards his phone, where a digital badge was scanned and his face appeared on one of their monitors. After that, he slowed his black SUV into a spot labeled "Spears" in thin yellow paint.

John passed pillars and parked cars, making for the guarded, glass sliding doors, where a cool blue light was bouncing off the dull grey garage floor. He waved his digital badge to the scanner and the guard let him pass through the doors.

In front of the garage and main entrances there were extra layers of security. A set of metal detectors and X-ray conveyer belts stood on black carpets like a TSA checkpoint. He pulled his cellphone and holstered pistol from his side and placed them into the basket, strategically sliding the old plastic phone underneath his other belongings so it couldn't be seen at first glance and taken directly to forensics. John stepped through the metal detectors without a sound, his eyes hesitantly meeting those of the guard behind the X-ray monitors. "All clear," he heard the officer say. He waited for the basket to come down the conveyer belt, tapping his finger anxiously. He took his belongings then passed under an archway with a golden seal reading the words, NATIONAL INTELLIGENCE BUREAU. He made for the right half of the atrium nonchalantly, around the pit of desks where Jennifer Nolan was eyeing him.

Henry was waiting, standing by his desk, his top button undone, his white sleeves rolled to his elbows. "John... you sure this is a good idea?"

John saw Assistant Director Michaels traipsing along the catwalk already. "Hurry," ordered John, passing Henry the cellphone he picked up from Mason Tower. Henry brought it onto his desk, pretending he was typing something on his computer. John nodded to greet Michaels as he approached from the grated metal stairs. The corner of his eye looked down to see what was taking Henry so long to switch the memory chip.

"Bison," said Michaels.

John faked a smile. "Told you, you can call me John, Sir."

"How about Agent Spears?" It was Michaels's attempt at a jest. "Come on upstairs, let's get this debrief over with." When he turned his big, suited back, Henry planted the phone with swapped memory in John's hand. "Oh, Bis— Spears." Michaels turned and continued, "That phone you found. Did you hand it in to forensics yet?"

John flashed the phone, saying, "Didn't get the chance yet."

Michaels snapped his fingers and another agent held out his hand for John to hand it over. He did, then Michaels waved for John to follow him. As he did he shared a glance with Henry, whose furtive expression could be read like a book.

When John reached Michaels's office, the assistant director held out a hand for him to take a seat across from his great leather chair. "So. Fill me in."

Where should I begin? John thought. "As you know, I followed Henry's intel on the ACT's right hand, Alec. He was using a textile mill to hide out and take inventory of a stockpile of weapons. Six or more crates. He wasn't the only one."

"Go on."

"Jeanne Leroux was there," said John. Michaels's face suggested Henry had already told him that information and that he was merely connecting his own dots in his head. "She escaped before I could question her."

"And Alec? Did he provide you with any further intel?" Michaels was blotching his dark cheeks with a handkerchief.

"No, Sir. Only that he planned to meet her again sometime later today. Maybe we can get more out of him during the interrogation."

"Interrogation?" said Michaels.

"I left him tied up at the textile mill." John's tone was flustered, impatient. "Nobody went to take him in?"

"Your brother sent a few agents but when they got there, the mill was empty. No crates, no weapons. No terrorists." Michaels explained it in a way that was condescending, as if John was making it all up.

"I knew I should've stayed. But then I probably would've missed the ones at the seaplane base." John stirred, scratching his head.

"And that was the ACT's work too, yes?" Michaels asked. He stood, turned his back to John, and stared down into the atrium below. He twisted a loose, golden wedding band around his finger, its decades-old imprint pinking his skin.

"I don't think so," John recalled. "Their accents were South American, maybe Brazilian."

"Don't you think we'd have intel on a Brazilian extremist group coming into New York, Spears?"

I would. But I'd've also thought we'd know if Jeanne Leroux stepped foot on American soil. John let out a sigh, seeing he was getting nowhere with this conversation. *Only tell him what he needs to know,* he thought. "They were heavily armed. They used some sort of signal jammer to bypass Air Traffic Control and Coast Guard's landing countermeasures. The signal was relayed through multiple satellites. But I tracked the origin to Mason Tower. That's where I found the hacker. I took his phone and brought it straight here."

"What else did you find? When you went to Mason Tower?"

Don't mention the bomb. "Nothing, Sir."

"I know you, Bison." *We're back to that name?* John thought, wishing he would be sent away already. "You're curious. You didn't inspect the phone? If you found something, that'd spare us the time it'll take forensics to sweep it." John shook his head. "I'll fill in the National Security Division. Let them deal with it. In the meantime, you head home. Henry will inform you when he gets a lead on Leroux and Alec's meeting location."

John shot out of his chair against that suggestion. "With respect, Sir, I ought to be in the field helping NSD."

"Our division is designed *only* to combat the ACT. It's not your job to meddle in separate affairs—"

"But they're not separate! Leroux knew they were coming—"

"That's enough, Bison!" Michaels interrupted. "I won't have another word of it."

After a moment of darting back and forth between Michaels's big back and a framed picture of him and his wife— formally dressed at some bureaucratic gala— John said brusquely, "Didn't your wife take a vacation to Brazil, Sir?"

Michaels half-turned, askance. His brows were perched, his nose scrunched. "Was that an insinuation, Bison?"

"No, Sir," John covered his tracks. "Just thought... maybe she'd heard anything about this group, is all."

"You keep my wife out of your thoughts and I'll refrain from reprimanding you." Michaels was more serious than John had ever seen him. "Go home," he ordered. John stood gladly and exited the office.

Michaels paced from file cabinet to vase for a moment, gnawing on his thumbnail. He sat at his desk, reached inside the drawer where an old phone quite like the one John found at Mason Tower lay under a careful spread of stapled papers. He held the send button and the phone turned on. Michaels's big fingers had trouble typing on the tiny plastic keys, but he made out a message:

To: Gabriel
Spears knows about the bomb.

Very quickly after that, the phone rang. GABRIEL. Michaels hit send again and put the phone to his ear. He heard a chilling, heavy breathing, but was the first to speak, "You said that you would be discrete. He knows too much!" There was a panic in Michaels's whispers.

"I don't want you to worry, James," a snakelike voice said in a thick South American accent.

"*'Don't worry?'* He *suspects* me!"

"John Spears will be dead within the hour," the voice hissed.

"And what of Henry Spears?"

"You simply wipe his station after you denounce his false allegations brought on by the grieving of his dear dead brother," the man assured Michaels. *"Should be of ease given your status as assistant director. If anyone inquires, there'll be no proof to corroborate his story."*

"This better work," Michaels remonstrated. He hung up the phone and tossed it into his desk, then then held his face in his hands.

John left the restroom with a washed face. He was still wearing his black thermal, blue jeans, black sneakers. His pistol was clipped into a scratched leather holster on his right hip. He lifted his charcoal chore coat from a rack in the hallway leading to the communications bullpen on his way to Henry's station.

"What's the word?" said Henry.

"When you sent the team to pick up Alec in Tribeca... was it Michaels who signed off on it?"

Henry looked puzzled at the question. "Well, yeah—"

"Alec was gone when they got there. I don't know if Michaels is involved or to what extent but there was something suspicious about our conversation," John observed.

"Think about this a minute, John," said Henry. "Why would he be working with the ACT *and* this Brazilian group?"

"Maybe if they're working together," proposed John, shrugging.

"Well, what's the plan now?" asked Henry.

John shook his head. "Michaels is sending me home to wait it out." Henry scowled, looking up to the office where he could see Michaels's shadow passing over the window blinds. "He wants you to continue tracking Leroux, while NSD handles the other group." John held his head in a defeated manner, turning towards the entrance.

Henry followed him a few steps and turned him by the shoulder. "Hold on," his brother persisted, leading him back to his desk. He got close to his monitor and keyboard, privately sectioned off from prying eyes. The schematics of the bomb appeared. "Take a look at this." He zoomed into the bottom right corner of the diagram, where a strange symbol was placed:

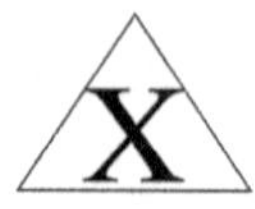

"What is it?" asked John.

"I was hoping *you* would recognize it." Henry sat down, running his fingers through his hair. He took a sip of his cold coffee and winced, immediately putting it down. "I'm running a search on the symbol now."

"Let me know what you find," said John.

Henry turned in his seat. "Are you really going home? Now?"

John glanced quickly at the AD office, feeling sure they were being watched with a close eye, then back to Henry. "No. I'm going back to Mason Tower to investigate that suite. There might be something there I missed."

"But Michaels sent a team there. How are you gonna explain it if you're stopped by them?"

John hadn't thought about it. "I'll figure it out."

"Don't forget this." Henry pulled the memory chip from the card reader attached to his computer and handed it to John. "I downloaded the data onto my station already. Not only were there schematics but contacts. I'm mining for deleted messages now. As for the phone itself... it must be a foreign model. There's nothing like that sold here in the States. I'll do more digging while the facial recognition looks for a match." John looked down at the tiny chip and put it in his jacket pocket. "Good luck," Henry whispered once again in a low voice.

"Yeah," said John under his breath. John went back the way he came, under the curved archway, around the metal detectors, through the sliding doors, and into the parking lot. He reached his scratched and bullet-ridden SUV, got in the car, and took off.

2:48 AM: MASON TOWER: MANHATTAN:

John was surprised to see no security out front of Mason Tower. When he entered for the second time, the gilded, glowing lobby was empty, save for two agents guarding the elevator, alongside the head of security John had spoken to before.

John approached and, flashing his badge and already reaching for the elevator button, said, "I'm gonna need to see the suite again."

One of the agents seized his hand before it could click the button. "What do you think you're doing?" he scrutinized.

"I was here during the explosion. National Intelligence Bureau, like you," scolded John.

The agent brandished the letters FBI on the shoulder of his blue jacket. John squinted, confused, as if doing so might rearrange the letters. "FBI?" *I thought Michaels was sending an NIB forensics unit,* John remembered.

"We have strict orders not to let anyone from NIB onto the scene," the FBI agent declared.

"What do you mean?"

"The crime scene's locked down. No one in no one out." The agent's word was final, his face closed in a manner that wanted to hear no more on the matter.

"On *whose* authority?" said John.

"Take it up with your superiors," the agent barked. "Now get out of here!"

I'm not getting in that room easily, thought John. He peered around the gilded lobby, at an exit sign, and to its left, a room in the back corner with a yellow electrical symbol sticker situated next to the bathroom. "Well, it's a long drive back." John nodded towards the restroom. The agent rolled his eyes and flicked his head to approve. John made for the restroom, turning his head ever so slightly to see through his peripheries if the agents were watching him. When he saw he was alone, he veered left, away from the white and gold restroom tiles and towards the black door across from the emergency exit.

The door led down a small set of stairs, where an entire floor was lined with pipes and levers and switches. At the end of the pump room floor were two adjacent doors, one with another electrical symbol, the other reading MAINTENANCE. John made for the one on the left, but before reaching it, a voice pursued him. "Hey! Who are you?"

Instead of turning slowly to see if there was a pistol aimed at his back, John impetuously spun and tackled the FBI agent to the ground. He slithered around the agent and took his back, wrapping his arm around his neck. The agent wriggled, struggling as his eyes darkened and he slipped into unconsciousness. John had held his breath but let it out, panting. He got up and continued towards the electrical room.

Inside, there were breakers and a bright yellow lever. John opened the breaker box and flipped them all simultaneously. *Darkness.* John reached inside his jacket pocket and took out the prototype TXPS. He fitted the glasses over his ears and pressed the green glowing buttons on the either side for night-vision. Emerald projections overlapped the lenses, the darkness proving not an issue now.

He stepped over the unconscious guard and headed back to the lobby. Before he reached the door, it opened unexpectedly. John leapt over the stair railing and tucked himself under the steps. The FBI agents charged towards the electrical room with flashlights, leaving the lobby unattended.

There was one agent on the ground floor in front of the stairwell, flashlight reflecting off of the gilded steel and glass of the lobby. John stayed close to the wall, away from the agents' lights, crossing in front of the elevators towards the staircase on the other side of the lobby from the restroom. The agent heard his footsteps, turned, shining his light in John's face. "Sir, you aren't allowed—" John cut off his sentence with a punch to the face, knocking the FBI agent out. John dragged him through the open doorway to the base of the stairs. He knelt beside the body, taking off the agent's jacket and fitting it around his own shoulders. John took the handcuffs from his belt and clicked them around the agent's wrists. He removed his TXPS glasses and instead took the agent's flashlight, flicking it back on.

John ascended the staircase. As he reached only the second floor, another agent was stationed and eyed him up and down. "Who are you?" the agent asked.

John stumbled to a response, "I- I was called up to the suite with the other agents."

"We were just called down to guard the lobby..." replied the agent.

John did not have a response to this. "I'm gonna need to see your badge!" Suddenly the lights shot back on, making the agent reel and shield his eyes. John whipped his heavy metal flashlight across the agent's face. As he fell, John caught him, gently placing him on the floor, but he had forgotten the *"we"* of it all—

The second agent stared frozen at his unconscious colleague. He drew his radio. "This is agent Samuel—" John ran up the half flight of stairs, swatted the radio out of the agent's hand with his flashlight and grabbed ahold of him. John shoved his hip into the agent's, tossing him back first down the steps to where the first agent was knocked out. John winced, knowing how much that must've hurt, but relatively unworried about the agent's safety. He was far more worried about the other agents waiting for him above, and the mission at hand.

CHAPTER FOUR:

3:05 AM: MASON TOWER: MANHATTAN:

John swung open the stairwell door on fifty-fifth floor. The hallway was quiet; the floor had been evacuated. Three doors to the left and he reached the obliterated entryway.

He entered quietly. Not an agent in sight, to his perplexion. There was no light in the room. It looked like the bulb in the ceiling fixture was cracked, but John did not remember it being shot in the exchange. There was bright city light coming in from the window wall across from the doorway. The suite was empty, save for caution tape and cases with plastic evidence bags. Did the agents posted there set a trap?

The signal jammer stood in the same spot John found it. It looked like someone had begun deconstructing the tower for transport, as if that were of greater import than removing the sheet-covered corpse that was starting to stink the room.

John knelt beside the body. He removed the sheet, pointing his phone camera and snapping a picture of his face. Next to the body were a set of unmoved belongings: a key ring with a single car key fob, the keycard to the suite, and a wallet. In it was an ID card. The face was the same. He sent pictures of the terrorist's face, along with a code that stretched on the back of the ID to Henry. *Jonathan Garcia. Definitely not French,* thought John.

Knelt beside the body, he saw a stream of red rolling towards him from the bathroom. John got up and slow stepped towards the blood. He turned the corner to see three FBI agents, dead and strewn across the floor and tub like they had been dragged. He backed away from the bodies, dread in his eyes.

Unexpectedly, rapid steps charged towards him and rammed into him from behind, forcing his neck to whip back painfully. John was driven into the bathroom mirror, cracking it, splintering the side of his head and the shoulder of his coat. The man tried to force his head down and through the sink, but John stopped himself, gripping the ceramic with his forearms. John sank his elbow into the man's ribs, then, whilst the assassin staggered, slapped the back of his neck and *pulled.* The man went colliding through the sink, glass shattering, water from exposed pipes shooting out. John went to pick him up by the collar but the man slipped under between his legs then sprang up and kicked forward.

John fell back into the main room of the suite, rolling swiftly to his feet. His arms raised to take the brunt of a roundhouse kick meant for his head. The force drove him into the window, cracking behind his weight. He ducked a punch and dropped to his knee, wrenching the assassin's leg and lifting. John spun, driving the heavy body *through* the window accidentally.

The two fell— John was sure to his death— but they crashed onto a window washer scaffold suspended outside the floor below. The wallet with the ID fell out of John's pocket. He made sure not to look down hundreds of feet through the grate, though vertigo still settled in. John reached for his pistol but the man grabbed his wrists, forcing the barrel away from him. He headbutted John and sent him tumbling backwards and the gun aside, then mounted him.

The wind was roaring loudly that high up; it was impossible for John to hear his own thoughts, especially as the full weight of a man's elbow pressed his esophagus. The scaffold started to creak and teeter, as if it were going to fall. John grabbed the man's collar and shoved him into the window of the suite beside them, the glass cracking and John's ribs getting pummeled by punches. He forced the man's head into the window and the glass cracked the second time, but the wires holding up the scaffold were about to burst. John, eyes about to fade, used the rest of his energy to force the man into the window again, this time the glass shattering. The two rolled into the empty suite just as the scaffold dropped onto its side, only being held up by two rather than four wires.

When they rose, they threw themselves at one another. John grabbed the man's arm, getting punched in the ribs. John spotted a gun behind the assassin's back and seized it, breaking apart from their clinch and pulling the trigger. There were no bullets. The man laughed, rushing forth and launching a haymaker that slid over John's head. John turned and kicked with his heel. The assassin fell backwards out of the shattered window.

John nervously stepped to the edge to look down the side of the tower as heavy gusts threatened to take him with. He winced, touching the side of his slashed head, breathing heavily. Who was that man? What did he want? And did he successfully keep John from finding whatever it was? The questions ran through his head nonstop, leaving little room for formulating a plan to get out of this place.

3:32 AM: MASON TOWER: MANHATTAN:

As John descended fifty floors of staircase, his phone rang. "John? What's going on?" Henry exclaimed. "There's an FBI warrant out for your arrest!"

"Already?" said John, unsurprised. "You're calling off your cell right?"

"What do you mean 'already?'" His brother was not in the mood for his risible phrasing and pretended the second question was rhetorical.

"I had to sneak into the tower, ended up knocking out four agents."

Henry sighed. "John—"

"But that's not all, is it? They must've found the dead agents."

"Who—"

"It was an assassin. Someone was there, in the suite," he explained. "He killed three of the agents before I made my way up there. He was waiting for me. It looked like he or the FBI was taking apart the signal jammer."

"So what did you do?" asked Henry.

"What I had to."

There was another sigh from the other line. "John, you have to turn yourself in to the FBI. We can explain—"

"Can't do that," John said, continuing down the staircase, now dimly lit by red emergency lights. "I can't go with the FBI. *Or* the NIB for that matter. Someone else besides you or me knew I would go back to Mason Tower. *They* sent the assassin after me. Must've slipped into the elevator right after the FBI flipped the power back on, beat me to the room." John's head was on a swivel even though he was the only one making his way down the quiet staircase.

"I don't need to ask who you have in mind. But, theoretically, it could be anybody." John could picture Henry looking over his shoulder, eyeing any analyst or agent that passed by with the look of a traitor.

"Have you got anything on the pictures I sent you?" John switched the subject.

"First the phone. It's not from the U.S., as we suspected. It was made by an English manufacturer, discontinued in 2009. Since then, they've been seen in poorer regions of South American countries like Brazil and Colombia."

"England isn't too far from France," John expanded. "Still can't rule out an ACT connection."

"There's more," Henry replied. "The phone had deleted flight plans from two weeks ago. He was in London and flew to an unknown airfield, probably in Brazil. Whatever's going on, one thing's for sure. You need to find the contact, Garcia."

"Already did. He's on the fifty-fifth floor."

"Yeah, that isn't him," Henry corrected.

"What do you mean it isn't him?" John's brows perched quizzically.

"The face you took a picture of belonged to a man named Joseph Rodrigues. The picture you took at the hangar— that was Raul Silva. Garcia's men must be covering his tracks for him, pretending to be him."

"None of this sounds right, Henry." John ran his fingers through his hair, wincing from the sting of the cut on his head.

"It gets worse," said Henry. "That signal jammer was only one of several. I analyzed the photo you took of it. It's doubling as a portable satellite, meaning—"

"They were using Mason Tower to bounce the signal from somewhere else."

"And who knows how many times?" added Henry.

"Any way you can trace the source?"

"I could, but it might take hours," said Henry. "Wherever they are, they're probably bouncing the signal off several more satellites. It can be a trap like Mason Tower, but this time even worse."

"Doesn't look like we have many other options," John replied regrettably as he neared the bottom of the staircase.

"What are you gonna do now? The building is on lockdown."

"Don't worry about me," said John.

"Worry about you? Wouldn't dream of it." That was the Henry John knew, unafraid of lifting their spirits with levity.

John hung up and stuck his phone in his pocket as he reached the bottom. The unconscious agent was no longer there, so he tread carefully. He peeked through the stairwell door into the main lobby, where the exit awaited him through a crowd of FBI agents.

John lowered his head and sauntered into the lobby, the collar of his cut up FBI jacket high beneath his cheeks. He plodded slowly through the lobby, avoiding glances his way and whispers that followed him. "Hey!" he heard one agent call. John ignored it, halfway through the lobby. "Who is that?" he heard, and "Hey, you! Get back here!"

John decided to make a break for the revolving door. It seemed the entire lobby chased after him, but he had made it through. John took the heavy flashlight from his waistband and wedged it between where the door met the frame. When the agents pushed through to get to the other side, the door was jammed temporarily.

John sprinted against the cold wind, ripping off the FBI jacket and tossing it on the sidewalk. He turned the corner where his SUV was parked and got in with a rush. Before he could take off, however, John felt metal brushing the back of his neck. *Won't be getting used to this feeling.* He was caught. At least, that was his initial thought, but he realized FBI agents would not break into a car and wait for their suspect as if they were about to assassinate him. He looked his rear view mirror. Immediately he remembered the man. *"Men you cannot touch,"* he had said at the seaplane base hangar. "A dozen FBI agents are gonna come storming around that corner any second now," said John.

The man pushed John's neck with the suppressed barrel of his pistol, fitted underneath the seat's headrest. "Drive," he said in a heavy accent.

John did as he bid. He glanced in the mirror again, at the man's sun spotted cheeks, his curly hair. "Garcia is it?" he said. John saw FBI vans lining the street to the right, agents crowding nearby.

"Shut up and look away," the man replied, tapping John on the temple with his pistol to ensure his face was hidden from agent on the sidewalk.

"I'll take that as a yes." John drove slowly down the clear road. "You won't be able to hide. It wasn't that hard to find you the first time," said John, glancing in the rearview mirror at him.

"I won't hiding much longer, Mr. Spears." Garcia had a faux bravado in his voice. Who could blame him for putting on a tough act, clearly being the one in control? "Make this right turn ahead," the terrorist ordered.

John looked in the rear mirror after taking the right, this time to see two black SUVs following them, one on either lane of the now empty road, where John was in the middle. "I was wondering where the rest of your friends were."

Garcia turned around, his eyes widening. "Call them off!" he shrilled. *"Call them off!"*

"They aren't with me," John insisted. At that moment, a volley of gunshots pelted the car like a hailstorm. John accelerated but the cars behind him compensated. The automatic fire zipped through the air, shredding John's SUV. Garcia turned around, shooting out of the broken rear window to no avail.

Suddenly hot liquid splattered the back of John's neck and a shriek ruptured his ears. Garcia was shot, wailing in the backseat of the car and grasping the wound on his shoulder.

"Put pressure on it!" shouted John. Just then a bullet destroyed the rearview mirror, and the side mirrors had already went. John yanked the steering wheel to the right, drifting around a corner, but the car's suspension *dropped* and the back tires *popped!*

The SUV flipped fully upside down. The roof of the car skidded along the middle of an intersection, sparks flying. John clutched his aching ribs, his eyes drooping. He looked out the broken window to see one of the black trucks coming for him and braced for another impact, but there wasn't one.

The SUVs stopped beside his, where John lay unconscious and upside down. From the back of each, four men came out with machine guns, speaking a foreign language. They wrenched open the crushed door and pulled Garcia, bloody and bruised, from the back of John's car. They pulled him by his arms, his knees dragging rigidly over glass shards before they ruthlessly tossed him into the back and climbed in.

Garcia looked up, trying to see through blurred eyes, breathing heavily and wheezing, clutching his gunshot wound.

It was *her*. He heard her velvety, sinister voice say, "Hello, Jonathan." It was the head of the ACT, Jeanne Leroux, with silver hair and deadly piercing eyes.

CHAPTER FIVE:

4:05 AM: MANHATTAN:

Through blurred eyes John saw city lights twinkling like stars in the reflections of tiny glass shards littering the ground. He was shifting between an upside down view of his car's front seats and the blackness of his eyelids. His ears were ringing, not by the remnants of gunfire (though that undoubtedly played a role), but by the din of whirring sirens. Red and blue lights splashed over him. Footsteps and admonishing voices came nearer, glass crunching beneath their boots.

A pair of FBI agents jimmied open the driver side door with a crowbar, then retrieved John a fair bit gentler than the way Garcia had been forced out, legs scraping over broken glass. That was about all John could remember of the incident, no faces nor voices of the terrorists who attacked them. His head pounded just thinking about it.

He was sat on the edge of an ambulance with both wrists cuffed in his lap. FBI and police crowded the street. A paramedic was swabbing blood from the cuts on his temple.

"You should've went home, Spears," a familiar voice of rebuke echoed in his ears. When he looked up he realized it wasn't in his head, but the assistant director of NIB was stood in front of him. "I told you to let the FBI deal with it. I've asked that you be detained at NIB headquarters since you're one of ours."

"You didn't say anything about FBI," said John, cognizant enough to correct Michaels where he purposefully misled.

"Doesn't matter. I gave you a direct order. You disobeyed. Shouldn't count myself surprised, though."

John stared at the ground beneath Michaels's feet, unable to look him in the eye. "You know I didn't kill those agents."

Michaels tiredly rubbed his eyes. "But you still snuck in and assaulted several. Of course, we found the man you did kill. Hardly anything left of him down there."

"Someone gave those agents an order to lock down the scene. Not to let in any NIB agents... to not let *me* in," John recounted. "What was I supposed to do?"

"Am I sounding like a broken record, Bison? I told you not to interfere with the investigation. *I* gave them the order not to let you in. Because I *suspected* you would try to!"

At this, John peered upwards and pierced Michaels's eyes with his own. "You and Henry were the only ones who knew where I'd be going."

"I have half the mind to let the FBI throw you in an unsanctioned black site!" Michaels growled. "Obviously, our enemies, as it were, knew you'd return also. Or else the assassin would have never found you."

"*'Obviously,'*" John mimicked, not buying it for a second.

"Witnesses saw another man being dragged out of your car," said Michaels. "Who was it?"

Like you don't know already, John thought, fixing his lips to speak to a man he presumed a traitor an onerous task. "Jonathan Garcia."

"Who the hell is that?"

"Don't know. But he's with the ones who came in at the seaplane base. The ACT must've kidnapped him." John explained only what he thought necessary to keep him from asking another question, but they kept coming.

"What was he doing in your vehicle?"

John's jaw clenched, which he had not expected to hurt as much as it did. "He was waiting for me. Don't know why. Said he wouldn't have to hide for much longer."

A stroke of luck, it must have been, that Michaels ended the interrogation there. "Take him to NIB," he ordered. John was pulled to his feet, placed in the back of a squad car by a police officer, then taken away.

Michaels scampered surreptitiously to the sidewalk, pulling out a cheap plastic phone and bringing it to his ear. "Yeah," he said in a low voice. "It's Michaels."

"Is he dead?" asked Gabriel.

"No, Spears's in my custody."

"What? Where is Jonathan? I expected to hear back from him by now." The slightest tinge of worry invaded the other line of the phone call.

"Apparently the ACT kidnapped Garcia," Michaels replied.

"The fool! *We expend our resources to cover his tracks and* this *is what we get for it?"*

"You shouldn't have let him go in the first place!" Michaels criticized. "What was he thinking, going after Spears himself?"

"Pride runs deep in our Hierarchy, James." Gabriel's voice seemed to have calmed, but Michaels was still pacing, nibbling his thumb.

"And why is the ACT interfering? What is your connection to Jeanne Leroux? Is she after..." his voice got even quieter, *"the bomb?* There's still things you aren't telling me, Gabriel!"

"Don't fret, James. Very soon, the ACT won't be a problem anymore. I will contact you shortly."

"Wait—" but Gabriel hung up abruptly. James chuntered a few curses then stuffed the phone back in his pocket.

4:13 AM: CONSTRUCTION SITE: MANHATTAN:

Screams of agony could be heard around an otherwise quiet city block, but any view of the goings on within the construction site was blocked by mullioned weather enclosures cordoning the scaffolds from the empty floors like scarlet checkerboards.

A punch like an iron ball buried into Garcia's blood-drenched cheeks. Another crossed his cheek, leaving a large, purple, swelling bruise and a gaping slash on the bridge of his nose. Red was dripping from his slacked jaw, his teeth shattered. Even tears streaming from the corners of his eyes stung as they met with the cuts on his face. His gunshot shoulder felt like a fire poker was being held against it.

There was a scalding work light aimed straight at his face so that he could hardly see the people surrounding him, which there were four. The one beating him was a large man with seemingly unbreakable skin on his knuckles. The one beside him was quite tall so that his pale features and spiked hair appeared more evidently as he towered over the work light.

As a woman approached, her expensive shoes clattering loudly over the unpolished concrete, the light was steered away from Garcia's face. It was like entering a building after spending an entire day in the sun: everything was dark, phosphenes dancing across every sector of his vision. When the woman forcibly lifted Garcia's chin, he was able to make out her face. It was Jeanne Leroux. Her pristine white skin and thin, glossy lips were seared by her evil grin. Without a word, she stepped away towards a table that Garcia hadn't been able to see before. He wriggled in his chair noticing that it was full of blades and tools lined meticulously on a metal tray. Leroux took a set of pliers and handed a pair to Alec, who bore a black eye from his earlier confrontation with John Spears.

Leroux bent close to Garcia and clamped down on his index finger lightly. His arms were zip tied to the chair so tightly that he couldn't move his wrists. Garcia's breathing became rapid, his heart battering against his chest. He shook his head, pleading under his breath, but to no benefit. Leroux clamped tighter and wrenched upwards on his finger. He let out an astonishingly dreadful scream. More pain than imaginable was channeling through his body and he was crying.

"How did that feel?" Leroux taunted after letting go of the shattered finger. "I want you to be ready. Because that will happen to every single finger, toe... and limb you possess. Unless you tell me where I can find Gabriel and his bomb." Her heavy, accented whispering would have been quite pleasant had her speech not been so vicious.

Leroux stared at the piteous shell of a man, awaiting an answer, only for him to spit a large glob of blood at her feet and pants. She sighed, playfully shrugged, then seized Garcia's middle finger. *Snap!* The excruciating cries continued. "Where is Gabriel? Where is your boss?" she repeated.

"I'm not telling you anything!" Garcia yelled back at her.

"This is going to get boring quick," Leroux whispered calmly into Garcia's ear. She leapt from her squatting position, gave a nod to Alec, then slunk back into the darkness again.

Alec took his pliers and clamped them down onto three of Garcia's fingers and wrenched. The pain was quite literally tripled, Garcia wheezing for breath and squeezing his jaw so hard his teeth were cracking. "Okay, I'll tell you! *I'll tell you!*" Garcia finally let out.

Alec smiled, staring at the weak shell beneath him. "Where is he?"

4:22 AM: NIB HEADQUARTERS: MANHATTAN:

Two FBI agents pulled John by his handcuffed wrists out of the back of the police car. The walkway was lined with garden plants and solar panels circling a central fountain. The windows of the dark-tinted headquarters were like the backs of cards dealt perfectly even along a square table; pick one and a room suited for a different purpose than every other awaited. They escorted him through the southern main entrance. With a simple wave of the badge they sidestepped the metal detectors and continued into the bullpen. The cool, blue-lit atrium was swimming with agents and analysts, including Henry, staring at John as he was paraded in restraints for everyone to see.

The agents shoved John into the farthest detaining room on the left, the ninth of nine that lined the hall straight across from atrium's entrance. Henry chased after the agents, holding the door before it shut, "John," he exclaimed upon entering the room. One man in FBI navy stood in the corner of the room, not speaking, not bothering to throw Henry out. For that, John assumed he was a respectable agent. "I'm already appealing a release request to get you out of here. Tell me what happened."

"Garcia was in my car waiting for me. We drove some little ways past Mason Tower when we were attacked by machine gunners. They took him." John was sat behind a metal table, his wrists chained through a loop in the center. The white light was dim, focused on single spot above them so that the rest of the room was shrouded in darkness.

"More of Garcia's men?" Henry asked.

"No, they could've killed him," replied John. "I think it was the ACT."

"You think the ACT is here in New York to steal..." Henry's eyes met with the impervious agent's, then continued in a more circumspect manner, "that thing?" He lacked any sort of subtlety, but that was one of the things that endeared him to John.

"Safe bet," John confirmed. "You need to find Garcia's location before he tells the ACT where to find it, Henry."

Henry shook his head. "I can't believe this."

"Believe it," said John coldly.

Not a heartbeat passed and there was a loud *pop* from outside, then two more, followed by hysteric screaming. *Gunshots.* Henry ducked but there was nowhere to take cover behind. The FBI agent, whose unbreakably stoic expression wavered, cracked open the detainment room door and unholstered his pistol.

Six men with machine guns and assault rifles stormed the atrium, the bodies of security agents at their feet and lying at the entrance. They shot haphazardly at desks and at the ceiling, sparks from electronics flying. Michaels was watching the chaos unfold through the blinds of his office. He ducked as a scattered bullet hit the corner of his window. He took out his cell phone and furiously dialed a number. *"I heard you have received your present, James,"* said Gabriel.

"What is this? Why are your men here, *in my building?"* Michaels yelled watching the analysts and agents crowding together helplessly and the security falling one after the other.

"Were you not the one that told me that Spears was figuring you out? That he and his brother were catching on? We need to eliminate him before he reveals our plans to the FBI. Reveals you to the FBI."

"It doesn't matter what he says, you idiot! He's in custody! He was going to be transferred in the morning! Now they'll let him go and your men won't stand a chance!" Michaels yelled again.

There was a conceited chuckle on the other line. *"We'll see about that, James."* The call clicked to an end, and Michaels threw his phone across the room.

At that moment, a terrorist walked into the office, keeping his weapon down. "Pretend you're my hostage," he commanded. Michaels pouted, reached into his dest drawer, and pulled out another burner phone. He put it in his pocket then led the way out the office, hands artfully raised.

John sat helpless in the detainment room as hostages were being held only rooms away. "Uncuff me. I can help," he pleaded to the FBI agent.

"That's not happening, Spears," he replied, weapon readied at the door. More bullets whizzed through the air nearby. The doors of the other detainments were shot open, the two-way mirrors in between the rooms shattered.

"They're coming. You can use my help! They'll kill all three of us if you don't let me go," John begged, but the agent didn't budge.

"Listen to him!" hissed Henry. The agent was sweating profusely, reeling from another glimpse outside. He unclipped the key ring from his belt and threw it on the metal table. John took the key and uncuffed his wrists.

He strode to the agape door and peeked down the hall. There were two black-clad men with rifles bursting through the detainment doors, likely searching for him. They had broken into room five. John was in nine.

"Henry, stay here." He turned towards the agent. "You come with me," he demanded. When the terrorists breached the next detainment room door, he and the agent hastened to the doorway of room six. They were out of sight of the terrorists taking over the main communications hub, who gathered hostages round the pit. John and the agent waited on either side of the doorway a moment.

When two rifles came protruding from the doorway, John nodded. Simultaneously he and the agent pushed the rifles into the air, the bodies of the guns swatting the terrorists' faces in perfect sequence. John took the gun from one of them and jabbed the stock of the rifle into the terrorist's face; the FBI agent did the same and looked out of the doorway to see if anyone noticed. "Clear," he said, taking out two pairs of handcuffs and tossing one to John. He cuffed a terrorist's hands, picking up his heavy assault weapon.

John looked up at the agent. "Let's go," he whispered.

The agent was first out of the detainment room, where a bullet met unceremoniously with his chest. John held out his arms for the agent to fall into. He checked his pulse, his eyes wide and devoid of light. John set him down gently and picked up the assault rifle, fury across his scrunched face.

John plopped down on his left shoulder, aiming and emptying the clip at the group of four terrorists. One dropped dead then the others scurried into cover.

He sprang behind the door, taking return fire. He knelt, took the other fallen terrorist's rifle and the agent's holstered pistol, stuffing it in the back of his jeans.

The gunfire ceased. A man with a heavy Brazilian accent spoke aloud from the atrium, "Spears! We have hostages! We will kill them if you don't give yourself up!" John knew there was nowhere left to go. He also knew that they would probably kill the hostages either way, and that they would most definitely kill him. John wondered if he'd ever faced a decision this delicate, but when he considered it, he realized the answer was not so difficult.

John tossed the rifle outside into the hallway. He walked out, hands in front of him. He made slowly down the hall towards the main communications hub. John was ready for anything, ready to be shot in the head spontaneously or forced to witness something worse.... He shut his eyes, prepared for his fate.

CHAPTER SIX:

5:04 AM: NIB HEADQUARTERS: MANHATTAN:

A caravan of police and FBI vehicles serenaded the street outside with wailing sirens, a small army of officers and agents carpeting the entrance walkway with weapons cast at the building's entrance.

John was on his knees amongst the other hostages, eyes flitting between each of the three terrorists, observing every detail. The two John and the fallen FBI agent had tied up were awake again, but had not rejoined the main group. One of them reached for his shoulder, pulled out a familiar obsolete, plastic phone from a pouch on his vest and dialed a number. "Gabriel, we have Spears." The terrorist-in-charge, as it were, was skinny and tan, his face sunken so that the shadows under his eyes were as black as his tactical uniform, like a skull with a curly afro tied in the back.

Gabriel? John contemplated if he had heard the name before. The hostages were staged in the center of the pit around the holotable, where the terrorist was pacing in a circle whilst the two of them were perched like gargoyles on the upper rings. From the lower level John could make out part of the tinted entrance doors. Outside the sky was turning violet, though it was hard to tell whether that was just the red and blue police lights meshing.

"What do you want us to do?" said the terrorist. Neither John— nor anyone for that matter— could hope to hear the other end of the conversation, especially as the terrorist climbed the stairs and lowered his tone. "Okay. Yes, Sir." He stuffed the phone in his vest pouch. When two of the terrorists returned with proud looks on their faces, the one in charge ordered they descend into the crowd like hawks and snatch two of the hostages: John and Assistant Director Michaels. *Why are they taking* him? Neither of the two put up much of a fight, for fear that the terrorists might air their frustrations on the agents and analysts in the crowd. John's thoughts quickly shifted to his brother, who was knelt with the rest of the hostages. There was little fear or doubt on Henry's face, but a steadfastness that told John he knew he would make it back alive. This determined John to make it so. But how and when could he slip away?

They forced John and Michaels through the front entrance of the headquarters, sidestepping the fountain and solar panel-lined garden, keeping their weapons fixed to the heads of their hostages so the police wouldn't fire. Two vans skidded to a halt with smoke under their tires. Two of the terrorists took John and Michaels in the same vehicle whilst the rest split with the other van, then they sped off in different directions.

The one in charge was sat across from John and Michaels, the other two in the driver and passenger seats behind him. He dialed again on his phone, cheap plastic buttons clicking. John assumed it to be the *actual* man in charge. *Gabriel....*"Yes, Sir," he said obediently. "The bombs are in place." John and Michaels shared a stunned look. *That's where those other two went,* John thought, but now was not the time to think. "With pleasure," said the terrorist, crooked smile across his skull-like face. He reached into another vest pouch and pulled out a small black box with a blinking red button on its side.

John's eyes widened as the terrorist's finger unreservedly inched for the trigger. John lurched his hips forward and kicked the terrorist's wrist, his own wrists bound in front of him. The bomb trigger flew out the window. John only hoped that that did not trigger an explosion, but there was not a second to spare waiting for the *boom*. John flung forward and latched onto the rifle across the terrorist's lap. They wrestled for control, John forcing the barrel towards the front, using his leg to kick away the pistol of the passenger. A few shots were flown, bouncing around the exposed metal roof of the van— Michaels ducked, shielding his head. The driver took a bullet to the head, the windshield smeared with red.

At the same time the terrorist in front of John shoved him away and aimed his gun at him and Michaels, the van was swerving out of control. The passenger jumped on the steering wheel but it was spinning wildly. The van toppled onto its side and slid through the street, its passengers rolling and contorting in the interior.

5:19 AM: MANHATTAN:

Déjà vu, thought John, hoping this was the last time he would be crawling out of the wreckage of a flipped car. He put one leg after another through the crushed opening, dragging his body over the glass and struggling with his bound hands. Michaels was pushing on the jammed sliding door on the other side of the wreckage. The passenger and one in charge were still alive too, forcing themselves out of the van, covered in shards and cuts.

When John was up he ran to the other side to help Michaels, kicking the door to pry it open and force it to slide. Once he pulled him out, John felt a large boot thrust into his back. John bounced off the side of the van and fell. The two terrorists had gotten up quicker and were kicking and beating him. Michaels watched, seemingly frozen, the terrorists not touching him.

When one of the terrorists had enough of pummeling John, he pulled a pistol from behind his back and aimed it. John was not defenseless from the ground, though. He wrapped his hands around the terrorist's ankle and tugged, while at the same time kicking his kneecap inwards. He flipped onto the grounded man and brought his elbow down hard onto the terrorist's nose, knocking him out. Immediately the passenger was throwing kicks to John's back. John spun around and used his arms to block a right punch. Propelling himself up from the ground, he wrapped his zip tied wrists around the terrorist's neck and, with a single swift maneuver, forced his knee up and through his chin. The terrorist collapsed, unconscious.

There was a ringing at his feet, from the pouch of the knocked out terrorist's vest. John reached down and grabbed the phone as well as a knife on the terrorist's person. After cutting himself and Michaels (reluctantly) loose, he pressed the send button on the phone and put it to his ear. *"Cesar?"* said the voice. *"Cesar?"*

"He's dead, Gabriel," John answered. "And the ACT are coming for you soon. I can help you, but only if you tell me where the bomb is." John kept a close eye on Michaels, who said and did nothing, and surely whose ears didn't prick at the mention of a bomb.

"Mr. Spears... I had hoped to have this conversation in person."

"We still can," said John. "Tell me where you are." John used a pistol he picked up to smash in the window of a parked rust-colored sedan. Red and blue lights and sirens were swelling in the distance.

"It seems my men really didn't stand a chance against such a capable *agent."* Gabriel's voice was darkly soft, seductive and charming to the right ear, but to John only a snakelike whisper.

"So you're the one behind this operation?" The question was said more like a definitive statement, though John himself was not sure how deep the well had been dug. After a moment without a reply, John, sat in the stolen car and poking together multicolor wires from under the wheel, asked again, "Are you gonna tell me what I want to know? Or do I have to track you down myself?"

"Don't worry yourself with our bomb."

"Sort of my job." John put the started car into gear and rolled away, Michaels watching him with no protest.

"Neither you nor Jeanne Leroux will be finding us. All is going quite according to schedule."

"I must've misplaced my schedule. Mind emailing me a copy?" Gabriel's slight chuff suggested he approved of John's humor. *"And I wouldn't underestimate Leroux's savagery if I were you. I'd be one the move now. Any place Garcia knew about will be compromised soon enough."*

"Garcia won't break." Gabriel hung up without another word. John used the terrorist's old plastic phone to dial a different number.

"John! Is that you?"

"Yeah, Henry."

Henry sighed with relief. *"I knew you'd get away."*

"Henry. Make sure they sweep headquarters. Who knows if those bombs I stopped are on a timer?"

"On it," Henry said soberly, refusing to linger on the shock of the situation. *"Did Michaels escape with you?"*

"Left him in the middle of the street for the police to scoop up."

"What did they want him for?"

John shook his head, doubling over the same question in his head. "I suspect they had orders to make it *look* like he was a hostage."

"You still think he's the traitor?" Henry asked, bemused.

"Either that or a coward. Although we shouldn't rule out *both*. When I was taking them on, he was of no help, and they didn't even *touch* him. See what you can find, Henry. There has to be something tying him to their organization.

Only thing I can think of was a trip his wife took to Brazil last year. I remember him telling me about it."

"I'll see what I can dig up. I have something for you, too," proffered Henry. *"When I got back to my station, the program Jen wrote to track Garcia by satellite was still running. I found him, John. Sending the location to your phone, now."*

"I better get there fast," said John. "I just spoke with the group's leader, Gabriel. Seemed pretty confident the ACT wouldn't find him. If Garcia doesn't talk they'll have no use for him."

"What else did this Gabriel guy say? Anything useful?"

"Afraid not," averred John. "I'll call you when I'm there. And your records, make sure you delete them just in case FBI tries to make you out as my accomplice."

"More running from the FBI..." Henry remarked. *"... Great."*

5:41 AM: MANHATTAN:

The police had arrived over fifteen minutes ago and were still questioning Michaels, the same way they had questioned John: sat on the edge of an ambulance, only Michaels' wrists were uncuffed. The two terrorists were hauled off by a second police cruiser promptly, the body of the driver zipped up and taken by a second ambulance.

Michaels winced as the paramedic pressed the bandage over the cut above his eye. She gave the officers the thumbs up, helped Michaels to his feet, aching, and stepped into the ambulance as it drove off. "I think that about covers it," said one of the officers, scribbling on a little leather-bound pad, "We can give you a ride back to headquarters, Director Michaels."

Michaels said nothing, merely nodded his head. When the officers turned towards their car, he rushed forth to the one on the right and seized the pistol from his belt. Before they knew it, one of them was on the ground, struck by the pommel of the gun, while the other was being pointed at. Michaels shook his head as if to say, "Don't move," then flicked the pistol sideways to signal the officer to drop his own. Michaels ambled around the car and bludgeoned the officer in the face with the pistol. He knelt and stole the keys to his cruiser, started it up, and made off.

"I'm here, Henry." John readied his pistol, weaving between concrete columns as he approached the stairwell of the under-construction building. It was dark. He put his fingers to his head, forgetting he didn't have the prototype glasses that Henry gave him. They were taken by the FBI along with his cell so he had to wedge one of the terrorist's cheap burner phones between his ear and shoulder. There was a purple-blue skylight rising along the open slits in the wall where windows would be placed, allowing some visibility. This time he would not have to analyze radio waves to know what floor to find Garcia. There were only two bright yellow work lights in the whole building, both on the third floor; that's where John crept up towards.

When he found the floor there was a white beam swiveling his way like the top of a lighthouse. John backed behind the hollow concrete doorway to avoid the light. When its holder had turned, John knelt and approached with short steps, shoving the phone in his pocket so that both of his hands were supporting the pistol between them. He stood and hammered the handle of his gun over the terrorist's head, quickly scooping the body to avoid an unwanted loud *thump*.

The terrorist had an earpiece dangling from his ear. John took it and plugged it into his own burner phone so he could communicate with Henry hands-free. He also took the terrorist's pistol and stuffed it behind his pants, then took his flashlight and aimed it under his pistol.

He walked in through a sectioned off part of the construction zone towards one of the work lights and found another two guards. They turned around at the bright blue light pointed at their backs. John turned his off and leapt behind a column to his left. They were approaching yelling curses his way in French. *Definitely the ACT,* John thought.

He stayed in cover waiting for them. They had their pistols in front of them, passing the column on either side. John sprang out and thwacked one of them square in the nose with his flashlight then kicked his heel into the other's chest. He grabbed the first by the throat and hurled him powerfully into the column, then finished with another battering with the flashlight.

"What's going on?" he heard Henry in his ear, undoubtedly alarmed by the groaning and rustling of clothes.

The second jumped up, snapping his gun onto John, but John grabbed the terrorist's arm and redirected the barrel. He forced the terrorist against the column by the neck, his forearm digging into his throat and pinning him to the concrete. John let go, wound back, and smashed him with an elbow. The terrorist fell, unconscious overtop the other.

He gathered himself again and neared the work light. Garcia wasn't there, merely an out-of-place bulletin board against the wall, with the hot yellow light pointed directly at it. John squinted at the pinnings. When his eyes adjusted they were wide with dismay.

"This is not good, Henry," John spoke into the earpiece.

"What is it? What do you see?"

"The bomb," John said.

"The bomb is there?" Henry could hardly keep his perturbed voice down.

"No," replied John. "But the picture is." John took out his phone and snapped pictures of the wall, too unsettled to marvel at the fact the cheap old thing could take pictures at all.

The board was plastered with the familiar schematics of the bomb, but one photograph stood out in the center, scratched by a large red X. It depicted a silver sphere with exposed, complex circuitry, red and blue wires sticking out and looping erratically across its metal surface. There was a glossy rectangular surface in the front of it, a flare from the camera's low-quality lens obscuring the red digital numbers ticking down on the timer. "I'm sending you the pictures now," said John.

A moment later when Henry had seen, he whispered, *"Oh...."*

"The ACT has known abut the bomb for a while now." John turned and beelined for the second work light across the floor. "I see Garcia." There was a body roped to a chair, shirt removed, bloody gashes trickling down his face and chest, the work light so close to his skin that it was peeling. As he encroached upon the scene, John had half the urge to put pressure on his wounds to quell the bleeding, but there were too many to manage.

"How is he?" probed Henry, but John did not answer.

"Garcia! Garcia!" John gently tapped Garcia on the cheek. He was breathing, but just barely, moaning as if he'd have rather stayed unconscious than awake and in agony. "Garcia, wake up! You have to tell me where the ACT went." Garcia merely slumped forward, unable to keep his eyes open. "No, No! Tell me where it is!" His soft whispers devolved into screams. *"Wake up!"* He lifted Garcia's chin, but he had taken his last breath, his eyes still open by John's doing. "He's dead." John gritted his teeth and slapped the tray of torture tools across the room.

5:57 AM: SHIPYARD: BROOKLYN:

In the lot beside a massive cargo ship, Gabriel and a half-dozen of his men awaited the lowering of a crane, attached to the wire a red cargo container.

He was as his voice indicated: attractive but with a full-of-himself slickness, his long dark hair combed back and his skin a young, unblemished gold.

Just as the shipping container scraped the ground, four trucks charged through the perimeter fence, where an already dead security officer lay at the gate. A barrage of bullets pelted nearly every terrorist in their path. Gabriel raced behind the container when a grenade was launched into the air. The explosion of one of his SUVs was close enough to burn his skin. His men were dropping like flies, fires blazing left and right.

When they had all fallen, Gabriel was dragged out from behind the container by Alec, the right-hand man, and forced to his knees.

From one of the trucks out stepped Jeanne Leroux. "Gabriel," she leered, bearing her crystal white teeth. Alec hoicked a handful of Gabriel's hair. He writhed, forced to look up to her. Leroux held open her palm and one of her men handed her a pistol. She lifted it and shot Gabriel in his left thigh; it was unclear whether she was aiming there or not, but she chuckled diabolically.

Gabriel's howling was unbearable. She aimed again to finish the job but her interested shifted. She drew towards the shipping container and unlocked the hatch. Alec, distracted, turned to chase a fleeing Gabriel, but Leroux said, "Let him limp away," with a smile, whilst two of her men swung open the heavy container doors. The inside made her bear her teeth again. It was a large metallic sphere, maybe twice her height, with red and blue wires strewn sloppily around it. The red timer on the front counted down the hours, minutes, and seconds:

18:00:01... 18:00:00.

6:05 AM: MANHATTAN:

"Set an agency-wide alert. Level ten priority on the ACT and Jeanne Leroux. We need all hands on this, not only CAD," John dictated.

"That's going to be tough," said Henry. "Apparently Michaels assaulted two police officers and stole their car. Now FBI's seizing control until Director Hall can sort everything out. They're poking their noses all over this place, especially looking for *you.*"

John descended the stairs of the construction site, slivers of blazing orange sunlight peeking between nearby towers. "Whatever way you can get the word out, Henry. We can't afford to keep this under wraps."

"In the meantime I might've found a lead. There're mass reports coming from near a shipyard in Brooklyn. Heavy assault weapons and explosions reported."

"They must've shipped the bomb in through there," said John. "I'm on my way. How much NYPD should I expect?"

"They don't have your face. *Yet.* The warrant for your arrest has only been passed around the FBI for now, so you should be able to get by showing them your badge."

"If only I *had* my badge," John irritably replied. He kept his chin up, sure he would find a way around his numerous dilemmas.

"Oh yeah."

John stepped out onto the street, where he felt warm golden light washing over him. "I'll think of something—" Suddenly there was a *zip* past John's ear followed by a metallic *clang;* the next indiscernible split second, the *crack* of a gun. John let go of the phone and dropped down behind a parked car as one bullet turned into many, tearing through his surroundings, skidding over car hoods and shattering windows. Concrete and metal became like paper.

When the shooting ceased, John popped out— everything but his shoulder and right side of his head still in cover— and let loose a few rounds, none of which hit their targets. He instead marked three men to the left, advancing across the street. John bent under the car, spotting what he believed to be a single terrorist to the right; he only got a second's glance before a bullet was striking the ground nearby and deflating the car's tires.

He pressed the mag release on the side of his pistol and the clip slid out of the handle. He had very little ammo. *Enough for two,* he thought, *maybe three,* remembering he picked up a pistol and then neglected it beside Garcia's body.

The car began to smoke. John leapt out from behind it, black smoke shrouding him from accuracy. He wisely went for the terrorist on the right, killing him with a couple of shots as he ran down the sidewalk. He slinked into an alley between the construction site and a residential building, between grey concrete and red brick that were being tattered by strays alike. He emerged from the alley with the rest of his ammo, missing every shot. He had managed to reach another parked car next to the sidewalk, though, closer to his target: the fallen terrorist's assault weapon in the middle of the street.

The smoke from two cars away was drifting into the street as the terrorists advanced blindly. John made it his opening to dive for the rifle. A few bullets hit the ground next to his body and whizzed over his head. Luckily, he was pressed to the ground shoulder-first, looking through the square reticle and opening fire. Beneath the cloud of smoke he saw the legs of one terrorist collapse. John rolled upright and strafed to the other end of the street, recklessly emptying the clip with two more terrorists advancing.

He was one car away from the one he had stolen before. John could leave now if he made a run for it, but he glimpsed at the front of the residential building across the road. He saw a child being pulled away from the window and picked up by his terrified mother. This imbued John with renewed spirit; he straightened himself, took in a sharp breath through his nose. As the terrorists advanced, he clung to the vehicle he hid behind as cover and wrapped around onto the sidewalk. They had no eyes on him. Before they knew it, John was behind them. He vaulted the rear hood and came behind the two. He used his shoulder to forcibly push the terrorist on the right out of his way. To the other John kicked behind the knee to lower him, then bashed his head through a door mirror. As the other rose with his rifle trained, John dropped behind the unconscious terrorist, picked up the grounded car mirror, and chucked it at his head. The man seized his swelling forehead long enough for John to lift the rifle strapped to the unconscious one's body and pierce the terrorist's vest.

John poured into the pocket of the unconscious terrorist next to him, knowing he'd find one of their plastic burner phones. When he did, he stood, dialing Henry's station. He had not taken a moment to observe the terrorists' features. Tan and dark skin, black tactical gear. They were Gabriel's men. "No doubt coming to rescue Garcia," John explained to Henry.

"Too late," Henry agreed. "Speaking of Gabriel's men, I've still been digging through the cellphone you picked up. The messages have to do with meeting places but don't give specifics, and questions about payment, but nothing that'll point us to any bank transactions just yet. There was one thing. You remember the symbol on the bomb schematics?" He spoke of the X with the triangle around it. "Sure enough, the same symbol has popped up, spray-painted in and around gang and terror attacks all over Brazil."

John had a feeling the news was rather inconsequential. "Any news on Michaels?" he asked as he entered his stolen car and dusted himself off, though nothing was going to take out the greasy black stain from his jeans.

Henry sighed. "He must've disabled the tracker in the police cruiser."

"He'd know how to do that." John was not surprised. "No satellite imaging?"

"I thought of that, too. The same signal jam frequency you encountered at Mason Tower is being used to block us. I'm still doing what I can to find the true source, but... you know."

"Could take hours," accepted John.

"Sorry I can't do more, John."

John shook his head, having the strange feeling that though Henry could not see it, that he could sense it. "You're doing everything you can. I'll be at that shipyard soon. Maybe then we can get some answers."

"Good luck," Henry said. John hung up the phone and dropped it on the seat next to him.

6:39 AM: NIB HEADQUARTERS: MANHATTAN:

Henry's fingers started to ache. He offered his hands a reprieve from attacking the black keys atop his desk; any longer and he was sure he would need a replacement keyboard. He massaged between his bent knuckles and tipped his head to crack his neck, though that was merely pretense to keep one eye over his shoulder. It proved necessary, too, since an FBI agent in a black and white suit was approaching his station. Henry closed the satellite interface on his monitor and replaced the screen with a police data sheet, pretending to get back to work without delay.

"Spears," the agent provoked.

Henry turned. The agent was handsome, too handsome, in fact. He had a slippery look to him, with gelled blond hair and a square jaw that concealed his crooked teeth with an overbite. "Yes, Agent Pool?" It had been the third time he came to Henry's station in the past hour, though he dared not question him on it.

"What are you working on?"

"Just analyzing the Brooklyn police reports." Henry started typing, hoping that would signal Pool to turn away and leave him alone.

"Come with me a moment," said Pool.

Henry had trouble hiding his vexation. "For what?" He knew what for: to prevent him from communicating with John. He was sure Pool knew. Perhaps he was about to arrest him for aiding and abetting.

"I've gathered some of my field office division in the conference room. We could use a debrief. Everything you can tell us about what we're up against." The request was regrettably reasonable. Henry got out of his swivel chair and followed the agent.

The conference room was a transparent box on the right end of the curved atrium. Five FBI agents sat around a pristine glass table, glancing at a television on the wall with files and satellite images displayed. When Pool entered first he held the door open for Henry, introducing him. "Team, this is Henry Spears. Chief analyst for the Counter ACT Division."

One of the agents, a woman with a sharp-shouldered blazer and blue shirt that clashed against her curly red hair, inserted, "Are we finally gonna learn what that is?" The agents around her laughed.

"That's the idea," said Pool, not sharing her jocular grin. He held out a hand for Henry to begin and took a seat.

"Right," started Henry. "Well, by now you'll have heard of the ACT. Not much is known about them publicly. But here, as you can imagine… we know damn near everything about them.

"They call themselves the Act to Change Tomorrow. ACT for short. A terror group based in France," Henry stood in front of the television, front and center to the agent audience, "their original roots began during the Cold War. After the fall of the Berlin Wall and the decline of communism, they fizzled out, went into hiding.

"That was until the mid-two-thousands, when my brother, NIB Agent John Spears, discovered resurging ACT cells in Europe. They were gearing up for something big, starting with the blackmail of French, Spanish, and English politicians with small scale attacks and by kidnapping prominent elite bankers. All designed to deter them from helping America in its war on terror in Iraq and Afghanistan. They partially succeeded, getting Spain and France to back down. Their entire mission was to shift the economic landscape, embed activists and spies in EU governments to resurge socialist sympathies and eventually spark regimes in which, according to their charter, wealth would be divided equally amongst the people."

"You'd think they'd've learned their lesson from Mao," said one agent.

"In twenty-twenty, after John foiled a plot to blow up the New York Stock Exchange, he followed their paper trail to Paris—"

"I didn't hear about any plot to blow up the stock exchange," another agent interjected.

"That was by design," said Henry. "He managed to stop them without alarming the public. Without even a single gunshot."

There were some impressed looks going around the faces of the agents at the table. Agent Pool's was not one of them. "Your big brother was more discrete back then," he remarked.

"Anyway," continued Henry, "after he unraveled their plans and found out about their leader, Jeanne Leroux: the daughter of original founder Henrique Leroux, the Counter ACT Division was formed, with John as the head. That was four years ago. Since then, the ACT has only seemed to grow in power and influence." Henry felt a lump in his throat admitting the last part.

"So why didn't Spears finish them for good when he was head of CAD?" asked the red-haired agent.

Henry chided, "You'll have to ask him. Got what you needed? Can I get back to work now?" Pool merely nodded. Henry left the conference room and made quickly for his table, hoping he had not missed a call from John. Sure enough, his phone was ringing, the alert on his computer monitor reading 2 MISSED CALLS.

Henry picked it up, his eyes mistakenly darting towards the conference room, where Pool was still watching him. "John," he trembled, noticing now Pool was coming out and walking towards him again.

"I'm here outside the shipyard. Swarming with NYPD."

Pool was at Henry's station. Henry turned away hoping to hide his face. "Yeah, I received the record invoice. I know Detective Johnston will want to find a way around the yellow tape, but as long as you call me back in the next couple of minutes and keep me up to speed—"

"What the hell are you talking about?" he heard John say. Apparently his disguised message did not get through.

"I'll make sure those reports are analyzed and sent back shortly, Detective."

"There's an agent next to you, isn't there?"

"Why, yes, actually, we're working closely with the FBI," indicated Henry. "Anyhow, I'll return your call—"

"Spears, give me the phone," said Pool, holding out his hand.

Henry thought the only option would be to strongarm his way out of this. "Don't you have anything better to do than harass me while I'm working?"

Agent Pool did not take kindly to that. "If you would prefer I arrest you and throw you into one of those comfy detainment rooms..."

"Give him the phone, Henry," said John. Henry reluctantly pulled the phone away from his ear as if it were magnetized.

"Spears, I presume?" Pool drawled confidently.

"If you arrest Henry, we're all gonna pay the price," cautioned John.

"Are we now?"

"There is a nuclear bomb in New York. The ACT is planning to steal it from the extremist group that smuggled it in. If they haven't already."

"Give me a break," scoffed Pool.

"Henry can't do much to help with the FBI over his shoulder. Send him home with a small group of agents to protect him while he helps me," advised John.

"Now why on Earth would I do that, Spears?"

"Because you know that I could be telling the truth. If I wanted to leave and never be found I could. I have no reason to lie about this. And if I can't get Henry's help to track down this threat, a lot of people are going to die."

Agent Pool looked down at Henry, phone idly buzzing at his ear. He shook his head, grappling with indecision. "Alright, Spears," he sighed. "I'll play ball for now."

"Get on dual coms with Henry," John said, not wasting a breath.

Pool parroted the order. Henry took two earpieces from his desk drawer and handed one to Pool. "I'm here, John."

"I'm at the shipyard in Williamsburg."

"Where those shooting reports came from?" said Pool, pulling up a chair next to Henry's station and ignoring the nosy looks from around the bullpen, especially in the pit from analysts like Jennifer Nolan.

"Still trying to find a way in past the police crawling all over the place," John explained.

"Well as long as you don't knock any of them unconscious," Pool derided. "What do you need in the shipyard?"

"I don't know. Some sort of clue. I'm willing to bet the bomb was here," said John. "If the police found it, we would have heard about it by now."

"Which means..." shuddered Henry.

"The ACT must've succeeded in stealing it," John finished the thought.

"What's the ACT want with a nuclear bomb anyway?" asked Pool.

"God only knows." John peered up at a tall white crane hanging over the shipyard. "I think I can distract some of the police. But you'll have to clear the rest, Agent...?"

"Agent Pool. And how would I—" the realization hit Pool immediately. "You want me to use my authority to send them away? I can be fired."

"We have a lot bigger concerns than keeping jobs, Agent Pool." John followed the shipyard fence down the sidewalk until he found a whole in the chain links.

Pool sighed again. "Get me the detective at the crime scene," he ordered Henry, reluctantly surprised that he had already gotten the information readied. The call line shifted and buzzed. When he received an answer, Pool responded, "This is FBI Agent Braxton Pool. Field identification number CT-one-five-one-oh-nine. I have a unit on the way to the shipyard now. Heavy assault weapons, grenade launchers, yes, I'd say this is an FBI matter. I'll need you and your team to clear out by time we get there. Yes, Sir. Thank you for your cooperation." The call was ended abruptly.

From the shipyard, John could see the officers mobilizing by the gate, though many were still crowded around a single shipping container in the center of the lot. John coolly crossed the lot, the police too busy with their investigation or evacuation to notice him. He reached one of the four wheeled bases of the enormous crane and climbed the ladder.

"You'd better not be messing around," said Pool.

"He's not!" Henry took a firmer tone with Pool now that they were on relatively the same page.

John reached the top of the crane, looking out at the city across the water, the sun nearly risen, looking down at the football field-length yard and the sea of shipping containers lining the edge of the river.

When he entered the control cabin, the buttons and console were still whirring from its last use, as he had suspected. He took a seat. "Okay... how do I work this thing?"

"Thought it would be harder to find the instruction manual for a gantry crane," said Henry. "Here it is. The right hoist controls forward and backwards motion, the one on the left controls the tilt and rotation of the spreader. The right trolley handle controls in and out extension of the crane arm, the left controls horizontal position—"

"I'm already hovering over the containers, I just need to grab one!" John sped him along.

"The left trolley joystick," said Henry patiently. "That's your left and right control."

John pushed the handle he hoped was the trolly control to the right. Slowly, the crane started shifting. "What next?"

"Right hoist controls to lower the spreader."

John pulled down the right stick on the control console. The claw-like spreader at the end of the crane lowered. He smiled, thinking he might have chosen the wrong line of work. "Alright, I'm over the container. How do I open the spreader?"

"The open button."

Of course. John tapped the yellow open button on the control console, then lowered the wide spreader around one of the containers. He hit the red close button next to it and was latched onto the container.

"Do try not to kill anyone, Spears," advised Pool.

John swiveled the crane head so that the hydraulic controls were chugging and the metal was grinding loudly. He heard panic from below. "Bombs away." He clicked the open button and the shipping container flung across the yard. The crash was monstrous, metal and concrete colliding in a heap.

"Hurry down there, John," said Henry.

John descended the ladder with haste, ducking between containers on his way to the crime scene. As he had hoped, the remaining police were investigating the sudden crash, some of them scattering towards the base of the crane, some towards the external power control, muttering curses about their failure to shut it off.

When he reached the scene, the air had shifted. There were bodies covered in tarps. There were black tire tracks, scorch marks and exploded bits of concrete, and too many bullet casings to count. John described the scene to Pool and Henry.

"What else do you see?" asked Henry.

There was a red trail leading to the opened doors of the shipping container. John was too aghast to respond. His heart rate increased, his breath rapid. Along the container door was a message written in what could only have been blood, dripping sloppily so that it was barely legible, though John could make out what it said:

WE HAVE THE BOMB

CHAPTER EIGHT:

7:00 AM: SHIPYARD: BROOKLYN:

Something was keeping John's legs from moving, keeping his shoulders so tight that their blades were touching. His heart was about ready to explode, bouncing against the inner cage of his chest like it wanted out. It was a sort of panic he was unaccustomed to, save for select moments of his life that vaguely flashed before him. Rather than a bright film coating his eyes, however, they came as brief charges of emotions that overcame him and went with rapidity. There was a guilt, embarrassment, and shame... then a dreadful trepidation closely pursuing. *"John? John?"* Henry's voice sounded like it was underwater; in fact, there was no sound at all. Everything was drowned out; even John's vision began to blur around the drooling, blood-writ lettering. He fell to a knee in front of the grey cargo container, his arms too weak to keep himself upright. *"John! Say something!"*

"*What's wrong with him?"* he heard Agent Pool as if he was shouting from a distant hill.

"Listen to me, John..." His demand was a tall task. All the lives John was sure he failed were attacking his senses, their shrieks and cries cast against a booming, scorching torrent of fire. *"You've been here before,"* said the feint voice.

"No matter how low it got, you were always there. You're my big brother. You always found a way to fix things. Come back to us." The more he spoke the louder Henry became. This time it sounded as though he were right next to him, like John could reach out and grab his hand to boost him back to his feet. The world stopped spinning. John let go of the short crop of his hair, his hand stiffening, and his heart started to find its normal pace.

"Thanks, Henry."

"Wanna fill us in, Spears?" said Agent Pool. There was a short quiet after his response, neither John nor Henry wishing to discuss the attack.

"The ACT has the bomb. It was here." John scurried away from the open lot as police officers made their way back to the crime scene.

"I'm attempting a reverse satellite track but it'll be a while," Henry made known. "I just left headquarters. A few agents are escorting me back to my apartment like you requested."

"Good, good," replied John, looking for the same hole in the shipyard fence that he squeezed through before. "I'll meet you there."

"And I'm still here holding things down," said Pool. "Probably about to be reprimanded for misleading the police. Not that that matters to you, Spears."

"Your help is appreciated," John averred. "Let's hope it was worth it."

7:23 AM: MANHATTAN:

John's stolen rust-colored sedan was jammed on the Williamsburg Bridge. He did his best to dodge the morning rush hour, angering nearly every driver who saw his headlights swerving abruptly in front of them. There was only so much he could advance, though; the cars filling the two lanes were glued together bumper-to-bumper.

He averted his eyes from the glare hitting the rearview mirror as he wove through the traffic. The burner phone he had picked up from a fallen terrorist started vibrating in his pocket. He picked it up. "Henry?"

"How did you like our present?" an unmistakable French inflection whispered.

"Leroux." John gritted his teeth, his fist clenching around the phone hard enough to crush it.

"Took a few dials to reach you," she said. *"I had a feeling you'd take one of their phones."*

John kept his rebuttal short. "Congrats."

"Whatever for?"

She wanted to hear him say it, but John would not indulge nor mince words. "What do you want, Leroux?"

"Would you believe me if I said I wanted to protect your city from Gabriel's barbarians?" Not for a second. It did not warrant a response from John but he contemplated the notion. If she did want the bomb to go off, why not side with Gabriel? It seemed they wanted the same thing. *And give all the glory to* him? John thought. *"Of course not, but what do I care what you believe?"*

"So you called to taunt. Or gloat?" said John.

"Maybe both. Maybe I want to help you. A healthy mixture never hurt," said Leroux. *"Haven't you yet wondered how his organization was able to get its hands on a nuclear bomb in the first place?"*

"You knew they were coming and you knew where," said John. "Earlier you helped them smuggle it in."

"On the first, you're correct, but to the second— you're mistaken. If you hadn't derailed us at the textile mill, we would've been there to stop them."

Somehow John failed to believe a word of that. "Then what do you know about them?" he followed up.

"Wouldn't you like to know?"

"I can figure it out on my own if you wanna play games."

"Oh, that I have no doubt," Leroux teased. *"But will you have the time to?"*

John's thoughts immediately brought him to the picture of the bomb posted on the bulletin board, to the glass square in the center of the metal sphere. "How long until that timer hits zero?"

"So you have *visited Mr. Garcia back in Manhattan?"* John could tell by her jubilant pitch she was smirking. *"How's he doing?"*

"I wasn't the only one. By time Gabriel's men arrived they were too late."

"They've an abundance of resources, it seems."

"More than you?"

She chuckled, not biting, not revealing more than she had to. *"It's light now, Spears. No more cowering in the shadows."*

"There's nowhere in this city we won't find you."

"I'm not the one hiding," she whispered wickedly.

John ignored her taunting. "Tell me where it is and I'll make sure your future cellmates to go easy on you."

"It's in safe hands. Anyway, I suspect you've got more pressing concerns. I'd give your brother a call when you can...."

"What are you talking about?" said John.

"Remember, Spears. I'm always *a step ahead of you. Call it a reprisal for beating on my dear Alec."*

The phone clicked and the call dropped into ambient buzzing. John quickly started dialing, eyes darting between the keyboard and the packed road. As he was about to hit send, however, the screen went black. John tapped it a few times to get it to come back on, but a red box with a slash through it was flashing. The battery was dead. John's nostrils flared. He threw the phone aside so it landed carelessly under the passenger seat, then stomped the gas pedal. The car clipped another's side mirror, wedging between two backed up lanes. He bumped into another car, smashing its rear taillight and squeezing off down the shoulder of the highway.

7:41 AM: MANHATTAN:

John clung so tightly to the steering wheel of the stolen sedan that he could have ripped it out of its column. His fingers were doing a dance along the faux leather, tapping rapidly. Sweat was beading down his forehead, despite the cold October air rushing through the broken window and biting his cheeks.

He veered right, escaping the traffic jam that had persisted ever since he left Brooklyn, but the East Village was not much better off. He slapped the wheel after he was forced to slam the breaks. He was so close, yet there was a slowness to the area. The buildings were more high-end than most parts of the city. Unique colors extended even to the fire escapes. Cleaner, more arched façades towered over the small streets. The people were in no particular rush, unlike the rest of the city, which made John swear under his breath. His car inched forward slowly but Henry's apartment was just up the block. He could even spot the greenery overtaking his copper-colored balcony. He also saw big black vehicles parked out front.

John had had enough. He got out of his car, not bothering to shut the door, then sprinted down the road. Horns were honking at him as he abandoned the vehicle and blocked the street. As he approached he thought he would see FBI agents posted at the base of the building, but there was no one, not even an agent sitting in the parked SUV. He entered the four-story building and drew a half-empty pistol from his jeans.

It was eerily quiet. The walls were grey, the stairs a polished black that did not creak as he slowly ascended. When he reached the second floor, an ACT terrorist was patrolling the hall. Unlike Gabriel's group, these men weren't clad in black tactical gear, but everyday street clothes. He could have been anyone, but John could tell the ACT from civilians. The brandless clothes, the sunken white cheeks, the militaristic high-held head; and the fact that he was pacing in front of Henry's apartment door. John tried to peek through the crack in the door but it was too slight. He crept up the last of the stairs as the terrorist's back was turned.

When the man turned again, John was there, pistol raking over his head. The body dropped like a ton of bricks. John snapped around towards the door in case another rushed out of the apartment to check. He knelt, one eye on the door, the other on the unconscious terrorist beside him. John lifted the man's jacket, took his pistol, and tucked it into his own jeans.

John stood and approached the apartment, heart pounding. He lightly nudged the door open, as much as needed for him to slip through. Immediately he heard muffled squirming from the living room on the left, and heavy foot-steps from the kitchen to the right. Across the foyer the hall continued, two open doors for the bed and bathrooms. John kept his gun forward, his legs knelt. He slightly rose and stared over the pastel green half wall. Henry and his fiancé, Danielle, were tied to wooden chairs next to each other. They were shoeless, their feet rubbing against the Indian rug in the center of the living room. Their beige coffee table, books, and television were toppled, wires and glass strewn about. Danielle was crying, her silvery-blonde hair frayed and messed. Henry was calm yet radically panting as though the rag tied around his mouth left little air to breath. Hovering over them was an ACT terrorist with his finger scratching the pommel of his pistol, just waiting for the chance to shoot. *Why haven't they?* John wondered, though he was glad they hadn't. *She wants me to watch. They're waiting for me.* John's hatred for Leroux intensified. He clenched his fists, wanting to let out a guttural roar or to unload his pistol into the man's back. John took a deep breath. If he acted too rashly, Henry and his fiancé would be killed. There was a terrorist in the living room, one on the balcony just next to him— where bright white sunlight was spilling inside— perhaps yet another in one of the rooms across from him. *Three or four. What's the play?*

John slowly backed away and retreated to the hallway outside the apartment, standing where the first terrorist stood. Be it by instinct or by reckless hope, he blurted out, *"Hey! Check this out!"* in French, then pressed against the wall nearest the staircase. He listed closely and heard one of them say, *"Go see what he wants."* The same heavy footsteps came thumping out of the apartment door. John was there with his pistol pressed against his skull. "Move or call for help and I blow your head off." John had known ACT recruits; he had studied them for years at this point. They were not like Gabriel's men, so easily willing to die. If threatened at gunpoint or tortured, they would break. "How many are in the apartment." The man lifted three fingers. "Where's the third? Bathroom?" The man shook his head. "Bedroom?" The terrorist nodded slowly. Henry's bedroom was also his office. "He's hacking into Henry's computer?" The terrorist was hesitant at first, but after John pushed the barrel of his gun deeper into his neck, he nodded. *This isn't merely to get back at me,* thought John. *They want what Henry knows to cover their tracks.*

They heard the terrorist in the living room call out to the hallway suspiciously. *"Reply to him,"* John said in French to indicate he'd know if the man was sending a warning.

"It's nothing!" the terrorist called back.

John pulled the man's shoulder and made him lead the way back into the apartment. John's hands were slippery with sweat. He wiped them on his jacket and fixed them back around his pistol tightly. There was a fluttering in the pit of his stomach so rapid he felt like he could vomit, but he forced down a gulp of air and pressed forward. *"There you are, what was that ab—"* the terrorist went quiet when he saw his companion come through the foyer, being held by the neck. John did not give him a chance to cower behind Henry and Danielle, though— he aimed around the man and fired three bullets square in the terrorist's chest. The one he held hostage immediately drove his body backwards, forcing John into the kitchen. John's spine bent around the marble counter, his brain jiggling from a hard back elbow to his temple. John did not have time to fight this one— the terrorist on the balcony was lifting his pistol at Henry and Danielle. John fired his gun, taking out the left leg of the man in front of him, then aimed and killed the terrorist on the balcony; he went careening over the banister and crashed onto a parked car.

Alarms and screaming came from the street below. John rushed to Henry and Danielle, nearly forgetting about the last terrorist holed up in Henry's bedroom to the right. Bullets landed next to him, shattering a vase and pelleting the wall plaster. John dove with his pistol forward and fired the rest of his magazine. The terrorist slid against the wall, blood trailing above him.

John stepped over the terrorist gushing from his leg and slid a knife out of its holder on the counter. He went to Henry and Danielle. He pulled the gags out of their mouths and began cutting through the zip ties behind their backs.

"John," sighed Henry.

"It's alright. You're alright." John was thanking every God there was in his head.

"You could've shot us!" Danielle whined. She had sparkling sea blue eyes and pink lips that were split and bleeding, leaking onto her white suit.

"So could he have," John replied, nodding at the dead terrorist at their feet. Danielle reluctantly took his hand and he helped her up. He grabbed Henry's shoulder and lightly gave him a shake to make sure he was okay.

"What is happening, John? What have you gotten Henry into?"

"He hasn't *gotten me* into anything, Dani," Henry stood up for his brother. "We're in this together. But you... you have to get out of the city— the *state,* even."

"*Me? Just* me?" she asked, tears streaming down her flushed cheeks. "What about you?"

"I need to stay here and help." Henry was even braver than John had realized. A part of him hesitated to ask Henry to stay, but he didn't have to.

"No, no, we were almost *killed!* We need to leave, you need to come *with me!*"

"Danielle," Henry said firmly, holding her arms, for if he hadn't they would be pounding on his chest. "I'm staying."

"If you do this, y—you *can die!*" she stuttered.

"It's better than letting more innocent people die today," Henry said. "Come on." He unhooked his and Danielle's keys from the half wall. "You drive to your mother's in PA. Farther if you can. Don't stop until you get there."

She hadn't the words to fight anymore. She kissed him tightly, arms wrapped around his neck. Henry turned to John. "Looks like NIB's the only safe place for us now. Coming?"

John looked down at the squirming terrorist, flopping like a fish in a pool of blood in the kitchen. "I'll meet you there," he said.

Henry and Danielle rushed out of the apartment building. John watched them kiss again, get in their separate cars, and drive off from the balcony. He turned again and walked towards the terrorist, bloody fist curled. The terrorist's angry mug stared up at him, almost challenging him to do something. John was happy to indulge. He lightly stepped on the terrorist's bleeding left leg and applied his weight. The man screamed and lurched back, swinging his arms uncontrollably. "Now you..." John knelt with his knee pressing more weight on the bleeding wound. "You're gonna tell me where Leroux is."

John saw in the teary eyes of the terrorist that he could hold on no lon-ger. He was about to tell him, but something bludgeoned the back of his head, and his eyes shut to black.

CHAPTER NINE:

8:05 AM: MANHATTAN:

John woke to an East River breeze whistling through a narrow window opening in the backseat. The car was winding down FDR Drive, bouncing as it squeezed in and out of the rocky shoulder lane. The beige concrete barriers drifted past like a strip of sand against the water. The smell of exhaust melded with brine ravaged John's nostrils. The slightest movement of his head felt like his brain was being juggled inside his skull. Through painfully squinted eyes he saw his wrists bound together by zip tie. He forced his eyes upward; the driver was the terrorist patrolling outside Henry's apartment, still rubbing the back of his head from where John pistol whipped him. The passenger was bleeding out all over the seats, his leg tied sloppily with a jacket tourniquet. The driver saw him in the rearview mirror, hollered, "He's awake!" then nudged the passenger, who winced with pain at the faintest shift and aimed his pistol at the backseat.

"Where... are you taking me?" muttered John weakly.

"Where do you zink?" said the driver. "To see zeh boss."

"And where would that be?"

The bleeding passenger chuffed— recoiled from pain— and declared, "You'll see."

"Tell me where you're keeping Gabriel."

The terrorists laughed, the passenger much gravellier. "'Keeping Gabriel?' Zat fool is no zreat to us anymore," the driver explained. "Madame Leroux shot 'im at zeh shipyard—" The passenger punched the driver in the arm with his pistol hand as if to say *shut up.*

"He's dead?" If he was that would necessarily simplify the investigation, but John did not want to imagine Gabriel's organization running around New York without a head.

John awaited the next moment. When the driver swore cut around a driver on the shoulder lane, the car bounced up. The passenger swore and lost focus on where his gun was pointing. In that instant, John sprang forward and forced the pistol into the air, simultaneously lashing an elbow across the passenger's nose. He slapped the gun away then drove his fists down like a hammer onto the bleeding leg, causing the terrorist to shriek in agony. The driver, distracted, was swerving. John wrestled him for control of the steering wheel, wrenching to the right. The car sparked against the metal railing atop the concrete barriers. John dug his elbow into the driver's leg, which stomped on the gas pedal. The car skidded forward, its tires bursting, its chassis sliding until, somehow, the car was in the air, *falling.*

The car hit the river like a misaimed cannonball. Immediately water was starting to rush in through the cracks. John was clicking the window switch in the backseat to no response. He started rapping the glass with his elbow but it wouldn't budge against the pressure. John lay back to start kicking the window, but the driver leapt to the backseat and started punching. Closed-in and without mobility of his wrists, he did what he could to block but took blows to the face and ribs. He kicked off the door behind him and plunged his head into the terrorist's nose. The driver's head bounced off the right window and cracked the glass.

Now the water was at their knees and filling quickly. John drove his shoulder into the terrorist's face, thrusting elbows wherever they could land, but he was kicked away with force. The terrorist pounced, hands wrapped around John's throat, pushing his head into the seat where water was overtaking it. John's eyes filled, his nose and mouth clogged with salt. He squirmed, hitting the driver's arms and clawing his face but he wouldn't relent.

John felt behind him, just above his head. He pulled on the seatbelt like a rope and wrapped it around the driver's neck. This offered John the slightest reprieve where he could lift from the water— which was now at the seats' headrests— and take a breath. The terrorist was the one clawing at him now, trying to twist himself free of the tight belt noose around his neck. John wrapped his legs around the driver's head and neck, trapping his arms in a triangle hold.

The terrorist faded slowly, too slowly, as when he was dead the water was just under John's chin. He pushed the body aside but there was little space. The first thing he did was free himself by wrapping his arms around the driver seat and yanking against the metal rods holding the headrest in place until the zip ties binding him snapped.

The passenger was submerged, unconscious or dead, John did not know. He got to work again on the cracked window in the backseat, but the pressure had increased, and water was spilling continuously over his eyes. *The gun,* he remembered. John felt around for it on the seat and below. The interior was almost completely flooded. He submerged himself to search for the pistol but could not find it. The river water was green and murky, filling rapidly with bubbles and being clouded with blood. He poked his head out, his lips kissing the roof of the car for spouts of air. Would this be the end? He had one more shot.

The car was filled. John sunk to the bottom, pushing the driver's contorted body away. He looked under the passenger seat, where he saw a metal glint from the front. That had to be it. John, letting out a pocket of air and pounding his chest to keep it in, swam between the two front seats. He reached over the passenger and his bleeding leg, which looked like red smoke rising and obscuring his vision. He patted the ground and finally felt it. John picked up the pistol and forced himself to the backseat.

John aimed the gun at the cracked window, shielded his eyes, and fired. The first bullet fizzled downward and barely scraped the glass. John started to panic, letting out another group of bubbles and fighting with everything he had to keep the water out of his lungs. He fired again. This time the bullet hit the glass but only spread the crack further. John pulled the trigger once more and the glass erupted into fragments.

John kicked off the door behind him to launch himself out of the car and towards the surface. The last breath of air escaped his lungs. There was perhaps twenty feet of water above him. He was not going to make it. John kicked and scratched at the water with every bit of energy that he possessed. *Almost there.* His eyes were fading, a vignette filling his sight. He started thrashing, taking in a gulp of water and choking on it.

By some miracle he broke the surface. Before he could draw in air, he vomited a quaff of green water. When it was cleared, he sucked in a gust of cold wind as if it were the first time. He filled his lungs so rapidly he thought he would burst like a balloon, but no amount seemed to be enough.

There were bystanders bellowing welfare checks from above. When his breathing was eased, John started swimming under the highway, towards a sidewalk railing. He climbed it, grunting and slipping, vaulted over and landed on his back. Happy to be on ground, John clung to it, panting heavily, taking in the sounds of horns and disgruntled passersby. It was the third vehicle crash he'd experienced in a matter of hours; his hope that the last time would in fact be the last was squashed, but a sense of divine intervention washed over him.

There was no time to linger though. John reluctantly got to his feet, soaked and freezing. He approached a citizen whose hand was raised for a taxi. When the taxi appeared, John shoved the man out of the way and stepped into the backseat. *"Hey!"* He shut the door and tuned out the furious protests.

"NIB headquarters," said John.

"NIB? What the hell is— *Hey!* You're getting my seats drenched!"

John pointed the soaked pistol at the driver. The citizen who was slapping the window and swearing loudly sprinted in the opposite direction. "Guggenheim Museum. *Fast.*" The taxi driver did not hesitate. John rested his head and let out a sigh of relief.

8:34 AM: MANHATTAN:

James Michaels was no longer driving the police cruiser. He had stolen a different car, more lowkey and suitable to the passengers in the back. He glanced in the rearview mirror. Two men sat wearing all black. "Where next?" he asked.

"Left here," one of them said calmly.

"It's been almost two hours. You don't expect me to play chauffeur all day, do you?"

"Well you can't be our spy anymore. That's for sure," said the other.

"I'd like to stop to make a call," said Michaels.

"Not yet."

Michaels scoffed. "At this pace we could've been well out of New York by now."

"We aren't going anywhere."

"You don't want to be here when that bomb goes off," Michaels pled.

"We have time."

Sweat was rolling down Michaels's bald head. He tightened his thick fingers around the steering wheel. There was no other course of action but to listen to them, do what they told him to.

Michaels's phone started to ring. "We said no calls!" one of the men hissed.

Michaels read the caller ID flashing in small text on the old plastic burner phone. "It's Gabriel," he said. The men were silent, unable to object to him answering. Michaels slid open the phone and put it to his ear. "Gabriel?"

"James. She took it," gasped Gabriel. *"Leroux took the bomb."*

"Do you know where they took it?"

"How would I know that, you imbecile!" Gabriel groaned as if in pain, breathing loudly and quickly. "We'll find it. But you'll need to regroup with the others." Michaels pouted, unwilling to make known his thoughts. "Did you hear me, James?"

"What happened to you?" said Michaels, hearing muffled moaning on the other end.

"I've been shot. Don't worry about me. Just do what I told you."

"Where are these 'others?'"

"The men you're with, they'll know where to go."

"You can't tell me?" Though Michaels did not wish to go anywhere for Gabriel, a part of him still felt outraged that he did not trust him with the information. "I've been driving all around the city for hours. Moving packages of God-knows-what—"

"I'm not entitled to tell you more than you're ready for, James... now do as I say. Or must I remind you—"

"No. You don't."

"Put him on speaker," barked one of the passengers. Michaels ignored him.

"I hope you haven't thought about doing something rash like fleeing the city. It'd be a shame if you lost your way. A shame for you... and your wife—"

"I haven't."

"Michaels, the phone." The terrorist behind Michaels slapped his shoulder and pinched.

"So you are clear on your duties?" asked Gabriel.

"Yes."

"And you are clear on your place in the Hierarchy?"

Michaels wavered, unwilling to answer the question, his face mushing like he ate something sour. "Give me the phone!" the terrorist grumbled.

"Yes," Michaels replied. He tossed the phone to the backseat.

One of the terrorists put the phone to his ear. *"Make sure Michaels goes directly to the meeting place,"* said Gabriel. *"If he strays or disobeys... shoot him in the head."*

The only part Michaels heard was *disobey*. Whether for or against his own good, he opted not to linger on the sentiment. It was not only *his* wellbeing on the line.... He kept driving and followed his orders to a tee.

8:50 AM: NIB HEADQUARTERS: MANHATTAN:

The taxi parked across the street from the museum where the ebony headquarters stood flanked by an array of solar panels and greenery. While the driver wasn't looking, John stuffed his pistol in the passenger seat pocket. He got out and immediately the cab drove off. He was still fairly damp, his shoes squeaking as he traipsed towards the entrance.

John raised his arm next to his head, for he expected a boost in security and that they would know he arrived before he even walked in. Sure enough, after pushing one of the doors open, he raised his other hand, met with a circle of NIB and FBI agents pointing guns at him.

"John!" he heard his brother racing to him. Henry ran through the beeping metal detectors and directly passed the agents pointing weapons. He did not care about the wet filth that covered John. He went in and hugged his brother tightly. "Thank God you're okay."

Thank God indeed, thought John.

"Get away from him, Spears!" called one of the agents. Another guided Henry away gently whilst the guns remained trained on John.

Barreling from the atrium in his black suit was the square-faced agent-in-charge: Braxton Pool. "Alright, that'll do. You all can lower your weapons." There was hesitance from the FBI agents, but the NIB agents knew John and did so without fuss. Pool shuffled towards John irresolutely, hand in his palm. "Sorry to have to do this, Spears." He took out a pair of handcuffs from a holster under his jacket. John did not put up a fight, instead raised his wrists, which bore marks from the zip ties he forced off previously.

John was escorted to a detainment room in the hall across the main communications hub; a familiar scene with quiet, inquisitive glances piercing him from every direction. Henry was there every step of the way and followed him inside.

"I may have a lead on Gabriel," John said as he was seated, his chains rerouted through the loop in the center of the table.

"That's a relief. Satellite imaging has never failed me in the past, but they have a talent for signal jamming." Henry crossed his arms and paced. Pool was standing beside him not quite sure what to make of the conversation.

"He was there at the shipyard."

"You saw him?" said Henry overexcitedly.

"No, before I got there. The terrorists who took me let slip that Leroux shot him. But they didn't say he was dead," explained John.

"So we do some searching for nurses, doctors, vets—" Pool put forth.

"Any medical practitioners in the shipyard's vicinity, yes," Henry agreed. "Could be wishful thinking, though, assuming Gabriel would go to an actual doctor for help."

"And if this Gabriel had an NIB director on his payroll, why not a doctor? It's smart." Pool had a point. Henry and John shared an appreciative look that said they were happy to have another agent on board.

"If you saw the scene at the shipyard..." John remembered the awful, bloody setting vividly. "I don't think he's got many more men he can rely on close at hand. If he does they'll be rallying for a move against the ACT. You're right about it being optimistic but it's all we've got right now."

"Not all," said a voice from outside the detainment room. In walked a tall man in a navy blue suit, with short, wavy brown hair and a strong face. His sapphire eyes had crow's feet, his plush cheeks laugh lines, though he was rather young looking, despite being of the same age and stature as James Michaels. He had big ears that made his head have to be supported by extra-broad shoulders, and he wore a bright white smile that emphasized his youthfulness. "Came up from the Washington office as soon as I heard about our friend's little situation," he said in reference to John.

"Is that what you'd call it?" John smiled, happier than ever to see an old friend.

"Let's get him out of those cuffs, Agent," the man said.

"Copy that, Director Hall." Pool was quick to follow the directive.

"And Pool, was it? You and your FBI friends are dismissed. I thank you for a job well done."

"He's been pretty helpful, actually," Henry vouched.

"Thanks, Spears." Pool bore a handsome grin. "But your boss has arrived. I'd say you're in good enough hands. Just keep me informed. Good luck. Director."

John tipped his head and Pool left, gathering the other FBI agents stationed around the atrium. His eyes returned to the director of NIB, Steven Hall, who extended a hand and a smile. "You don't look so hot, John." The three shared a much needed laugh. "Right, then," Hall began. "What have I missed?"

CHAPTER TEN:

John quickly changed into some new clothes in Michaels's office. He put on a clean set of jeans and a thin black sweater with sleeves too long so he rolled them up his forearms. He winced as the shirt was sliding over him and ran his fingers over the desiccated blood from the wound on the crown of his head.

There was an almost ghostly feeling to the office. The shutters let in dashes of blue light where there was otherwise shadow. Under the golden desk lamp there was a framed photograph. John picked it up. It was Michaels, Hawaiian shirt, his big arms wrapped around a woman who seemed happier than ever in her fiery sundress. John wondered again how Gabriel got to him.

The thought was briefly interrupted when Steven Hall entered. It was his office now. "There he is," Hall cheered, a fresh glance at John up and down.

"Good as new," said John. Hall eyed the photograph in John's hand. "I'm still tryna wrap my head around it."

"Michaels is like you, John. Seen things in the army that would send any man to a shrink's couch for a decade. Instead he was quiet. Stoic. Got right to work after I offered him the job. Never made a big deal out of taking orders from someone his age." Hall sat in Michaels's chair, rubbing the leather armrests in a sort of sentimental way. "I never imagined he'd betray his country. Part of me still refuses to believe it."

"I don't think it's a coincidence his wife and sister-in-law took a trip to Brazil over a year ago." John placed the photo back down on the desk. "Even so… no blackmail is excuse for what he allowed to happen."

"Agreed."

"What's the plan, Hall?" asked John.

The dread on Hall's face quickly subsided and his dimpled smile returned. "While Henry searches for Gabriel *his* way…" Hall got up and opened the office door, waving for John to head out first. "*You* have another avenue to pursue." John curiously left the office and started down the metal catwalk. Hall walked at his side down the staircase. "After those terrorists attacked this building and took you away, whether it was foresight or sheer luck, you left two of them alive. The police scooped them up, brought them back here." The two stopped in the hallway branching from the atrium in front of the rows of detainment rooms. "And seeing as you're the one who uncovered these guys— and nobody's been able to break them thus far—you get to interrogate them." John was pleased, which in turn increased the grin across Hall's lips. "Go get 'em, Tiger. Or was it *Bison?*" John rolled his eyes, despising that alias. Hall tapped him on the shoulder then went back out to the atrium.

John pressed a replacement badge he was given against a scanner next to the door and the lock disengaged. He entered. Two terrorists sat across a metal table from one another. There was the one who lead the attack on NIB headquarters four hours prior, the one from whose mouth John had first heard the name *Gabriel.* His face was more sunken than before, maybe because John had caved it in after he caused the van to crash. He shared the same puffy, curly hair as the man across from him. John remembered kneeing him in the face, which explained his lopsided broken nose stuffed with dried blood. John wasted no time beginning the questioning. "Where's Gabriel?" As expected, they kept shut. "We know about the bomb. The shipyard. It might surprise you to hear he got shot by Jeanne Leroux. She stole the bomb within the same hour you attacked this place." There was a tightening of the terrorists' jaws, a twisting of the lips to keep from speaking, as if forcing themselves not to believe a word of John's tale. "You two are already looking at life in prison for murder and attacking a federal headquarters. Give me something worthwhile... and we might be able to shorten that." Still there was no response, no changing of their faces. "Of course, you aren't afraid of prison. Or death. You're not like the ACT. Not cowards. You're willing to die for the cause. Only tricky thing is... the *why*. What's Gabriel offering his little gang to keep them in line?"

That seemed to trigger a glance by the terrorist in charge of the attack. "The Hierarchy is no gang, Spears," Gabriel reviled.

"The Hierarchy... that's what you call it?" said John. "You sure Gabriel's not actually a comic book villain?"

"We have no weakness for you to exploit!" The terrorist rattled his chains, the one across from him shaking his head hoping he'd stop talking. "No limit to our scope."

"Nuclear weapons, I get it. But you showed your hand to the wrong crowd."

"Leroux is nothing. Gabriel will find her and cut her heart out," the one on the right viciously snarled.

"Now this is a conversation," John invited the second terrorist. Neither of them was amused. "Now... in the event your mission failed. Where would Gabriel go to hide? Tell me now."

"You are a fool! We'll say nothing! No matter what you do to us!"

"Shall we test that theory?" John grabbed the legs of the chair in which the terrorist on the left sat in and yanked. The man flew out of the chair, his arms still looped through the table whilst his body was bent on the ground. "I know you aren't afraid of dying, but *everyone* is afraid of pain," said John, taking a hold of one of the terrorist's arms and shoulder.

"You idiot! He won't talk!" said the one on the right, still sitting helplessly in his chair.

"Maybe *you* will." John *twisted* until he heard a *pop*. The terrorist shrieked, unable to reach for his dislocated shoulder to cradle it. The other was quiet still, a look of derision bending his brows. "No?" John walked to the other side of the table and forced the other arm of the terrorist against the table. *"Tell me!"*

"DON'T!"

John *popped* the other shoulder out of its socket. The terrorist was shedding tears and wailing. He looked across the table with little sympathy. John pinned the terrorist's wrist to the table, wrapped his palm around one of his fingers, and started bending backwards, all the while locking eyes with the man across from him. *They won't talk. There's no time for this,* thought John. He let go of the terrorist's hand. There was a smug lip curling from the one across the table as if he'd succeeded. John frustratedly shoved open the detainment room door.

He trudged through the atrium. Before he could reach him, Henry was already meeting him halfway. "Tell me you've found something," said John.

"I found something." Henry nodded to Hall, who was talking to another analyst at her station on the outside of the center pit.

The director approached and said, "Talk to me, Gentlemen."

"It's not much," started Henry, "but there are a handful of hospitals near the shipyard. Only one of them, however, is missing a surgeon. Doctor Wells didn't come into work this morning. Could be a stretch, but—"

Hall interrupted him with a plan already set in motion. "Get down there, John. I'll approve a tac team. Set a five block perimeter around the surgeon's home. See if you can't spot a sign of Gabriel or his men."

"Yes, Sir."

John and Henry started to walk off, but Hall called out, "John, hold up." John turned back while Henry went back to his desk. "Before you go... I spoke to Agent Pool while you were interrogating those two in there, to see if there was anything else useful from his perspective. He told me something."

"What is it?"

"At the shipyard, he said something happened to you. You froze. Had a sort of... blank moment." Hall inched closer and lowered his voice. "I hate to ask, but what you're getting into is no walk in the park. This is the most serious threat we've ever faced. So are you—"

"I'm fine, Hall." John eyes evaded Hall's, instead darting across the blue and black-specked floor.

"I know you are. If I doubted that, I never would've recruited you." John looked up at him with widened eyes. "Yeah, I've always known. I figured, you were a capable soldier. A good agent. You could manage an attack if it was rare. After all, no spurs of anxiety could stand a chance against *the* John Spears."

"I thought Henry was the only one who knew. Since we were kids—"

"Psych evals are more accurate than you might think, John. Even to the most highly trained. Don't worry. I never told anyone then. I'm not in a rush to now. Just make sure you keep your eye on the ball. We can't afford any missteps, not when the stakes are this high." Hall's voice was grave, his hands in his pockets. "Now get going. Keep contact with Henry. I'll be on the phone with the DOJ and White House. They should have been informed hours ago, but... Michaels." Hall shrugged and scoffed with a certain disgust, then walked away back towards the grated metal stairs.

9:38 AM: MANHATTAN:

Four tactical vehicles were spread out, weaving between every street in a five block radius, the northern corridor of Kips Bay. Coordinated with the police, there were blockades around every corner. The perimeter was set.

"Listen everyone," John said into an earpiece. "We don't know what this man looks like, just that he's of South American descent. We know that Gabriel suffered a gunshot wound to the leg."

"...J...John?" the signal was patchy and full of static, but he heard Henry calling for him.

"Yeah, Henry?"

"*Tac van four scanned a few parked SUVs on a residential block. I ran the plates. They all belong to South American migrants, some from Brazil some from—*"

"That's profiling, Spears," said an agent in the backseat beside John. "If that's our criteria to move in—"

"Frankly I find a nuclear bomb threat a tad more problematic. Agent?"

"Collins." The agent had curly red hair and light, freckled skin. His jaw was tightly set. He did not care for Henry's intel tactics or John's willingness to act on them, and it was written across his face.

"I know it doesn't sound very moral—"

"Screw morals. It's against the law. Suppose we charge in there and find a bunch of men looking after their grandmas?" Collins had a point, but John was determined to see the plan through.

"Suppose we find the terrorists in there," John rebutted. "We don't have a choice." Collins kept to himself after that. Their truck grouped with the others in the middle of a blocked road. "This it?" John got out and looked up a short red brick building. "How many floors, Henry?"

"Ten. Safe to assume they're holed up in the doctor's apartment on the tenth floor, but safer to clear each as you make your way up."

"If things get out of hand, we need to make sure nobody gets too far. Vehicle one group, stay here," commanded John. He fastened a bulletproof vest around his chest and armed his pistol. "Remember. We need Gabriel alive. Let's move."

John was the first in the building, followed by at least fifteen Emergency Services Unit officers— SWAT and hostage negotiators— and NIB agents split into two lines filing up the steps. The walls were a peeling green, the stairs a newly painted chestnut. As pairs of agents broke off to search each floor, John continued ascending.

Collins had John's back when they reached the top floor. "You take that side," said John, back pressed to the right of the first apartment. Door-by-door, that was the only way. John gave the nod, then stepped back and *kicked* the door down. There was a shriek from the kitchen. It was a small albeit charming apartment ornamented with china cabinets and multicolor ribbons strewn from the ceiling. John, pistol aimed, and Collins, with his rifle, scanned the entire apartment within moments. The woman who lived there, seemingly alone, was cowering in the corner by her refrigerator. John had no time to console her, merely shushed her and went back out into the hallway.

About to search the next room down, they were interrupted by some light *pops* from downstairs, which quickly turned into booming automatic fire.

"Where is it coming from, Henry?" said John. Suddenly droves of tenants were shoving past him and Collins and fleeing down the stairwell.

"I can't tell!"

"One of the agents' heart rate monitors went flat," said Steven Hall, who had joined in on comms. *"He's down. Fourth floor."*

Collins promptly clicked the radio on his shoulder and addressed the agents, "All units, there is heavy fire coming from the fourth floor. We have an agent down and another under fire. I repeat, the fourth floor is red! Civilians are running out in waves, so check your fire and let escape—"

"Top priority is the Hierarchy leader," amended John. "He could be blended in with a civilian crowd!"

"Spears!" yelled Collins. "We have to get the civilians *out!* We can't force them to stay in the building!"

"I know that! Tac team outside should facilitate their evacuation but *don't* let them past the police blockade!"

Collins shot a disapproving look John's way before continuing down the steps, nudging between the panicking crowd of tenants. When they reached the fourth floor, they were joined by about a dozen SWAT officers lining the wall and stairs along the hallway, where the bullets were coming from. John made the first move to pop around the corner and send a couple of shots at two terrorists halfway down the hall. He sidestepped into an open apartment on the left, Collins across from him on the right, backs to the doors as a volley came their way. Officers were yelling and advancing, firing off shots then following John and Collins further up into the apartments.

John nodded and he and Collins came out at the same time, knelt low to force an adjustment to the terrorists' aim. They fired a few bullets each and took down both of the terrorists. They advanced, SWAT behind them.

The door of one of the apartments suddenly burst open and a terrorist with a knife was slashing at John. He evaded in the nick of time for Collins to plant a bullet in the enemy's chest. "Thanks," panted John.

There was little time to settle in as three more terrorists erupted from the end of the hall. John's eyes flitted to Collins's feet. There was something rolling on the floor between them. *"GRENADE!"* John pushed Collins through an apartment doorway and leapt backwards into the one behind him.

The shockwave might have exploded John's eardrums as well as the ground in the center of the hall. John saw Collins rearing, hands covering his ears. John's were ringing loudly. He saw one terrorist coming into the doorway, rifle aimed. John lurched for his pistol in front of him, but the terrorist went tumbling over him, dead. Collins had fired a shot off, saving John again. In the blink of an eye, John was too late, too filled with shock to return the favor. Another of the terrorists entered the apartment Collins was in to clear it and shot a couple of rounds. Collins's head dropped back lifelessly. *"No!"* yelled John. He got up, pistol in hand, and unloaded in the terrorist's back. Walking out into the hall, he had forgotten there was a third. He whipped his gun to the left but the terrorist struck with the stock of his rifle, knocking the pistol out of John's hands. He lifted his gun to fire but John pushed the barrel away from him and hurled himself forward headfirst. The terrorist's nose crumpled in a bloody mess. John wrapped his arms around him, lifted with his hips, and spun, tossing the terrorist through the hole in the ground; the terrorist landed with a violent crash on the floor below.

John got up, eyeing the downed SWAT officers gathering themselves and helping their wounded to the right. Across from him, he lifted the dead terrorist off of Collins, who was panting like there was little air in his lungs. John knelt, patted his chest. There was no moisture, no redness of blood. Two bullets were lodged in the front of Collins's vest. "You're gonna be alright. Stay down," said John. "Henry?" John tapped his earpiece, bits of static coming in and out. "Send paramedics."

"Already on their way, John," replied Director Hall.

"Go get... Gabriel," Collins gasped for air.

John put a hand on Collins's shoulder then stood, dust and debris kicking up under his steps. He dropped his empty magazine and loaded his pistol again. This time it was he alone who charted the rest of the hallway lined with bodies. He quickly glanced left— the room was clear— then right— there was a man. John entered the apartment carefully peering around each corner. It was only John and *him.*

Gabriel had to have been younger than John, his golden cheeks unblemished. His hair was scraggly rather than slick, his face drenched with sweat. He was sitting in a purple velvet couch and clutching his elevated left leg. A thick bandage that at one point might have been white was now brown and disgusting, wrapped tightly around his thigh. Had he been anybody else, John might have pitied him. Instead he was wary and still alert as he approached, gun pointed.

Gabriel sluggishly, weakly reached for a machine pistol on the coffee table where his leg was heightened. "Don't even think about it," said John.

Gabriel's hand fell at his side. He couldn't if he tried. "You've found me," he spluttered. "Happy?"

"John? Did you find him?" John heard Henry's voice in his ear.

He went closer, looking down at Gabriel's leg and cringing. "He's here. His wound is infected. Badly."

"Paramedics are still four minutes out," said Hall.

John sat on the coffee table a few inches away from Gabriel. His teeth were grinding, his fingers turning claw-like. "You're dying," he told Gabriel. "You can still do the right thing. Your men must have orders. If you die, what are they to do?"

Gabriel let out a brittle laugh like a breath of air. "I don't matter as much as you think, Spears."

"You're in charge," replied John. Gabriel shook his head. "Then who is?" The man before him looked away, eyes shut, ready to pass, but John scooted in closer. "If you tell me what I need to know, when I find Leroux I'll hand her over to your people. So you can get justice—"

"Justice is reserved for weak wills," coughed Gabriel.

"Then revenge."

"That woman..." Gabriel couldn't help but smile, showing a sort of respect for the woman who bested him and brought him to this place. "She'll never get what she wants. He always has a plan."

"He?"

"The man behind the veil. You'll never find him. But he always leaves a trace."

John's mind was brought to the symbol on the schematics of the nuclear bomb. "The X...." Gabriel nodded to confirm.

"The symbol of the Hierarchy."

"And everywhere that symbol is left behind... people die," said John. Somehow the fact made Gabriel smile with pride. "What's his name? Who's the one in charge?"

"I don't know any names." Gabriel faltered, his voice weaker.

"I don't believe you."

"I'm telling you the truth." Gabriel's skin was pale and clammy. "Garcia was the only one who ever met him. For over a decade we've followed the shadow's every wish. Every time we asked for more, he gave it. Not just money but resources. He improved our families' lives...." Each word was quieter and more breath-like than the last.

"I'm losing him, Henry," urged John. He patted Gabriel's cheeks, trying to keep his eyes open. "Stay with me a little longer, come on!"

"But now... he's *here*. Your nation will burn... for what it did to us." Gabriel's body stopped shaking and eyes rolled to the side. John let out a defeated sigh. As paramedics came barreling through the apartment door, John stood and walked out.

Michaels was escorted into the warehouse by his entourage of Hierarchy terrorists. There were long rows of shelves filled with boxes and draped with plastic. Standing between every row were men in groups of five or six. All-in-all, dozens filled the area. They were crowded around a central point of the warehouse where there was nothing and no one save a man in a perfectly tailored, all black suit. He was of a lighter complexion than the rest of the Hierarchy, freckled and wearing an uncharacteristic black combover and a pair of round tortoise shell glasses. The silver watch and cufflinks around his wrists spangled. He was taller than Michaels but thinner, fit and well put together. When he turned his face was half in shadow, but his cheekbones were high and pronounced, his jawline marvelously sculpted and worthy of a prince. "James," he said invitingly. He had a posh English accent, the kind befitting a member of nobility.

"Who are you?" Michaels was surrounded by Hierarchy members. His unease was palpable, sweat beading down his neck.

"I must say I regret the way we've gone about recruiting you to our ranks. Your wife... she is a lovely woman."

"What have you done with her?" Michaels stepped forward but a member of the Hierarchy stopped him with a stiff arm.

"Nothing at all, James. She's still at work, where she should be." The man was so calm it added to Michaels's unease. "And that shall remain. Granted you follow through with the next phase."

"Which is?"

"John Spears."

"What about him?" said Michaels.

"I think you know. Spears has gotten too close to uncovering everything I've worked so hard to accomplish. He must be terminated. You will do this, James."

"You want *me* to kill Spears? Why not get one of your hundred goons to do it?" He waved his hands, bringing attention to the dozens of Hierarchy around him.

"Because you still haven't proven yourself entirely. Do this, James... and you get to decide your future."

The offer was sound yet prompted hesitation in Michaels still. He twiddled his thumbs, staring at the man's expensive-looking shoes. Finally his head rose, and he agreed, "Fine... I'll kill him."

CHAPTER ELEVEN:

10:05 AM: MANHATTAN:

John's NIB-issue truck was shuffling between three lanes dragging north up first avenue, just beyond the neighborhood Kips Bay. *"Now that we've clued in the president's cabinet, naturally, CIA's got their fingers in the pot."* Director Hall was hiding a discontent in his voice, attempting to sound hopeful, but John caught a few sighs during the pauses between his sentences. *"They've offered up some information. Who knows why, but we'll take what we can get."*

"What've they got?" said John.

"Images. From over fifteen countries in Europe and mostly South America. Taken over the last ten years," Henry chimed in.

"Let me guess." John's mind brought him to the Hierarchy's symbol: the X centered within a triangle.

"What's worse," Henry began, *"they're usually preceded by bombings or assassinations. The most recent was in Panama four months ago."*

"That's when they shut down the canal for a day," recalled John.

"Supply chains were sabotaged, global trade bottlenecked. Prices of fuel fluctuated unexpectedly," Hall explained. *"And this is the first we're hearing of this symbol appearing."*

"You think CIA knew about the Hierarchy then?" asked John.

"Oh, I'm certain of it. The question is to what extent? And what else aren't they sharing with us? We're hunting a nuke in the most populated city in America, for God's sake!" Hall made no effort to hide his frustration now.

"Let's just make sure we beat them to any new information, yeah?" John seemed to reassure them.

"That's why we're calling," said Henry. *"I've been monitoring police reports for hours now. Forensics photographed a crime scene just thirty minutes ago and uploaded them to the NYPD server... there's a drawing on the wall in marker. It's the Hierarchy's symbol."*

"Where?"

"Super close to you. Take a left on east thirty-ninth street. Police blocked off the corner of second ave. Looks like a murder took place in front of a convenience store."

"I don't like it," Hall protested. *"Minutes after Gabriel spills the truth about the Hierarchy and their symbol, it shows up close by?"*

"Could be a trap," John agreed.

"But you're going anyway." Henry knew without having to ask.

"Good luck, John," said Hall.

John hung up and set his phone aside, turning onto the narrow thirty-ninth street. He passed a tall black apartment tower that looked like a blade, sharp on one end and blunted in the back. Directly ahead he could see police cruisers and an ambulance. Yellow tape cordoned off the street corner, where onlookers were crowding behind it with terrified faces.

John parked behind an ambulance just outside the crime scene boundary. When he got out he was quickly met by a police officer. "Sir. You can't be here."

John flashed his replacement NIB badge and that was enough. The officer lifted the caution tape for John to duck under. "Detectives," he called. Two men turned, one wearing a black suit and having short, shaggy hair, the other in a brown peacoat with a gelled combover and thin, monolid eyes. John showed them his badge. "John Spears, NIB."

The one in brown offered his hand to shake. "Detective Park," he said. "This is Detective Jordan."

"I half expected FBI to be here," said the other quietly. "But National Intelligence...."

"I expect they'll get here too," replied John. "I'm here for a specific reason." Just then his eye caught it. Beyond the two detectives was a white sheet barely covering a pool of blood that was attempting to spill off into the street. Lining the sidewalk to the left was a convenience store with a flickering LED sign and graffiti-painted columns between its windows. On one of the columns was the mark, so engrained in John's head that he could spot it a mile away. John approached the column and ran his finger along the Hierarchy's symbol. His eyes narrowed and his jaw set. He turned and looked upon the sheet. "Who was he?"

"Avery Latimer," said Detective Park. "Witnesses say he was just minding his business. Next second, *pop!* Suspect wore all black, drove off before anyone could ID him."

John pointed at the symbol on the wall. "Still had time to draw *this.*" He knelt by the body. "May I?" Detective Park extended a hand to allow John access to the body. Detective Jordan was mindful to block the sidewalk so that the onlookers were obscured.

John lifted the sheet and inspected the corpse. The man's eyes were still open. John felt a chill go down his neck, but the sight had not seemed to alarm him. The blood was coming from square in the man's chest. John handed the corner of the sheet to Park, who held it whilst John lifted the man's shirt. "Had to be a three-oh-eight round at least," he said, covering his nose and promptly dropping the sheet over the grotesque sight. *"A sniper." The one on the ground was only here to mark the kill....*

John's eyes widened. His head snapped to his right. The bullet must have come from that way, the way he came. He scanned over the ebony tower at the end of thirty-ninth street. As his eyes rose up the balconies along the corner of the building, he saw a glint— *"SNIPER!"*

John leapt behind one of the convenience store columns just as a bullet came *whizzing* by and pierced Detective Jordan in the chest. *"JORDAN!"* Detective Park dove to his partner and cradled his head, but he was gone.

"GET OUT OF THE OPEN!" yelled John. Another bullet came *snapping* through the column a millimeter from John's nose. That was his queue to find better cover. John sprinted out onto the sidewalk and Park followed him, another bullet shattering one of the store windows. John and Park leapt into the store as a bullet like a red hot light came spinning past them and exploded a bag of chips. Another shot burst a jug of juice to John's right, splattering like blood.

The two raced through the convenience store, the aisles around them being splintered with debris and destroyed everyday objects. Bullets even came through the wall— more inaccurately than before when the sniper had windows to see— but still close enough to be worried.

John and Detective Park plowed through an aisle towards the back of the store, where there was a passage connected to the hotel lobby next-door. *"MOVE!"* John yelled at the guests crouched and screaming in the middle of the dim gilded passage. A police officer had his pistol out and looking out onto the street. A shot came straight through the front doors and laid him out.

John's breathing was a whirlwind, his heart ravaging his chest. He pressed against the wall just beside the exit doors. The firing had stopped but it was merely a waiting game for the sniper. He glanced around the lobby of the hotel; the walls and furnishings were trimmed with gold, as was the mirror framed on the wall behind the concierge's desk. John took out his phone and dialed Henry. When he picked up he panted, "Henry! Quickly, there's a sniper. I'm gonna send you a picture, I need you to figure out what floor and room he's on!" He did not wait for a response. He opened his camera app and pointed at the mirror, where, from its low angle, he could see the glinting of the sniper's scope in its high-up balcony. He took the photo and sent it, just as another bullet— presumably a warning shot so that he would stay put— landed on the welcome mat just by his feet. "Did you get it? East corner of the tower!"

"It's hard to tell from the picture alone but matching with GPS images... that's the thirty-second floor, John!"

John wasted no time. He got up, put his phone in his pocket, and made for the bellhop cowering on the floor. Detective Park caught his drift when he started rolling the gilded luggage cart towards the entrance. "You don't have to come with me," said John, but Park knew well the risks, and scowled, standing behind John with his hands wrapped around the cart.

The two pushed forward, crouching behind the luggage as the cart rolled out onto the sidewalk. A bullet came and *pinged* off the top of the cart, the vibration intense enough to make Park remove his hand and shake feeling back into it. The cart rattled onto the street and another bullet tore through one of its suitcases.

"GO!" John and Park sprang out from opposite sides of the cart, guns aimed high enough to miss the tower and still deter the sniper from letting off another shot. The two emptied their magazines until they reached a point of the sidewalk where the view from the balcony was too steep to fire from. Out of breath, they pressed on, reloading and entering the building.

There was a security guard in the lobby surrounded by cowering civilians. *"NYPD!"* yelled Park. "Lock this place down! Nobody in or out!" He and John called for the elevators, for which there were two adjacent ones. When the first came, John told Park to go on, while he smartly waited for the second, so that the sniper could not descend whilst they were going up.

They did not account for the stairs, where the sniper was already well on his way down, carrying a large bag around his shoulder, all black like his attire. He was looking at his phone screen, where a camera feed showed the elevators and lobby in four squares, John and Detective Park ascending in the top two. When he reached the base of the grey stairs, his face became evident. His skin was rather pallid, his hair a sloppy texture, short and militaristic. He had brown eyes so dark they might as well have been black. The sniper wore an arrogant, prideful smirk as he ambled through the lobby paying no mind to the citizens eyeing him down. His tranquilizing lack of alarm seemed to panic them even more.

When the sniper reached the back exit, there was a guard waiting for him with his hand out. "Where do you think you're going? Nobody in or—" The guard was unable to finish his words before the sniper latched onto his arm and twisted. He forced the guard into a wall in the alley and drove his elbow into his head, crushing his face against the bricks.

The smile on the sniper's face expanded. He put away the touch screen phone in exchange for an old plastic burner. He put the phone to his ear and said, in a deep English accent, "Spears is on east thirty-ninth street. Get him before he goes."

John and Detective Park reached the thirty-second floor. Park had waited for John outside his elevator, gun pointed at the corner condo down the left hall. They each took a side of the door. John gave the nod for Park to kick the door in. They spread left and right but the condo was quiet. It was a sleek, luxurious apartment with a high-rise view and modern silver and grey décor. The two met back up in the main room, where the only thing they saw in common was the balcony door, cracked open.

John slid open the glass and walked out onto the balcony, cool autumn winds gusting and whistling. John noticed subtle scratch marks on the top of the balcony railing. "He was here," he muttered. "His rifle was...." For a moment he imagined he was the sniper, his line of sight identical, seeing the crime scene down below, and the body of the fallen detective. "Let's go. He can't have gotten far—" After John turned to leave, he noticed something else. Etched in the grey separation between the glass sliding doors was a mark: the symbol of the Hierarchy.

10:45 AM: MANHATTAN:

A squadron of police officers and FBI agents was scouring the blocks around the apartment building. John had been standing at the entrance beside Detective Park, but when the body of his partner rolled past on a stretcher covered by a sheet, Park got in his car and made off to follow the coroner's van. John was dialing a number on his phone whilst walking back to his vehicle. "Henry," he said dejectedly.

"*Did the hotel staff give you anything?*" Henry inquired.

"Yeah, the name of the guest renting out the apartment."

"*Who was he?*"

"Jonathan Garcia." John and Henry shared the same sigh. "They've gone beyond keeping a low profile. The Hierarchy's more spread out, setting traps hoping to take me out." John got in his car and started it, taking off without a moment's waste.

"*They're far more organized than we imagined hours ago,*" agreed Henry. "*Too much was going on, we must've looked past it. The license plates from the trucks outside where Gabriel was hiding out... the Hierarchy members were U.S. citizens."*

"They've been embedding themselves in our society for years."

"Maybe over a decade, according to Gabriel," said Henry.

"I'm not returning to headquarters just yet." John made a left onto second avenue headed south. "I'll remain active in the area just in case something pops off."

"Sounds good." The line clicked and John set his phone aside. In his rear-view mirror he eyed a suspicious brown van tailing close behind. He wanted to get a closer look at the front seat but the window was lightly tinted. John veered into the right line, seeing if the van would follow. Side-by-side with it now, he could see the passenger, his window rolling down, and a *gun* pointing out of it.

John slammed the breaks, but at the rear of the van was an even worse place to be. The rear doors swung open; three men in all black starting firing assault rifles out of the back. John yanked his wheel and turned, bullets chasing after him down the short road. He swerved to the left into an oncoming lane. He dodged between the vehicles head-on and parked, fearful horns blaring.

The van attempted to align with him but John shifted around to maintain a distance. Gunfire began showering the windshields of innocent bystanders. John pulled out his pistol and waited for the opportune shots but could not find them. Cars began to spin out of control and flip left and right. Suddenly the terrorists' van came sliding to the left side of the street and smashed into John's car. He regained control, only now he was on the sidewalk, honking for civilians to get out of the way.

He wrenched to his right and got back on the road, colliding with the terrorist van. The passenger was reaching over the driver with his gun and pelting John's bulletproof window. The two vehicles were in the dead center of the road, with all oncoming cars doing their best to veer out of the way now. Down the street, however, was an eighteen wheeler semi chugging towards them. John and the driver of the terrorist van locked gazes. It was now a game of chicken. They each pushed against the other truck, grinding and sparking metal. They were at a stalemate, pushing each other against the center of the street as the semi-truck threatened to decimate them both.

John unbuckled his seatbelt, one hand on the wheel. "Well here goes nothing," he sighed. The trunk's horn was louder and louder, yards away now—John opened his door and *leapt.* The sinister grins on the martyrs' faces dropped as John hit the ground and tumbled harshly. The next second, a ball of fire erupted from the two obliterated vehicles. The semi, still somewhat intact, screeched to a halt, its cargo unlatching and skidding across the asphalt and sending debris flying into the bases of buildings and sidewalks all around. John was sprawled on the ground, scratches torn through his clothes, his head leaking blood. Through hazy eyes he saw nothing but fire and carnage. Slowly he faded, whilst the terrified screams of the innocent filled his ears.

CHAPTER TWELVE:

11:10 AM: BELLEVUE HOSPITAL: MANHATTAN:

The outside of the building was rather ordinary and plain, a black glass structure no taller or more special than its surroundings. The inside, however, boasted an extraordinary brick and marble façade as though the outside of the building were decades older and flipped into the interior. Its white archways and cornices were bound by a semicircle of four curved floors leveled atop one another. Above, clouded sunlight shone through a grid-like canopy of glass and steel. It looked more like an ornate train station fused with today's technology rather than a hospital. Dozens were crowding the ground floor, looks of angst and deprivation and despair to go around.

Henry Spears was among the many clamoring towards the reception desk. He was out of breath, outpacing the two NIB agents following him. His black suit jacket was wrinkled and large enough to make one think he had lost ten extra pounds on top of his already skinny frame. Henry pushed to the front of the line, brushing back his hair, which was damp with gel and sweat. The receptionist, wearing purple scrubs with pink ribbons, shared the same disapproving glare as the visitors in line. "Sir, you have to wait your turn like everyone else—"

"National Intelligence!" Henry slapped his badge on her desk but she was not having it.

"*Analyst,*" she chided, waving back over the visitor who was speaking to her before Henry bumped into him.

"You don't understand—" Henry was aided by the two special agents at his side, throwing their badges on the receptionist's desk. These were men she would not deny. "I'm looking for my brother. John Spears."

John lay in a white bed in the ambulatory wing on the second floor. The TV against the beige wall was broadcasting the ALN network at a low volume. "*The upsurge in violent attacks, vehicle crashes, and police activity has people speculating...*" reported a woman with wavy, dirty blonde hair with streaks of black, wearing a vibrant red suit that matched the slanted ALN logo on her microphone. "*... local officials and the mayor's office are apparently overwhelmed by callers trying to find out what's going on, but as of yet, no new information has been provided. To many, it seems far outside the realm of coincidence for all these events to be occurring within such a short window. We spoke with witnesses to a crash in which a vehicle spilled over the railing on FDR Drive, leading to a yet unspecified number of victims...*"

The ALN logo swirled past the screen, transitioning to another segment with the same reporter holding a microphone to a woman's chin. "*They must've been going fast! How else would they have gone over that rail?*"

"*You didn't see the crash directly?*"

"*Nah, it happened so suddenly! One second I was driving, then the car next to me got rear-ended. Next I saw, people were getting out of their cars and looking over the rail in the water.*"

"*And what did you see in the water?*"

"*There was a car that was sinking. But eventually one man came out! We all saw him swimming underneath the highway, ain't nobody knew where!*"

"What did this man look like?"

The door was thrown open frantically. Henry entered the patient room and bent over his knees, letting go a sigh of relief and simultaneously catching his breath. He came around the edge of the bed to John's side and put a hand on his arm. "John..." he muttered. "How long until he wakes up?"

A doctor wearing almond-colored glasses and a long white coat stood on the other side of the bed, where the heart rate monitor was steadily beeping away. "He's been through a lot of trauma, your brother. The sedative will keep him out for maybe six, eight hours."

"No, that won't do. You need to wake him up now," demanded Henry.

"That really wouldn't be advisable—"

"Doctor. This man is instrumental to a national security investigation. You have to cooperate with us and wake him up—"

"I don't *have* to do anything. This man's health is within the purview of his doctors, not you, Mr. Spears." The doctor was firm and started walking towards the two NIB agents in the doorway.

Henry, however, was still up for a fight, "Doctor—"

"I'm sorry," the doctor said more tenderly this time. "*When* he wakes up, we'll ask *him* if he's willing to discharge early. Until then, I can't help you." Henry nodded, but the doctor wanted to leave on a hopeful note, not realizing the more he spoke the more Henry wanted to strike him with his fist, "I understand whatever investigation you're undergoing is urgent. But pressuring John into waking up and resuming his duties... it's cruel. There's always someone else for the job."

Henry shook his head, unintentionally squeezing John's arm so tightly that he left a white handprint on it as the doctor left. "If only that were the case." He turned to the NIB agents, standing quietly with their hands folded like a pair of secret service bodyguards. "They're gonna come after him," Henry declared. "Everyone in this hospital is in danger. Is there nothing we can do?"

"We can't force the hospital to turn away patients in need all for one agent," replied one of the agents. "But we can bolster security on this floor."

"Get on that," ordered Henry, not meaning to sound as authoritarian as he did. He looked at his brother, lying palely and battered. "Let's hope our backup isn't too late."

11:28 AM: BELLEVUE HOSPITAL: MANHATTAN:

Henry paced the end of John's bed, hands wrapped around his cellphone. His laptop was opened on the chair at his bedside, with Henry's eyes darting for it every few seconds. One of the NIB agents poked his head in. "Well?" said Henry, desperate for news.

"Agents are still ten minutes out."

"The hell is taking them?" Henry huffed again.

Not taking it to heart, the agent calmly replied, "Traffic." Understandable enough, Henry supposed, nodding. The agent departed from the wing, giving a nod to another suited guard posted outside the patient room. He descended a set of stairs until he reached the semicircle colonnade that flanked the ground level two floors down. He wore a grave expression across his face, eyes suspiciously dancing between the ill citizenry, the front door, the healthy visitors, and back to the door. One hand gripped his radio, the other tickled the leather of his hip holster.

A second lapsed before he was able to compute, upon which time there were ten Hierarchy terrorists in black flooding the hospital atrium. The agent seized his pistol and yelled, *"STOP RIGHT THERE!"* To the man in the front, a familiar face, James Michaels. The agent was so taken aback that his legs tottered, his pistol lowering slightly. In that moment a terrorist to Michaels's left opened fire with a suppressed submachine gun. The agent fell and screams ensued; people began pouring out of the hospital in throngs. The terrorists ignored them, only here for one purpose.

Henry and the agent guarding him and John both looked at each other, alarmed by the shrieking from below. "I'll go check it out," said the agent. Henry gesticulated as if he was about to stop him, about to say, *"Don't go, you fool!"* but he faltered.

Henry peeked out into the bright white hallway and saw John's doctor, hurrying from room to room. Henry called for him when he popped out again. "Hey!" The doctor approached like a headless animal, licking his lips madly like he was trying to sand them down. "We're under attack," said Henry, composed. "You have to wake him up."

"Mr. Spears, I told you—"

Henry took ahold of the doctor by his arms and whispered with an air of desperate urgency, "By time the other agents show up, we'll be *dead!*"

The doctor needed no more convincing. *"Flumazenil!"* he spouted. The doctor rushed to a locked cabinet in the corner of John's room and twisted his key into a drawer. He pulled out a small, clear bottle with a white label, and inserted a syringe.

"Is that enough?" said Henry, observing the small dose.

"Well, not exactly... the counter-sedative has a shorter duration than the benzodiazepine—"

"Meaning what?" blurted Henry, losing any sort of patience.

"It'll take multiple doses spread over a several minutes and monitored over several hours to—"

"Just give him a full dose!" yelled Henry. At the same time two loud gunshots rang out from down the hall, and a scream, presumably of the agent who went out there.

"If I inject your brother with a milligram of flumazenil, the risk of seizures, rebound sedation, withdrawal symptoms skyrockets! It can put him in a coma!"

Henry, breathing heavily and feeling his chest as if it were going to implode, bent and held the end of John's bed. He looked at his brother, trembling. "The risk is greater if we do nothing," he decided. "Do it."

The doctor was shaking trying to extract the liquid. Henry gripped his hand to keep it still, a gesture that seemed to calm the doctor if only slightly. He approached John and injected him directly in the vein. "How long?"

"A minute. Two tops. If not...." The doctor did not care to express what that meant, for Henry already knew.

On the ground floor, Michaels made only a gesture for the terrorists to file out. One of them grabbed the receptionist who Michaels pointed at, picking her up by her hair with little remorse. "Where is John Spears?" Michaels said calmly. The woman's lips were glued, the only sounds coming out of her the painful breathing from her nose as her hair was nearly plucked out the back of her head. "If you tell us, no harm will come to you. If you don't—"

One of the terrorists took that as a queue to shoot and kill one of the hostages cowering beside a white column. Michaels's face shared the same horror as the receptionist, who started to weep. Michaels truly had no interest in harming anyone else, an aberration that the woman read on his face. "Second floor," she cried.

Michaels nodded, his eyes falling to the floor with relief. "Let her go," he ordered. The woman was roughly pushed aside and she collapsed. At the same time, bullets started flying from behind Michaels. He ducked and turned towards the entrance door, where a half-dozen suited NIB agents were pouring in. Outnumbering and outgunning them, the terrorists still scuttled behind columns and the reception desk, popping out only to exchange fire with the agents.

Michaels pointed at two terrorists and yelled, *"You two with me! Let's go!"* The three ran the opposite direction of the agents, making for the stairwell beneath the semicircle ceiling.

Upstairs, John's eyes opened. Henry finally took in air again. He lightly tapped John's face and shoulder, for he was groggy and addled. "H... Henry," he moaned.

"That's right," said Henry as though a miracle had taken place. "Look, John, there's not a lot of time. I need you wake up, get on your feet, come on!" Henry pulled John upright with little care, John groaning and aching, the doctor biting his coat as if he felt the pain himself. "Come on, John!" Henry slung John's arm around his shoulder, which seemed to hurt John the most. He stood, and John was forced to follow suit.

"W-what's h-happening?" John stuttered. "I f-f-feel... c-cold."

"That's the withdrawal," said the doctor. "I told you we shouldn't have—"

"It's too late for all of that!" said Henry with a raised voice. He let go of John and grabbed his shoulders as the doctor shone and inspected his eyes with an ophthalmoscope. The bit of light across his irises seemed to help wake John a little, but he was still reaching for supports as he limped across the room, stirring. "They're coming, John. The Hierarchy. They're coming for *you.*"

John did not respond but he slammed against the drug cabinet to keep himself upright. He opened the drawer and pulled out a bottle and syringe. "Oh no," the doctor urged, "you *cannot* inject yourself with *anything else!*"

"It's not... for me," said John weakly. He filled a syringe to the brim with some clear liquid, then tossed the bottle aside. "Get in the bathroom." Henry and the doctor did as he said, hiding away whilst John pressed his back against the wall next to the hospital room door. He took deep breaths, slapped his cheeks trying to fire back up his senses. John peered through the door's window and his eyes widened at the sight of Michaels, he and two terrorists splitting up to clear patient rooms in search of him. John backed away, waiting.

When his door finally opened, John was there. He pushed the door shut with his foot while his hand was jabbing the syringe into the terrorist's neck. He plunged the cold liquid into the man's veins, wrapped his arm around him as the drug laced his system, as he slipped away.

John guided his body gently to the floor. He tried to lift the machine gun strapped to the terrorist's shoulder, but it felt like a knife was being wedged between his ribs. There was surely a fracture there. He set the weapon back down and pushed the body over, taking instead the pistol from behind his back. *"Henry!"* he whispered, picking up his pile of worn, asphalt-stained clothes from the corner of the room. As Henry and the doctor came out of the bathroom, laying eyes over John's work, they heard one of the other terrorists yelling out a name. John slipped on his pants and shirt and approached the door. Again they heard the Hierarchy member calling something in Portuguese.

Impetuously, John sprang from behind the door and opened fire through the window, loud snaps and shattering noises forcing Henry and the doctor to shield their ears. When the terrorist had fallen, John was eye-to-eye with Michaels halfway down the hallway. In a flash, Michaels dashed the other way, making for the staircase. John forced the door open and ran after him. *"JOHN!"* Henry yelled, but there was no reaching him now.

As John turned the hallway corner to the stairs, he suddenly forgot how to use his legs and tumbled down them. He had to ignore the pain, though, and get up again. Punching his thighs to get them to work properly, he raced down the steps towards the first floor.

When he reached the ground level, bullets immediately started flying his way from the terrorists in cover on his side of the semicircle, and indirectly from the NIB agents battling them. John dropped and followed Michaels, who was striding down a hallway towards the back exit.

John reached the sliding door, gun pointed. When he stepped outside into the cold wind tunnel of the grey alley, he felt metal against his temple. "Drop it, Bison."

John did as Michaels ordered. "What are you waiting for?"

"I'm no murderer, John."

"Tell that to the agents and officers that have died today."

"You can't put that on me. I'm only doing what I have to, to keep my family safe—" John was in no mood to hear his excuses. He turned with expert swiftness, misdirecting Michaels's pistol and kicking out his feet from under him. Now it was John with the gun, aiming down at Michaels on the ground. "Well done," he complimented.

Michaels reached for John's pistol on the ground next to him but John yelled, *"Don't try it!"*

Michaels surrendered, hands by his head. "What now, John? Gonna take me back to NIB?"

John looked at an ambulance glowing, already on and chugging exhaust into the alley. "I have a better idea," he said. "You're gonna take me to your boss." John tugged Michaels by his vest and forced him to his feet.

"I can't do that."

"You say you're not a murderer. Neither am I. But don't think after everything you've done today, I won't put a bullet in you." There was fury in John's voice.

"Just calm down, okay—"

"This isn't a negotiation. *Director.*"

The look of discomfiture was apparent upon Michaels's face and low shoulders. He nodded, then mumbled with defeat, "Alright, John. I'll take you to him."

11:52 AM: MANHATTAN:

Michaels was forced to drive the ambulance at gunpoint. "We're nearly there," he said. "Can I... make a request?"

John was hardly willing to grant the request, so he saw no point in declining his speech. "Sure."

"Can I... can I call my wife?"

"No," John immediately shot it down.

"At least promise me you won't involve her. She doesn't deserve all I've brought upon us."

"*Is* she involved?"

"Not by choice." Michaels's voice shook, his eyes watering. "She was just... minding her business. Her and her sister. On vacation. I figured there were more dangerous places, but... at that point nothing I said would have changed her mind. Our marriage had been falling apart for years. Entire weeks passed where I didn't see her, didn't hear from her. It was normal. And yet, when a month passed and there was no ransom to be paid, no way of getting her back...." Michael's eyes were glassy and bulging. "She thought I was a monster. She thought I didn't love her enough to rescue her. My son... wondering why his mother hadn't come home...." His fingers tightened over the steering wheel. "The reason they didn't ask for money was because they wanted something more. They only released her when I agreed to work for them."

"How long ago was this?" John asked.

"Over a year ago. Ever since I've done what they've told me to. Using NIB resources to help them smuggle in their bomb."

"And you're okay with that? With them blowing up New York?" John looked at the man with disgust.

"If it meant keeping my wife and son alive and safe..." Michaels did not finish the sentiment. "That was the only reason she stayed with me. I had her convinced that if she left, she'd be taken again, or worse."

"Hell of a way to keep a marriage together," said John.

"She saw things in me that no one else did." A single tear rolled down Michaels's cheek. "She revived a part of me I didn't know was still there, not knowing or even caring if I was a good man or not. She made me one. I owe her everything. But even she would rather die than be a coward like I am. I tried to set up an escape, to make plans to get out, but she wouldn't go for it. And *now...* that'll never happen. I just hope God is merciful. That when that bomb goes off, she's far from it—"

"That bomb is *not* going off," John contended.

Michaels chuffed, as if it were merely wishful thinking. He then stopped the ambulance midway down the street from a tall grey and brown warehouse. "He's in there."

"You better not be lying to me, Michaels—"

"I have no reason to. Either in jail, or helping you, everything I care about is doomed. I'm no use to him anymore."

"Who is he?"

Before Michaels could answer, his phone began to ring. He took it out of his pocket, one of the Hierarchy's plastic burners, and answered it on speakerphone. *"Hello, James,"* an English accent hissed.

"We just left the hospital. We got him. Spears is dead," said Michaels shakily.

"If only I could believe you, James. I know he's with you right now."

"W-what are you talking about?" pleaded Michaels.

"I see you."

John and Michaels shared a look of shock. They both saw the glimmering scope from atop the warehouse. "Wait, *don't!—*" Michaels's sputtering was interjected by a bullet *zipping* through the ambulance window and *cracking*. A hole in his chest burst with red.

John, eyes swollen and startled, hurried out of the ambulance as sniper bullets pursued him, splitting the ground and *pinging* the vehicle. He hid behind the back of the ambulance, flinching with each *plink* against the metal.

After a moment without gunfire, John had to make a move. Would it be like last time at the crime scene? Was the sniper merely waiting for him to come out again? It was a risk he had to take. Pistol-first he peeked slowly around the ambulance. The glimmering was gone.

John cautiously made up the sidewalk and towards the warehouse. Upon entry, there were only boxes. Shelves and aisles lined with cardboard and metal, but no people, no terrorists or their English leader. John kicked over a box, letting out a growl of frustration.

He left the warehouse with the same discretion, making his way back to the ambulance and rubbing his sore ribs.

There he saw Michaels, dead and sprawled over the dash. He opened the driver door and pulled him out. He gently brought his heavy body to the ground. He looked at him for a moment, not with disgust now, but with pity, and with dread. John closed Michaels's eyelids and lay his hand over his stomach, patting it before he stood.

John got in the ambulance, blood smearing the seat, window, steering wheel and his clothes. Before putting it in drive, he stared another moment at the body. He lifted his head doggedly, shifted gears, and drove off.

CHAPTER THIRTEEN:

John left the restroom wearing a clean grey thermal and a green army jacket, his worn jeans still stained with black asphalt and specks of blood. After disposing of the old clothes he approached a desk on the top ring of the bullpen. A woman sat clacking her keyboard, rigorously chewing a wad of pink gum. "Excuse me," said John. "I wanted to know the status of someone. Agent Collins, he was leading a team a few hours ago at Kips Bay and was taken to the hospital."

The woman rattled the keyboard with a flurry. "Yes, there he is, Gregory Collins."

"What's his condition?"

"Hang on," she replied. After a moment her fingers were sprawled across the keys, dormant, unmoving. Her eyes met John's, twinkling in a sympathetic way. "It says here... Agent Collins passed away."

"*What? How?* He was wearing a vest, he couldn't have had more than a few broken ribs—"

"Doctor's report says he had internal bleeding. They didn't detect it until they were too late," the woman explained. "I'm sorry."

John hung his head, rubbing his eyes. "I'd like to speak to the family later, if possible."

"Of course," she said, staring icily at her computer monitor.

"Thank you," John said with a low breath. He saw Henry sitting at his station not far away and waved him over. Henry followed him to the hallway across from the main entrance of the communications hub.

"Where are you going?" Henry asked.

"Armory," John put simply. "Did you get anything off Michaels's phone?"

"It's too soon to know for sure. There are no messages, only calls back and forth between him and Gabriel." John carried on down the hall as though he hadn't heard a word Henry said. When they turned the corner to a brightly lit corridor, he added, "If I was there with you, I could've maybe heard something on that call you didn't."

"Sorry," John muttered disingenuously.

"Hey." Henry pulled John's arm and spun him around before he entered a white door. "You're not gonna acknowledge what happened at the hospital back there?" John seemed out of it, searching his memory but not finding an answer. "You abandoned me there in the middle of a firefight."

"Henry, I—"

"I'm not gonna hold it against you, I'm not ten. I know Michaels needed to be caught, but...." Henry had no way of expressing just what he was feeling, but John understood.

"I acted impulsively," admitted John. "I got eyes on Michaels and... I saw red. I'm sorry. I shouldn't have left you there—"

"No, you did the right thing, just... we're in this together, yeah?"

John needed no time to think that one through. He set aside his lament for Agent Collins, heartily tapped Henry on the shoulder and said, "A thousand percent."

Henry grinned and followed John into a pearlescent room with blinding fluorescents lining the ceilings. "What was he like? The Hierarchy's leader."

"English." John approached the armorer, standing in a glass vestibule that separated the white room from the armory. "The connection makes sense now. Garcia was the only one to meet him in person, and he was in London before returning to Brazil. Whether or not the bomb was smuggled from England is up in the air, but we're closer to finding out who's funding the group."

"That's progress, I suppose," said Henry, walking into the black room after John. Rifles, pistols, shotguns, and crates of ammunition lined rows of racks and shelves along the walls. "But there's nothing left to go on."

"There has to be something." John clicked a magazine into a black forty-caliber pistol and thrust it into his hip holster.

"There isn't," insisted Henry. "They cover their tracks well. Even the warehouse. The man who rented it out owns another business out of state so he's not around. Seemingly no affiliation but of course I'll keep digging." John puffed open a black duffel bag and loaded it with magazines a submachine gun. "Why do you need all these guns?"

"Better safe than sorry," John quipped.

He wrapped the duffel around his shoulder and left the armory, Henry trailing close behind. "What'll you do now?" John was at a loss; the more he asked himself the question the deeper his mind sank into a sort of fugue whiteness. "There's no point rushing out the door," said Henry. "Stay here. I'll get Hall, we can go over everything we've gathered thus far. It's really the only thing we can do to piece together the investigation." John nodded in agreement. Letting the duffel strap loosen around his shoulder, he followed Henry out of the armory, and back to the atrium.

12:30 PM: NIB HEADQUARTERS: MANHATTAN:

John was bent with arms spread across the side of the glass table in the conference room. The blinds were opened, through which he often saw the same pair of fuchsia glasses glancing at them inquisitively. Jennifer's auburn hair made her stand out, but she wasn't the only set of eyes watching them with intent.

"What about the ACT?" said John.

"It's been seven hours without a sign of them." John's gaze at Henry for stating the obvious was pointed. "They're doing the smart thing. Laying low, not moving around. Which makes them impossible to find."

"Not impossible," said Hall. "It's too late to reverse track them with satellites, and they've been careful enough not to do anything stupid like running red lights." Running a red light was what alerted the NIB to Alec's presence in the first place. "But we can make our business known through more public measures." He shook his cellphone in his hand, standing up and walking towards the glass door. "I'll have NYPD set out an APB for Leroux and her man. Frankly should've done it hours ago, but... secret intelligence." With those words he waved his hands to behold the great main communications hub, then left the conference room dialing a number.

"Why don't we try getting in contact with CIA?" proposed John. "They're bound to know more that we don't, considering they've been gathering intel on the Hierarchy for God-knows how long."

"We can try, but I wouldn't get our hopes up," replied Henry. "You know how they are."

"Compartmentalize," John spoke of the CIA's basic precept. "Worth a try. Why don't you see if you can get in contact with someone over there?" Henry nodded and left the conference room for his station. John turned towards the television mounted against the curving wall, where images of Hierarchy members were sliding by: Garcia, Gabriel, and other deceased and captured ones. He had half the mind to interrogate some of them himself but remembered what happened last time. For one, he preferred not to lose control again, and for another, knew they would not break. There were other agents better suited who had yet to get the job done, so John considered the crusade a waste of precious minutes.

After a moment of staring at the sliding pictures, he felt his phone vibrating against his thigh. It was an unknown number. John picked it up. *"Agent Spears,"* he heard the priggish, evil voice he had heard in the ambulance. It was the head of the Hierarchy, dark and malicious. John felt the best course was reticence, which attracted further probing by the Englishman, *"I know you're alone. I wouldn't attempt to trace the call or gather your brother and director."*

How could he possibly know that? John thought. "What's this about?"

"You don't know who I am, but I know exactly *who you are."*

"Care to enlighten?" John said.

"About myself? Hmm, I'm afraid not. Don't want to make it that *easy, do we?"* the Englishman taunted. *"But about you? There is so much. Thirty-two— turning thirty-three tomorrow, happy birthday. Columbia University, twenty-ten, criminal justice degree. Four years in the United States Army, a veteran of the Syrian Civil War. Trained in military strategy by the Israeli army to combat the Caliphate—"*

"So you have the same intelligence on me as the ACT. So what?"

"I have more than that, John. I have omniscience.*"* John let out a scoff, but the Englishman continued, undeterred, *"We are at the halfway mark today, it appears. The past twelve hours have proven a challenge."*

"Sorry about that."

"That's quite alright," said the Englishman, *"because now, you're going to make me a much happier man."*

He was sure of himself, John would have to give him that; yet peering around the bullpen he could not help but sneer at the Englishman's overconfidence. "And how's that?" he asked.

"NIB headquarters is approximately fifteen minutes from Cathedral Parkway, one hundred-tenth street subway station. You are to go there and catch the twelve-fifty-two C train to Columbus Circle—"

John interrupted him with an involuntary cackle. "Why the hell would I do all that?"

"Because if you don't," drawled the Englishman, *"I will blow up a police precinct."*

John looked at his watch: 12:35. "You're bluffing."

"Are you willing to take the chance?"

John stirred, considering the ramifications. If he waited too long to decide.... "Let's say I do this. There's no way I'll make it. I'm in the Upper East Side, I'll be better off driving directly to Columbus Circle—"

"No!" the Englishman raised his voice, then lowered it to a calm again. *"No, that won't do. Why, you ask? Well, I want to make sure you know how to follow instructions, John."* John wanted to smash his phone. He was not keen on taking orders from a faceless terrorist. *"You will do this, and you will tell no one, not even your brother. If you do, I will know."*

"How?" asked John, this time out loud rather than in his head.

"Twelve-fifty-two, John. You're running out of time. Lives are on the line. Save your boys in blue." The phone hung up with a muffled click. John grabbed his green jacket slung around a chair and fast-walked out of the conference room. Rushing through the atrium he felt Jennifer's pink-framed eyes over him again, as well as Henry's, and Hall's from up in his office.

Henry put on hold his phone call and stepped in front of John with a hand to his chest, saying, "Where are you going?"

John scrambled for an excuse, anything, his mind failing him. "I'm... going home, I have a headache."

Henry did not buy it for a second. "Headache, what are you talking about? We have a job to do—"

"I have to get out of here." John shoved past Henry, who looked stupefied. John hustled past the side security checkpoint to the parking garage, Henry's befuddled eyes chasing him.

John got in the agency SUV, started it, and drove off post-haste.

12:51 PM: 110TH STREET STATION: MANHATTAN:

John sprinted down the steps heaving his duffel bag behind his back. The train platform was grey and silver, with the pocked yellow line before the track. John's head swiveled, reading the signs to see which one was the C train. There was a man with the typical characteristics of a Hierarchy member walking towards him, only he was wearing a public service jumpsuit, a custodian holding a trash bag. John reeled, awaiting a knife or a gun to come out of the man's pocket as the train was screeching loudly into position. "Get on the train," said the man, shoving John's shoulder.

John was about to miss it, the doors sliding shut. He leapt onto the train, surrounded by a dozen-or-so citizens holding onto silver poles and sitting in orange and yellow seats trimmed with dull grey.

John held one of the warm handrails, his eyes darting around for anything or anyone that appeared suspicious. In every direction there were voices, people on phones or talking amongst each other, a lot of the chatter having to do with the events of the past twelve hours. Many of the people on the train,

John had deduced, were on their way to Penn Station, where they would take the transit to New Jersey or the rail to Long Island.

As the train chugged into dark tunnels, John panted, overwhelmed by the noise and expecting at any moment something terrible would happen. *I hate trains,* his mind viciously told him, over and over again. He stared at every face, watched every lip move, listened to every word and conversation he could.

Through a window to the next car over, John spotted a man with black hair and sunglasses staring back at him. At the same time, John's phone rang. It was Henry again. He looked back up at the man and saw him shake his head with disapproval. John ignored the call, the notification on his screen reading seven missed calls.

John anxiously tapped the railing. There had to be a way to get the message to Henry without tipping off the Hierarchy. There was a woman sitting to his left texting. He cleared his throat to get her attention, but she wouldn't look up. John's eyes shifted between the terrorist watching him and the woman to his left. He was free to use his left hand to tap her shoulder. "What?" she carped.

"Listen to me," John whispered through the corner of his pursed lips. "I'm a federal agent."

"Yeah? Good for you," she said, ticked off.

"You don't understand. People are in danger!" John tried to emphasize *danger* but it was difficult whilst trying to pretend he wasn't speaking.

"No kidding. We all know what's been going on today. Why are you talking like that?"

"I'm being watched. I can't dial for backup so I need you to do it." John knew he was taking a gamble. If the head of the Hierarchy hacked his phone, he could be listening to him now, regardless of it being a phone call. As an extra precaution he pressed a hand against his right pants pocket where the phone was, in the hopes of muffling its microphone. "This is a matter of life and death."

He was slowly coaxing the woman but she still seemed skeptical. "What's in it for me?"

John's face pinched lividly. "You get to *survive, Lady!* Now please! Take down this number!"

"Alright, alright!" It was simple enough to get her to use the phone she was already glued to. She dialed the number as John gave it to her.

"Tell him John is the one calling. Tell him a police precinct..." John tried to lower his voice even more so nobody around him would be alarmed and start talking to him, "... is going to be destroyed if I don't do what they say."

At NIB headquarters, Director Hall was pacing in Michaels's old office behind the desk. Henry was sitting across from him, a still stunned look written on his face. Suddenly, the phone rang. Hall stuck out his hand, beckoning Henry to answer it. "National Intelligence Bureau, Director Steven Hall's office...." His face turned, his brows raising. *"What?"* This caught Hall's attention. He stood over Henry, watching his eyes enlarge. "A police precinct? This doesn't make sense, *who's watching him?"*

"What's going on, Henry?"

"Okay... okay. Thank you." Henry hung up the phone. Hall's squeezed brow line begged for more information. "It's John. He's under duress somehow."

"Duress?"

"The Hierarchy's making him take a train to Columbus Circle. If he doesn't follow their orders, a police precinct is gonna blow up," Henry explained.

Hall's hand covered his mouth, a horrified expression crossing him. "Which precinct?"

"I don't know."

"Well, it could be any! There are seventy-seven in Manhattan alone!"

"I know!" Henry retorted with equal alarm.

"We have to get every analyst we have on this," said Hall, rushing doggedly out of the office with Henry behind him. "Contact every precinct. We have to find out where they're targeting... before it's too late."

CHAPTER FOURTEEN:

The silver train slowed to a screeching stop. *"Fifty-ninth street, Columbus Cir-cle,"* the disconnected voice addressed through the speakers. The train was more packed-in than it was when John first came on. Though a crowd of departing passengers obscured him from the terrorist's line of sight, he advanced towards him rather than getting off the train. John slid open the door to the next car, reaching for something small in the side pocket of his duffel bag.

His eyes met with the terrorist's; he dropped his bag in between the train doors just as they were about to close. A loud *ding* came from the speakers, and the voice, *"Stand clear of the closing doors."* With the man's gaze momentarily averted, John lunged towards him. His knife slid cleanly between the man's ribs, but he squeezed and pushed John's face and arms, grappling, fighting back. John punched him in the side but was pushed away. Screaming citizens were rushing off the train while there were onlookers from the platform.

The terrorist was wide and intimidating enough to show little pain pulling the blade out of his torso. This time it was John against the knife. He dodged a swipe and a thrust, blocked a punch with his forearm but was pushed back, tripping atop a set of tricolored seats. John used the backwards momentum to flick the knife away with his foot, flexing downwards on the return to kick the man in the chest. John got up, dodging another punch, flitting side-to-side around a handrail. The next attack he caught and pulled. The terrorist's head hit the rail, his skull giving off a resonant ring. John held onto the wrist and side-stepped, wrapping his arm around the rail and the around the terrorist's neck. Squeezing, he kicked out the terrorist's knee from under him so that his counter-elbows were uselessly slapping John's thighs. The terrorist was flopping now, fading. When his unconscious eyes dropped beneath his lids, John loosened his grip.

He set the man into one of the seats and tapped his pockets. He found what he expected: one of the Hierarchy's burners. John slipped it into his jeans and reached for his duffel bag. He got off the train, the doors closed, and it made off.

John hurried away from the platform, away from prying eyes and the bystanders yelling after him and calling the police. The lights were a sickly green, the brown bricks beneath his feet worn and cracked. It was a larger station than normal, with two tracks next to him and another two across the way. Between them was a dim golden concourse where flocks of people were sat, walking, and waiting in lines at small box-shaped food stalls. The underground market was a steaming food court with a diverse level of variety becoming of New York. The smells were a strange but savory fusion in certain parts, a sweet, attractive scent in others. The hall was replete with chatter, the scraping of spatulas, the fiery swirling of pans. It was hot, unlike the cool surface above; a sea of irradiating bodies John had to wade through to get to the exit on the other end.

He barely made it halfway there when he saw a man in all black— not in the usual tactical armor— but catching his inmate-like stare John knew instantly he was Hierarchy. John turned around. Maybe he'd try the other end of the market. Alas, another one was waiting for him. John was fortunate to find a party of passersby that could shield him. He squeezed in between the group and stepped on a few feet, roiling a few of them who then cussed at him in a different language. Swimming amidst the group like a severely slow jet stream, he came side-to-side with the terrorist. John sprang out from the group, knocking over a few but tackling the one that mattered. John slapped away the terrorist's gun, which, sliding across the floor, caused a few people to scream and start storming the opposite way. The second half of the concourse John had left behind was merely ogling the scene. It was from that direction that the second terrorist came barreling towards him.

John silenced the squirming terrorist beneath him with his elbow, then launched back to his feet to meet the second, but was pounced upon before he could guard himself. The two rolled across the floor, John's duffel bag being left behind yards away. The terrorist reached for a pistol in his jacket but John held his wrist at the jacket zipper. With his other hand John pulled the man in by the neck, meeting his nose with his forehead, breaking it. He felt the warm blood bubble and land on his head as he shoved the terrorist off of him.

John did him the same way he did the other terrorist, knocking him out cold. When he picked up his bag and made for the stairs, two more terrorists were descending, this time not bothering to hide their guns. *"Get down!"* John yelled at the people not yet panicking, as if they were used to seeing fights. He leapt into one of the food stalls, a couple of bullets zipping his way and shattering the storefront.

John could not fire back at them towards the crowd of innocents. He had no choice but to run the other way while the terrorists were preoccupied with the rushing droves of citizens blocking their aim.

There was more trouble the other way, though, as a duo of police officers were running towards him. *Oh great!* John stuck his hand out to stop the officers, whose guns were finding him as their target— bullets belted from behind him and one of the officers fell. John flinched again and sprinted past the second cop, who was recklessly returning shots until he fell to a blitz of automatic fire.

John reached the end of the concourse, where the yellowing lights returned overtop broken white tiles and graffitied columns. The stairs were close, but he couldn't make it without taking a bullet in the back. He reached into his duffel bag and pulled out a submachine gun. He inserted the clip and pulled back the black charging handle. John turned, the lane clear enough of civilians that he knew he couldn't hit one. He shot but the bullets hit the ground next to one of the terrorists, prompting them to jump into cover behind columns like John. He advanced a little closer to the steps, hiding behind one of the painted beams that was being chipped away by a return volley.

Before John could peek round the corner, a loud opening of gunfire made his left ear like tin. He reached to cover it as two other men were firing, not at him, but at the Hierarchy terrorists in front of the market concourse. John went around the column he was standing behind; it was some miracle they did not see him, for they were focused on another target. As they pushed forward, John saw no better opportunity. He ran out of cover trailed by ground-splitting bullets and up the stairs to the sidewalk, where the gunfire was echoing onto the street and crowds of people were running away, sirens coming closer. John stuffed his machine gun back into the duffel bag, tightened the strap so it fit like a backpack, then ran across the intersection to blend in with the crowd.

He reached inside his pocket, pulled out the terrorist's burner phone, and started dialing. *"Come on, come on, pick up!"* John was walking along an entryway to Central Park, its memorial arch and marble structures standing rather insignificantly across a familiar tall black building. Mason Tower bordered a plaza with a globe in its center, like a birdcage made of wiry metal.

"John?" he heard his brother exclaim.

"Henry! I'm at Columbus Circle! It was a trap!" *Of course it was,* he thought, his hand surprisingly steady; he did not like that he was getting used to this. "There's more. There were ACT terrorists down there too, in the subway. They were trying to kill the Hierarchy ones." He did not wish to share the ironic fact that he might have been dead had it not been for the ACT. "Tell me you got my message."

"*We did,*" said Henry. "*We contacted every police precinct in Manhattan. Only one had their communications blocked, probably by the same signal jammer we've been encountering all day.*"

"That must be it!" John crossed at the light, shifting the phone from his right to the left as blaring sirens were shooting past, wincing from the gunfire still ringing in his ear.

"*It's the twenty-fourth. One hundredth and Columbus! We have the bomb squad and NIB teams on the way. Right now, you're only an eleven minute drive away!*" said Henry.

That's almost back where I came from! John thought. "They're locking down the roads! It'll be an hour before I get there by car! And once they realize I'm not dead, they'll blow the precinct!"

"*It's a forty-five minute walk otherwise!*"

"Twenty if I run like hell," said John, picking up his pace.

"*You'd better run, then, John. Hurry!*"

John hung up the phone and darted down the sidewalk, shoving past any and all civilians with little regard. He drew a sharp, cold breath, his heart beginning to pace.

In a high rise apartment elsewhere in the city, the head of the Hierarchy sat tapping his expensive leather chukkas repeatedly. It was the one anxious stain across his otherwise cool visage, his demeanor that of a patient predator with prey as good as in his jaws. "I must say," he chirped with his usual soft projection. He was sipping a dry sherry the color of chestnut, which seemed to bring him even more satisfaction. "This is historic. A union of the ages. Even after all you've done."

"And all you've done as well," a voice like velvet replied. Jeanne Leroux was there, her face bathed in the cool, diffuse light coming from the wall of windows. Together they sat at a dining table, the Hierarchy's leader naturally at the head, Leroux beside him, though at a distance, closer to her second-in-command, Alec.

"Sure, we've had spats back and forth," the Englishman retorted, "but *you*... you killed Garcia. You killed Gabriel. You somehow managed to steal the bomb right from under them. And all you've had to do the past, what, eight hours? Is lie in wait. Fascinating."

"I told you once, I'd be a worthy adversary."

"So you did. And so you were. But *now....*"

"Before I can consider us allies, *Meyers,*" there was a derisive emphasis in the way she said his name, "I must know your plans."

Meyers twiddled his fingers, his lip curling as if the answer to the question were too obvious to mutter. Nonetheless he said, "To detonate the bomb."

Leroux shot him an unappreciative look. "You know what I meant," she hissed.

"I know you don't approve of my methods."

"Killing millions was never on the table for us. If there's another way to get what we want—"

"There isn't," Meyers said decisively. "I know you prefer the subtler arts. Espionage, blackmail, government infiltration. Trades I'm all too familiar with. I wish to create a need for global conflict. Which begs military contraction. That creates a shift in the prices of commodities that *I* help to speculate. So while the socialist, egalitarian ends you seek directly contradict my own, I think you realize the opportunity I've presented us here. When we destroy their beacon, their great silver city… when we've destabilized their trade, their currency, their whole nation— nay, the entire west— well, my people will reap the benefits. With the corruption and inequality you so desperately wish to uproot in question, so too will you be in a position to change things the way you want."

"Many words to say you crave riches."

"Oh, but it's so much more than that, Jeanne. While our enemies are busy picking up the pieces of their fallen civilizations, the former glory… the *respect* Great Britain once had around the world will be restored. I'm not merely hurting this country for the fun of it. I'm *saving* mine. Don't you see? You can do the same for yours."

"I'm no politician, Meyers."

Meyers laughed, sipping his brown drink. "Nor am I. But to make the difference we seek that is what we must become. Yes?" Leroux did not respond. She turned towards Alec, who had no say in the matter but whom she looked to for a sign her considerations were sound. "If you want to play the benevolent third party, be my guest. My South American proxy will happily take the credit. But this bomb *will* go off, Miss Leroux. The question remains, will you reap the benefits with us?"

Leroux let out a deep contemplative breath through her nostrils. "Alright, then."

"Excellent."

"You should know," she continued, "I have men all across the city, hunting your men down to kill them." Meyers laughed again. "Don't you care?"

"Not in the slightest, my dear." He did not appear much older than her, perhaps in his mid-forties, to Leroux's late thirties, yet spoke to her with avuncular condescension. "Our people are all working towards the same goal at the moment. To kill Spears. As long as that happens... as long as our little *alliance* remains a secret... we cannot be thwarted."

1:36 PM: NYPD 24ᵀᴴ PRECINCT: MANHATTAN:

By time John got there, it was too late. The front of the grey building was blown to bits, blackening the mortar with scorch marks, blanketing the sidewalk with glass.

John had not run that much since the military. His heart was likely to burst through his sternum and run off on its own. He panted, bent, hands clutching his knees between attempts at slapping the ineluctable plague of failure out of his thoughts. He looked up, sweat dripping from his nose. All around officers were cramming the street, helping each other where they could, coughing and shrouded in soot.

John ignored the officers shoving past, as they did him, instead approaching a man wiping sweat and soot off his brow, holding a blue peaked cap and star-insignia on his collar. "Captain," John shuddered, winded. He clutched his ribs, which were aching more than they were after he leapt out of that car and landed himself in the hospital.

"Who are you?"

"National Intelligence Bureau," John began.

Two blocks and parking lots down one hundredth street was a brick apartment building taller than the police station. A man was knelt on the rooftop, aiming a sniper rifle over the ledge. John was in his crosshairs, only barely though, as officers, paramedics, and now firefighters were racing past, leaving hardly a half-second between each to maintain a shot on him.

He was the same man who had attacked John on thirty-ninth street... and the same who killed James Michaels, having the same pallid skin, choppy, soldier-like hair, and ebony eyes.

He saw John finish his conversation with the police captain then trail off behind a line of ambulances and fire trucks. There was no getting him back in his crosshairs. The sniper did not fret, though. He took out his burner phone and dialed a number. After a moment he said, "Spears showed but I couldn't get a shot on him."

There was no reply, merely the disappointed click of the phone being hung up.

From his apartment, the head of the Hierarchy tossed the phone to a terrorist standing guard at the door. Jeanne Leroux was gone. It was only him and the door-watcher, a thirty-something Englishman quite like the sniper, bearing his resemblance so much so that they could be brothers. Only, this man was not so pale, his cheek and jaw bones pronounced, his thin eyes a magnetic shade of green, and his hair a sophisticated, well-kempt undercut.

"Kenneth?" said Meyers.

"Yes, sir?" he replied in an accent much thicker than Meyers's.

"You've waited long enough, I think."

Kenneth Parsons stood, taller and more bodily defined than Meyers, nonetheless ready to fall in line at his behest. "What do you want me to do?"

"Isn't it obvious? I want you to kill John Spears. I had hoped Bell would have completed the job but... he's like the rest. You aren't. Would you carry out this task for me?"

Parsons turned towards a table that was set up against the wall under a golden lamp. Pristinely sharp knives and an automatic pistol spread atop a black cloth glimmered in the light. His bloodthirsty grin was aglow as if by a flicker-free fire. He turned back to Meyers and replied, "Aye, sir. Gladly."

CHAPTER FIFTEEN:

Had John been acting irascible, unwilling to perform the doctor's checkups, peeved or pushing away, Henry would have understood. Instead, sitting on the examination table, his dangling legs statuesque, John was staring catatonically at one of the grey walls of the infirmary. Henry was watching from the corridor outside, dim blue lights illuminating him from overhead. Director Hall was turning the corner, Henry saw in his peripheral. "How is he?" Hall asked.

"Damaged," said Henry tersely. "I haven't seen him this low since...."

Hall remembered it just as well. "Since relinquishing his directorship of CAD. John was never great at dealing with failure."

"That failure wasn't only on him," Henry confided. "We both could have saved those people that day. I could've stopped the train, ordered an evacuation—"

"Oh, God, not you too. Henry, stop it. It's a miracle only *twelve* died. A miracle your brother survived. You did all that you could. Besides, that was four years ago. It's safe to let it go—"

"How can I let it go if he still bears the weight of it? I think *because* he survived he felt so bad. And now it's all rushing back to him. Forced onto that subway train, helpless to stop that precinct from...." Henry's eyes circled the same spot on the ground as if it contained all the answers, or rather, it was the only place that did not cause his thoughts to wander.

"We're all to blame. It's part of the job. John just... he takes these things the hardest. I remember scooping him up from the army, one foot in death's door," Hall reminisced. "He was inconsolable. But he came around. I'm sure he'll come around again."

In the infirmary, John's only show of feeling was the dagger in his side he felt when the doctor stroked his bare ribs, one at a time. "No new fractures," said the doctor. It was the same squirrelly, almond-colored glasses-wearing doctor who treated John at Bellevue hospital. "That's good at least, huh?" He did a poor job at trying to up John's mood. John was as numb as he could be with fractured ribs, as taciturn as a shy little boy hoping to be alone. When the doctor was finished, John slipped back on his grey thermal, hiding the distress he felt in his side.

"He's not as bad as he was three hours ago," the doctor admitted to Henry, standing in the sliding glass doors of the infirmary.

"Is he well enough to get back out there?" said Henry.

The doctor gave a half-hearted curl of his lips. "You know what *I'd* say to that. But... if he wants to, nothing's stopping him, I suppose."

"Thanks, Doc." Henry shook the man's hand and he was alone with John. He approached as a hunter would slowly approach a skittish deer, fearful a flight response might kick in or John would explode with pent-up emotion. Henry actually preferred the latter. At least he wouldn't be sitting there, looking half-dead or wishing he was. "John?"

His brother did not respond, did not look in his direction, which said all that needed saying. "I know what you're feeling right now. It's not fair. It's not right. Doesn't matter how few got hurt, because even one person getting hurt is enough to feel like you've failed. But John..." Henry scraped a chair across the dotted white floor and sat in front of his brother, in the place where he was vacantly staring, so that his eyes were now on him. "You don't need me to tell you. A lot more people are gonna get hurt today if we don't do something. They don't need pity, they need strength. They need you, out there, doing what you do best."

John's mouth slightly tilted open like he was going to say something, but he backed down after a beat. Henry continued, "I miss my fiancé, John. I have to get back to her. But I won't leave you here. I'll never let you fight alone. But I need you to actually *fight*."

After a moment, John drew in a heavy breath that made his chest and chin rise. "What can we do?" he whispered.

That was enough to make Henry grin. He got his brother back. "The symbol. It's been spotted again."

"Another murder?"

Henry nodded, regrettably. "This time there were witnesses. They say the guy had an automatic pistol and body armor, all black. A few officers were there but... he got away."

"The last symbol led to a trap," John recalled.

"Yeah," said Henry uncertainly. "You're right. We should wait for another lead—"

"No," John declared austerely. "I'll go check it out. I just... need a couple of minutes."

Henry nodded and left John without protest. He sat on the examination table, back bent, attempting to straighten out but folding to the pressure he felt in his spine. John reached for the NIB-issue cellphone on the end table in front of him. He began dialing a number— pausing for a moment's hesitation, thinking *could the head of the Hierarchy be listening? Does she even want to hear from me?* None of that mattered, though. His heart skipped as he pressed call, his breath stopping short of every buzz of the line until someone finally picked up.

"Hello?" It was a woman's voice. To John, it might've sounded like music, enough to revivify his spirits and set his heart to standstill. *"Hello?"*

John had forgotten to greet her, and suddenly, with a stutter, said, "St-Steph?"

"John?"

"Yeah. Yeah, it's me."

"I had a feeling you'd call today. After everything that's been going on." The sound of Stephanie's voice pierced his emotionless carapace, forcing him to stumble into his next words, but she beat him to it, *"I'm okay. I was enjoying a nice day off but they called me in. Did you hear about the twenty-fourth precinct?"*

The reminder was bound to come. John fought through the oppressing wave of guilt and failure as his brother commanded of him. "Yeah."

"Too close for comfort," she sounded like she was trying to make a joke, but the sentiment was genuine. *"Anyway, you don't have to worry. I'm okay."*

"I just..." John put his fist in his mouth, not wanting the words to come out wrong. "I just wanted to hear your voice, is all."

There was a silence from the other end that made him nervous. The shy little boy briefly returned, until he realized that Stephanie knew something was amiss. *"What's wrong?"*

Everything, John wanted to say. *Everything except for the voice I'm hearing now. That could make anything right.* He did not say that. He took in a sharp breath through his nose to calm himself and replied, "Nothing. Just a... long day."

"Where are you?" she asked.

"NIB headquarters. But I'm about to leave. There's a crime scene I have to check out."

"Send me the location. I'll meet you there."

John's eyes widened. That had not been his intention. "What? No, that's— you can't—"

"Why not? You said you're investigating a crime scene. I'm a detective."

"I didn't— it's too dangerous," said John.

"More dangerous than standing in a police station?" argued Stephanie.

She had him beat there, and yet John would never forgive himself if he walked Stephanie into a trap. "I don't know, Steph. I don't want—"

"Save it, John. You were always overprotective. Let me do this. We're starving for leads down here. FBI's quiet. NIB's quiet. Anything that can help us figure out what's going on, I need to see it through."

John scratched his head, finally exhaling and giving up trying to order Stephanie around. "Alright," he said. "I'll send you the location."

2:32 PM: MANHATTAN:

John's NIB vehicle slowed to a halt along a Harlem street corner. The buildings were all of a similar reddish brick, with bulging, curvaceous façades and flat roofs. Leaving his phone in the car, John stepped out and a whiff of char and metal hit his nostrils. At first he looked to the rooftops. Not a glint, no black-clad body, no snipers. *So far, so good,* was the thought, until he saw the scene. There was a café. Its windows were gone, scattered into thousands of bits beneath the toppled tables and chairs of its outside seating. The bright sun that warmed John's face and hands was unbecoming of the gruesome sight before him. There was blood, a preponderance of it. He saw rubble from a small explosion, then two white-shrouded bodies on the sidewalk. On the ground to the right of the bodies, spray-painted in red, was the Hierarchy's seal.

"Agent Spears," a familiar voice broke John free of his trancelike concentration. It was Detective Park, one of the two detectives John had met on thirty-ninth street, his brown peacoat slightly stained with the blood of his partner, but kept on, perhaps as a reminder. His gelled combover was rougher, more unkempt since he last saw it. "Director Hall called. Told me to expect you."

John tried to prevent his pity for the detective from showing through. "I'm sorry about your partner, Detective Park."

Park's thin eyes fell to the floor, then back up again with tenacity. "I reckon his family has it harder. Would've been worse had you not been there."

Not so sure about that, thought John. *That sniper was waiting for me.* He opted to not linger on the subject. "What's the story here?"

"One cop shot, still alive. Two civilians dead and four injured by explosive shrapnel."

"What caused the explosion?" John asked. Just then a black SUV quite like his NIB issue was parking just beyond the scene. John backtracked, lifted the yellow tape to meet her halfway, his chest rising and falling rapidly. "Stephanie," he said in a low voice.

She stepped out of her truck wearing a dark blue suit with rounded shoulders on her blazer, not that John would have noticed that right away. His immediate impression was how beautiful she looked. It was true, the pictures of her on John's phone did Stephanie little justice. She was immensely pretty, her tan skin shimmering in the sun, her almond irises and wavy, cascading hair sweet confections that danced irresistibly in John's direction.

The awkward part was how they would greet each other, but Stephanie made it easy by pulling John in for a warm embrace. *Still the same shampoo,* John thought, immediately regretting he had assessed her coconutty scent. When they broke apart— after what felt like much more than a couple of seconds— she said simply, "Shall we?"

John nodded and guided her under the tape. "Detective Park, this is Detective Stephanie Diaz." The two shook hands. "Tell her what you were telling me." As Park filled Stephanie in, John's eyes hadn't left her. He found himself resisting, thinking she was a sight he did not deserve right now.

"Did you pick up the shells the suspect used?" Stephanie's mind was strictly on the scene. John knew if his lingered any longer he would be doing a disservice to her and Park. The detective flashed a plastic bag containing a dozen bullet casings, which Stephanie took and inspected. "Nine millimeter."

"And the explosion," said John attentively. "Didn't happen to pick up a grenade pin, did you?"

"Good eye." Park walked the two to the covered bodies. Like on thirty-ninth street he paid a considerate amount of attention to the onlookers, the citizens just beyond the perimeter of ambulances, police cars, and caution tape, wishing for them to be spared the sight.

Stephanie was slipping on a pair of black latex gloves, handing a pair to John as Park lifted one of the cloths. "How many times did he shoot this guy?" she said, her face scrunched and disgusted.

"Witnesses and officers on the scene claimed he was using an automatic pistol. That's why he was able to let off so many rounds so quickly."

"He disperses the people with the grenade," murmured John, "then executes two of them from... how far?"

Park pointed to an X made with tape in the center of the street, not seven yards away.

Stephanie was running her fingers along a wound on the second body. "This guy was stabbed. It wasn't the killing blow but these perforations... the knife had a serrated edge. A tactical blade."

"Grenades, body armor, automatic weapons," John concurred. "Only soldiers carry around that kind of stuff."

Stephanie, knelt, started towards something else, the red-painted symbol nearest the second body. "And what's this supposed to be? Was it here before?"

"No. The killer drew that," said Park. "And I've been wondering the same thing. Especially considering that symbol was there earlier. In the place my partner was killed."

Stephanie rose, a shocked look in her eye. "I'm so sorry." She looked at John, whose head was hung regretfully. "Do you know what it means?"

Park looked at John in a way that expected answers, as if he deserved them. *He does deserve to know. So does she,* thought John. "You can't tell anyone. The information has been compartmentalized to prevent panic. Only higher circles of FBI, CIA, NIB, and the White House know."

"Know what?" Park was impatient, askance.

"The symbol," John divulged, "it belongs to a terrorist group."

"The ACT?" Stephanie knew all about them.

"What's the ACT?" asked Park.

"Not them. Although they *are* partially behind some of the stuff that's been going on today. They're called the Hierarchy. Brazilian terror group. Likely a proxy paid off by an English man or organization." John spoke in a low register so that the officers, paramedics, and certainly the citizens were none the wiser. "We don't have much on them. In fact, the same way the police has been kept in the dark, we're *sure* the CIA knows more than they're telling us. But Henry and I are working with what we've got."

"And so, this man, the one who killed these people," Stephanie began, "he's working with the Hierarchy?"

"As what, some sort of mercenary?" Park speculated.

"An *assassin,*" John revealed. "Probably stringing me along for a trap." Park's face suggested he did not fully believe John, like there was more he was leaving out, and John could not blame him. "There's nothing left here. Detective." John extended a hand to which Park reluctantly shook.

"Where will you go?" asked Park.

John looked at Stephanie over his shoulder and avowed, "We're gonna find this guy."

"I've got nowhere to be. I'll look with you."

2:56 PM: MANHATTAN:

John and Stephanie drove their separate trucks, Stephanie slowly trailing him as they patrolled the streets, which were, to nobody's surprise, more devoid of traffic than perhaps John had ever seen them. Park had insisted on a police escort, so his car was in the back, and John followed a cruiser that was slowing to a stop in front of him.

Gunshots. The officers in front of John got out of their car and immediately fell. John raced out of his SUV, seeing Stephanie already out of hers with her pistol aimed. The two met behind his car door then inched up to the back of the police cruiser. Park's car swerved around them and came to a halt. The three were out now, pointing their guns at a man dressed in all black, with elbow and knee pads, a belt looped around his waist with grenades and combat knives. In his hand was a pistol with a huge drum magazine sticking out the bottom. He was the Hierarchy's assassin, Ken Parsons, a jaw so sharp it looked to cut, his eyes a powerfully bright green, his black undercut rife with simple sophistication.

Parsons approached John, Stephanie and Detective Park, who were standing behind car doors as cover. "Stop right there!" John yelled. Parsons singled him out and held out his other hand. In it was a grenade, its pin unhooked by his thumb and falling with a *tink.*

John pulled Stephanie down as Parsons launched the grenade to his left, towards Park's unmarked cruiser. The car exploded in a great fiery plume and flipped onto its side, forcing Park to the ground where he lay unconscious.

Another police cruiser swung to a stop behind the assassin and the officers came out. Parsons's gun was already fixed though. He sprayed a hail of automatic bullets at the officers that sprang through glass and metal. One of the officers fell, dead. The other managed to hit Parsons with two bullets in his vest, prompting a painful groan, but that was all. Parsons walked calmly towards the officer, who was pathetically trying to reload his pistol. Parsons slipped his knife from his waist and thrust it into the officer's chest.

When the officer dropped, Parsons reloaded his pistol and holstered it coolly. He turned to the first police cruiser, where John and Stephanie were rising, ears ringing from the explosion. Parsons wiped the bloody knife on his pants then twirled it garishly. He looked directly at John, held out his hand, and waved him over, as if to say, *"Show me what you've got,"* a challenge John was ready to take him up on.

CHAPTER SIXTEEN:

3:00 PM: MANHATTAN:

John barely let off a shot before Parsons rolled to his front and vised John's wrist with a forcible grip. With the other hand he swiped his blade; John dodged left but was blocking Stephanie's line of fire, no doubt in purposeful position for Parsons to follow up with a kick that felt like an anvil crushing his radius. John's gun was flung under a car. Parsons was weaving from side to side to avoid a bullet, threshing John with repeated strikes.

John missed a punch then it was his turn to maneuver away from a thrusting knife. Stephanie decided to step in but would immediately regret it, taking a slash through her blue blazer that sent droplets of blood leaking onto the pavement from her forearm. This did not deter her. She stepped in again as John got a hold of Parsons's blade arm. With his elbow Parsons blocked and simultaneously struck Stephanie, who initiated a punch. At the same time John smashed his head into the assassin's, forcing him to fall back onto the ground, his knife clanking on the concrete.

With a swift circling of the feet he was back up, sweeping Stephanie's shins from under her. The cracking thud of her back against the pavement was such that John's attention was misdirected towards his aching companion, giving Parsons the opening to attack John with a tall kick to the temple. Disoriented, John was barely able to raise his forearm to block a second kick, but a third made its mark in his fractured ribs and stung worse than any pain he'd experienced today. John returned with a front kick that all but pierced Parsons in the gut, then followed by punching him across his cheek.

Lip swelling with scarlet, Parsons's face contorted into a masochistic smile. With separation between them, Parsons reached for the automatic pistol at his hip, but John wasn't about to let it be done unceremoniously. John seized the wrist and redirected the gun, away from himself and from Stephanie, who was still writhing on the ground, perhaps seriously hurt. Bullets split the air by John's ear and forced them to ring, stripping the coats of paint off of parked cars, shattering glass storefronts and windows.

When the pistol's magazine ran out, John pulled Parsons in, elbowed him in the nose then palmed the gun out of his hand. Parsons reacted by reaching low, sliding another, smaller knife out of its scabbard in his boot and slashing. John backed away, making distance with a powerful punt.

Parsons sprang towards him and rolled under a punch, finding his other knife on the ground and snipping a trace of John's forearm. John winced, blood dripping, quickly put on the defensive again. His reflexes had to be astounding as the bigger knife was savagely cleaving for his head, the smaller dashing with fiendish quickness for his arms and hands.

Parsons switched from the unsuccessful series of slashes by thrusting forward with legs bent in a lunge, cutting John just above his waist.

John's side singed from the wound and a matching lancination from his ribs was yelling out at him to cease fighting.

"Not bad, Spears," jeered the Englishman. "No wonder nobody's killed you yet." John did not reply, only circled the same tract of skid marked street,

Parsons matching his slow heedfulness with a grin and lack of prudence. "That's 'bout to change." He twirled his knife between his fingers.

Parsons charged, blades lashing, just missing John's chest, severing the leather zipper from his green army jacket. The knife flipped in his hand and he returned right with a backhand strike, but John's forearms met with Parsons's and he shoved the assassin off. Parsons whipped around and thrust again, this time John catching him and holding one knife at bay. The other came low; John seized the other arm. It was a test of pure strength, John pushing against one blade that was close enough to scrape his nose, and another that was one nudge from entering his gut.

John was first to use his legs, beating Parsons to it. He forced the assassin down by driving a foot into Parsons's knee, then wrenched the fingers on his left hand. The knife threatening his stomach dropped. With both hands he heaved Parsons by his right wrist and forced his knife to the assassin's throat— but Parsons swiftly evaded, dropping the blade and using his own legs against John's.

The two were on the ground now, both reaching for the knife in between them. John seized it first and came down with it. The blade wedged into Parsons's elbow pad. With merciless force the assassin kicked John in the abdomen and launched him several feet away.

Parsons unstuck the knife from his plastic padding and approached John, who was on the ground panting and recoiling from pain in his ribs. Parsons came down the same way John did but John rolled out of the way— the knife *plinked* off the concrete and split apart from its handle. John rolled to a crouched position and sprang forth with impressive dynamism, smashing Parsons in the side of the head with his knee.

Parsons tumbled. John pounced. Mounting the assassin John turned his face into a pulp. He would not stop. He wanted to kill him. It took for Stephanie's bleeding hand to touch his own for him to take a beat, to realize Parsons was their only lead, and that he lay half-dead under him. John's eyes were red with fury, shooting daggers at the assassin.

Stephanie reached for the neck of the inert Parsons and pressed two fingers to it. "He's alive," she said.

John gave a smile of relief, not for him, but for *her*. She was still intact, and yet the wound on her forearm, the dizzying crash of her fall, they made John glower again. "He shouldn't be," he replied. The two rose, Stephanie flinging John's arm over her shoulder as the police and ambulances rounded the corner.

3:24 PM: MANHATTAN:

They were both wearing tattered clothes that were covered in blood. Stephanie peered to her left. John was in worse shape than she was yet he squeezed the steering wheel with split open knuckles as if they didn't sting. There was a police escort following them, the closest cruiser carrying Ken Parsons in the back, cuffed and immobilized.

John's phone started to ring. He picked it up and set it down on the armrest between them on speaker. "Spears," he answered.

"I must give you credit for your resilience." It was the eerily soft tone John had heard before, the signature English accent he was getting used to. *"Tell me, what is your secret?"*

"Only if you tell me," said John, "who you are."

"Ah, why not? Call me... Eric."

"Alright, Eric. Next question—"

"Oh, but you must allow me one first," sang Meyers, sounding like he was salivating. *"My man. Is he alive?"*

"You'll have to be more specific."

"Don't be coy, John... the game's no fun that way," Meyers intoned.

"So this is a game to you?"

"Oh, yes, John. A game of choice. If we're exercising formality, call it a test. Multiple choice."

"What if I choose not to play?"

"I fear that's not an option," said Meyers. *"Now. Kenneth Parsons. Is he alive?"*

John found it in him to smirk. "It must kill you that I know something you don't," he taunted.

"A trait we have in common. Tell me, how close are you to finding my bomb?"

"About as close as you, I'd assume. Or let me guess," John speculated, "Leroux's come over to the dark side... or the... *darker* side."

There was a stale, smarmy laugh from the other end. *"Very good. Very good,"* Meyers emphasized. *"It took some convincing. Eviscerating millions isn't exactly on the ACT's founding charter."*

"And what's the Hierarchy's charter read like? Shakespeare?"

"We simply do what we must," Meyers replied. *"The loss of life is... tragic. But unavoidable in the long run."*

"Do I have to ask why?" John knew he would not get an unenigmatic response.

"What kind of test would this be if I gave you all the answers?" laughed Meyers.

"Sorry. Forgot to study."

John's interplay with the terrorist turned Stephanie off entirely. She frowned, and whispered, *"Hang up already!* He could be tracking us!"

"Ah, there's the ex... Stephanie Diaz. A vision indeed. How are we, Detective?"

There was a smugness in his voice that made John want to fling his phone out the window. "You leave her out of this, you hear me?"

"I didn't bring her into it." Meyers gave a final sinister chuckle then hung up with a click. John and Stephanie locked gazes, uncertainty swimming across both of their faces.

3:47 PM: NIB HEADQUARTERS: MANHATTAN:

John and Stephanie were met at the garage entrance of headquarters by Henry. He escorted them past the security terminal and back into the main communications hub. "Hall told me you two were together. Hi, Stephanie," Henry said, his gaze furtively evading hers.

Together. John thought it was an overly simplistic choice of phrase. The eye contact Henry was avoiding was evidence he felt the same way and regretted it. "What do we have on the guy with the knives?" John asked, hoping to put a stopper in the eventual awkwardness of standing around Henry's station.

"Kenneth Parsons," Stephanie amended. "Here's his phone." She handed the outdated plastic burner to Henry, who began sifting through it whilst briefing the two.

"Former SAS, British Special Air Service. The UK government's rather tight-lipped about the whole affair but Hall is slowly getting through to the higher ups at Langley."

"CIA knows all," said John.

"They said they're willing to give us info on the Hierarchy," explained Henry. "They agree too many dots are connecting to keep it quiet from the rest of the DOJ.... That *and* Hall is threatening to have them investigated and held liable if the bomb goes off. For now, they were kind enough to share with us Parsons's military records. He was deployed to Syria, same time as you, John."

"From fighting terrorists to joining up with them," grumbled John. He glanced at Parsons's picture on Henry's screen, looked up, and saw the same man— though visibly more beaten up, thanks to John's bloodied knuckles—

strolling past with two armed officers at his sides. He grinned through puffed cheeks as he was hauled to his detainment room across the atrium.

"Oh, God," muttered Henry, his face glued to Parsons's phone though seeming like he wanted nothing more than to look away.

"What is it?" John looked at the phone screen and quickly understood. He and Henry glared up at Hall, who was calmly meting out orders to Jennifer Nolan at the top of the pit. John stepped away, Stephanie not knowing what to make of Henry's worried face. *"Hall!"* John called out loud enough for the surrounding analysts and agents to stop what they were doing.

Hall's head tipped with a look of puzzlement. "John," he awkwardly exclaimed as if John's howling was a form of excited greeting.

John got in Hall's face, scowling up at his bright sapphire irises. "You have some explaining to do."

"I do?"

"That man we just brought in. Only one call was made from his phone in the past six hours. Only one number in his contacts. *Yours.*"

Hall twitched, his youthful white smile brightening the room, though everyone around was biting their nails. "There's gotta be some mistake—"

"I don't want to believe it, Hall. Don't make me the fool again today."

Hall saw John's fist was clenched and his smile faded at once. He reached slowly into his jacket pocket and took out his phone. He handed it to John. "Take a look for yourself."

John took the phone and brought it to Henry. Stephanie whispered in John's ear, *"What's going on?"*

"We're about to find out."

Henry swiped through the phone, typed on his computer to which the device was plugged in, then back to John. "He did receive a call from Parsons."

John was ready to return to Hall and deck him, but Henry continued, "But it only lasted a three seconds."

Hall approached which made John take a step back, arms shielding Stephanie. "You know me, John. I've never spoken to that guy, *or* the Hierarchy head. I swear I have nothing to do with this."

"The call was close to three hours ago," added Henry.

"I know what you're talking about," said Hall. "It was a dud. Nobody on the other end so I hung up, assumed it was a wrong number. I'm a busy guy. Honestly, if I were in contact with the Hierarchy what could I possibly talk to them about in three seconds?"

John was sure he was telling the truth, but the last thing he needed was another Michaels situation on his hands. After all, *he left the conference room and seconds later I get a call from Eric,* thought John. *But that was hours ago... three seconds could be plenty to give a name... to order a hit. Who do I believe?* John scratched his head hard enough to cut his skin. "John..." Hall pleaded.

They would have to table the matter, as suddenly agents were pouring into the conference room and crowding around the TV. Others were building small groups around desks and tuning into the news station on their computers. "What's happening?"

"*ALN network!*" an analyst called out to Henry. He typed quickly on his keyboard and brought up a news feed, where Meyers's cold face shone on the screen, his tortoise shell glasses glinting under the studio lights. The crimson ALN logo was spinning in the bottom corner.

"*New York City. My name is Eric Meyers. In the past sixteen hours, the people of this city have witnessed rather minor attacks. I am the one coordinating those attacks. My last stroke of 'terror,' as you might call it, was the twenty-fourth NYPD precinct in the Upper West Side.*" John's lips were pursed furiously and his nails dug into his palms. Stephanie was squeezing his arm just as tightly. "*But*

I have not done this in secret, no. Agencies such as the FBI, CIA, and National In-telligence Bureau— which many of you don't *know of— have been the ones keeping these secrets from you, the people, and even from the police themselves. Such shame-ful behavior."*

Hall scoffed. "Is this guy for real?"

"Yeah, he is," said John.

"One major secret is this." A visual appeared on screen, an image that had scourged John's thoughts all day, of a silver sphere with a red timer on its face. *"This is a thermonuclear fusion device. Unfortunately the bomb is impervious to tampering or preemptive detonation. The only way it goes off is when the clock runs to zero in..."* Meyers checked his silver watch, *"eight hours and nine minutes, at midnight, tonight.*

The entire atrium flooded with murmurs. "Oh my God," gasped Steph-anie. John felt more regret than in that moment for not telling her than he cared to express even in his thoughts.

"This man, John Spears," John's face flashed on screen as Meyers contin-ued his memorandum, *"was the first to know about this bomb. He is a special agent for the NIB's Counter ACT Division, an agency* within *an agency you haven't heard of. He has tried for sixteen hours to stop me and this bomb from terrorizing this city, and he has failed."* Everyone around John was staring his way. He hung his head, a fermenting mixture of hate, vexation, and shame swirling inside of him. *"He, along with failing to stop the ACT, also failed to stop my organization, the Hierarchy. So, people of New York, when this bomb goes off in eight hours, John Spears is the one to blame... and he again will be to blame for what is about to come."*

What next? John thought. *"A game of choice,"* he remembered Meyers saying over the phone.

"I have planted two bombs," the Englishman disclosed as two camera feeds came on screen. *"One is in Penn Station. And one is in a police station. The way I see it, if the NIB keeps secrets from the people and the police, then who's more important to John Spears? Call within the next thirty seconds, John, or I detonate both. And choose well. The people... or the police."*

John pulled out his phone and immediately scrolled though his call history. "What are you thinking, John?" asked Hall. *I don't know,* he wanted to say.

"I'm thinking we only have thirty seconds to make a choice, or more people are gonna die than have to."

"You have to choose the people, John," Stephanie declared, her eyes twinkling with welling tears. "They don't deserve this."

"But we also need as many cops as we can get to hunt these animals down," contested Hall. *Fifteen seconds* left, ticking down on the screen. John dialed the number.

"I'm a cop," said Stephanie. "When we took oaths we were prepared for something like this. To lay down our lives to protect the people—"

"Nothing 'like this' has ever happened before! This city will erupt into chaos!" *Five seconds.*

Chaos is inevitable, thought John morbidly. "Shut up!" he yelled, phone buzzing in his ear.

"Have you decided?" said Meyers. John hesitated, breathing heavily. *"Well?"*

"The people." John watched Stephanie burst into tears and Hall hang his head over the outcome of the impossible decision.

After a moment of eerie silence, Meyers replied, *"The people it is."*

The camera feed on screen zoomed into the Penn Station terminal. John's heart stopped. A blaze of fire and the camera cut out. The atrium descended into weeping and wailing, the sound of deathly lament. John's own eyes were red and watering. "You're a monster."

Meyers smiled devilishly, a new image that would haunt the blacks of John's eyes. *"Do take care of Mr. Parsons for me."*

CHAPTER SEVENTEEN:

4:00 PM: MANHATTAN:

"Everyone get back to work." Hall's voice wavered, his characteristically bright patina replaced with a sort of surly unease. His high shoulders had shrunk, his sapphire eyes blackened. "Forget about what he said." *Unlikely,* thought John. "Let's find this guy." Hall clapped his hands together and turned towards Henry's station. Stephanie and Henry were still there, heads lowered with disbelief, but John was gone.

John's fingers drifted along the wall as he stumbled towards the right detainment room, cold blue like moonlight spilling onto his back and leaving his face in deathly shadow. When he found a door he opened it and entered. The world was warped, as if a scarlet lens were plastered over his eyes, especially bright when he found Kenneth Parsons chained to the table.

"Hey, you can't be in here," ordered an agent in the corner of the room. Without the slightest vacillation John pulled the agent by the collar, forced him out of the room, and slammed closed the door. He picked up one of the metal chairs opposite Parsons and wedged its front leg between the door and its handle. Suspended against the door, the entry became barred, the agent finding this firsthand as he rattled the handle trying to get back in.

John's burning sights spun to Parsons, who gave a desultory, "Nice to see you too—" but was interrupted by a large fist rearranging the brokenness of his face. John's knuckles split again but what was a little blood? A little flick of his wrist and the pain went; with his other hand wrapped around Parsons's throat he drove him against the wall, the chains tightening, the assassin's arms practically bolted to the table. Another punch burst Parsons's nose again, wet blood mixing with the dried, peeling splotches around his mouth. *"Wait—"* Parsons bubbled, but yet another punch whipped his head back against the concrete wall.

"How did he know you were here?" demanded John.

"What?"

"Meyers thought I killed you, but now he knows I brought you here. *How?"* thundered John.

"How should I know? Bruv's got plenty ways of getting information—" John growled, squeezing Parsons's throat and raising his fist again. *"Wait! Just wait, alrigh'?"* Parsons's lifted his hands as far as they could but that was just below his neck; he could not protect his face if he wanted. "You don't have to torture me, Spears. I'll tell you what I know."

If the simple Hierarchy terrorists NIB had kept for hours under interrogation would not break, why would Parsons? John was doubtful, his fist still scrunched and leaking. "Why?"

"Simple, init?" Parsons spat. "I'm not one of his. I'm a merc. I go where the money is. And seeing as there ain't no money coming since I'm caught...."

John somehow found himself having more respect for the Hierarchy members, yet he loosened his grip around Parsons's throat and backed away. "How does he know so much? How is he able to *call* me, and know where I am at all times?"

"Got an insider dun he?" Parsons had a habit of contracting nearly every word, not because of his wounded mouth and snout, but because of his thick cockney accent.

"Michaels is dead," said John.

"Nah, not Michaels. There's anuva. Dunno who, though. Certain things Eric likes to keep close to the chest."

"If you don't know anything, what use are you to me?" asked John coldly.

"Did I say I know nuffin?" Parsons barked gruffly. "Bet ya ain't know that Leroux broad is working for Meyers now."

"Actually he confirmed that himself over the phone."

Parsons's face contorted as though the piece of information was important enough to win him a few years off his eventual sentence. "How 'bout where the bloke's hiding? Bet ya ain't know that?"

John's face flared with enmity. "Tell me," he said.

"Safe 'ouse. Closer than you think. I'll write you down the address, long as you get me some water." A simple enough bargain.

"How do I know he hasn't already relocated?"

"I'm not one of his, I told ya. But that's not what *he* thinks. He thinks I'll keep shut as long as I'm in custody," Parsons explained.

"And how do I know Meyers won't be expecting me?"

"Ya don't. Got a contingency for everything, Meyers does."

"If you're lying to me," said John, now face-to-face with the mercenary, "I will come back here. And I *will* kill you."

Parsons grinned smugly. "Well then, Spears. How 'bout that water?"

4:22 PM: MANHATTAN:

A caravan of two SUVs and an armored ESU truck came tearing down fifth avenue towards Midtown, the vastness of Central Park warping past with an autumn palette of emerald, gold, bronze, and ruby.

The trucks reached their stop at the southeastern edge of the park. The glistening statued soldier astride a gilded horse pointed at their destination across from Grand Army Plaza. It was a narrow grey spire that protruded towards the low-forming clouds, standing adjacent the landmark Plaza Hotel.

John and Stephanie, rather than leading the charge, were in two files wedged between the front rifle-carrying tactical team and the suited pistol-wielding agents in the rear. Coming up on the apartment building the streets were quiet, devoid of the massive gatherings one would come to expect of this part of the city.

Meyers was watching. He was already coming down the elevator, the fingernails on his free hand scraping together with angst. One of the Hierarchy members beside him was holding a tablet that showed the rows of agents gathering round the base of the building. Meyers checked his watch, its ebony hands not ticking quickly enough.

When the elevator *ding* went off and the doors slid open, he hesitated. A lobby-full of agents was waiting for him, quietly, guns trained.

Suddenly bullets started flying, not at Meyers but at the SWAT team from the emergency exit across the grey ground floor. At the forefront of the terror counter-offensive was a woman, silvery hair and jade eyes, firing a pistol with shocking accuracy, hitting the agent nearest Stephanie.

Stephanie and John dropped into cover behind the concierge's desk, where the hotel's employees were in armadillo position on the ground. Meyers used the crossfire as opportunity to come out of the elevator, surrounded by a wall of Hierarchy human shields firing towards the entrance.

"That's Meyers!" John hollered, peeking around the desk just before a bullet crumbled its ceramic tiling. Leroux and Meyers were almost too calm as they walked towards the building's back exit.

"You take the right, I'll go left!" yelled Stephanie, pointing her pistol back at the front entrance.

"Now!" John held an arm around Stephanie and used his body to shield her as they ran past the agents advancing the lobby. They went back on the street and split up quicker than John could say, *"Be careful."*

The ACT, Hierarchy, and NIB exchange was heard all the way down the block, where John was sprinting for the intersection. Before going all the way, he cut left into an alleyway between the apartments and another, shorter brick building. Meyers was sprinting now out of the back of the tower, Leroux going the other way where she would be cut off by Stephanie.

Meyers shot an entire magazine of pistol bullets blindly behind his back, but John was crouched behind a dumpster. He made for the other end of the alley, John chasing.

Meanwhile, Leroux was climbing up a rusted red fire escape away from Stephanie, the detective right on her heels. Leroux kicked down from the ladder but only hit Stephanie's shoulder. She whipped around with her pistol aimed but Stephanie swatted it away, shoving herself onto Leroux on the first platform. Leroux wrestled away and started running up the stairs to the second floor but Stephanie was right after her.

John managed to leap and tackle Meyers. The two fell with a sickening crack; John hoped he broke something in Meyers. He postured up and clinched a handful of the Englishman's tailored black collar, fist raised. Meyers popped up his hips and staggered, tossing John off of the mount. *He knows what he's doing,* John observed. The two got to their feet and immediately began exchanging blows.

Atop the fire escape, Stephanie stuffed a kick with a sharp inhalation, being driven back into a wobbly railing she feared might break apart under her weight. Leroux continued to flee upwards, but Stephanie was at her heels. She nipped her foot and Leroux tripped. Stephanie ascended and dodged the incoming kick. Leroux stood up and started raining strikes, Stephanie not quick enough to dodge them but considerably taller, stronger, and more durable than the nimble, foxlike ACT leader. With a bleeding lip, Stephanie wound back a powerful fist that disappeared Leroux's cocky grin.

At the same time, John's punch was blocked with an expertly timed elbow, sliding across Meyers's ear. Meyers countered with a roundhouse to John's fractured ribs, and a punch of his own that bruised John's right cheek and sent him to all fours. "Pleasure to finally meet you in person, John," Meyers taunted, kicking John's forearms from under him. "A bit sooner than I'd expected, though." As John tried to push himself up, Meyers drove his knee hard into his side and forced him on his back. "No doubt the last sixteen hours have made you weaker. It's a shame I can't face you at your best."

He allowed John to his feet. John winced, wiping blood away from his cheek with his already reopened knuckles. "Strong enough to take down Parsons," he jabbed.

"But not strong enough to *kill* him," said Meyers. "I should have known you couldn't do it. Not in front of *her.*" Stephanie's face flashed in John's mind. He hoped desperately that she was okay. "Perhaps it isn't merely the events of today... perhaps *she* is making you weaker too."

Enough, thought John. He charged forth to get back in the fight.

Stephanie threw two more punches, blocking and avoiding Leroux's strikes. She latched onto Leroux's arm, kicked at her side and forced her onto her back. Stephanie wrapped her legs around Leroux's neck and midsection— the arm still trapped in a triangle hold— and squeezed.

Leroux kicked and tore at the rusty red grates beneath her, enough pressure on her right arm for it to break. With her free hand Leroux twisted Stephanie's ankle. Stephanie's hold broke but she propped herself up quickly, limping. Leroux shot back up at the same time and threw a kick that wildly undershot. Stephanie, getting Leroux's back, captured one of her arms. Leroux, missing a backwards elbow, had her other wrist seized. Before she knew it, Stephanie had her in handcuffs.

"Let me go you bi—" Stephanie squeezed the cuffs tighter around Leroux's wrists and made her shriek with pain. "If you think arresting me solves anything, you're sadly mistaken—"

"Shut up," said Stephanie calmly, dialing a number on her phone.

John and Meyers were less than a block away, still exchanging with speed and sharpness. Meyers's flurry of punches became too unpredictable for him dodge, too onerous to block. Each retaliation was met with even more power, and even more pain.

John barely blocked a kick with his forearms, which felt like they might break if he held them out again, then he threw a punch that went over Meyers's head. Meyers brought his knee up; the strike felt like a stab, like John's ribs fully dislodged and pierced his lung.

John slowly dropped to one knee, each breath feeling sharp and unbearable. "Such fun," laughed Meyers. Sirens blared as the gunshots slowly dwindled and a troupe of Hierarchy and ACT terrorists were visible down the alley. "But I really must be going now, John. Maybe I'll see you around."

"Where is it?" John groaned. "You tell me where it is!"

Meyers merely smirked, then jogged towards his underlings.

John panted short, agonizing breaths, ordering his legs to push and get himself upright. Stephanie came striding to his aid, forcing a handcuffed Leroux against the brick alley wall. *"John!* Where's Meyers?"

"He got away," he grumbled.

"I'm running satellite imaging now!" he heard a feint voice coming from Stephanie's cellphone.

"Was that Henry?"

"It's me, John." She raised the phone and turned up the volume.

"Keep me updated on Meyers's location." John's face squinched and he fell back against the wall opposite Leroux. She seemed pleased to see him in pain but made no motion to speak or act. "I'm gonna go after him."

Stephanie helped him straighten up, saying, "I'll go with you—"

"No," John interrupted. "You get *her* back to NIB." He got closer and whispered to Stephanie, "You have to force the bomb's location out of her."

"Then what?" said Stephanie, desperation in her voice. "What happens when you find the bomb? If what Meyers said is true, can't manually detonate it and *you* can't disarm it."

"I have an idea," said John, "but I need Henry's help." Stephanie and John shared an untrusting look Leroux's way. She handed John her phone and he stepped away to speak to Henry alone. "We have eight hours. Barely enough time to get what we need."

"What are you talking about?"

"Listen. When I visited Hall at D.C. headquarters a few months back, I gained access to the NIB's experimental equipment vault. The same place they sent you those glasses from. They've been trying to develop miniature electromagnetic pulse devices."

"Why didn't you mention this before?" said Henry.

"I— I didn't *think* about it," quavered John. "Last I saw they never got them to work, and *certainly* never applied them to nuclear weapons."

"For good reason, I'd imagine. Fifty-fifty chance an EMP will make the bomb go off sooner."

"It's the only option we've got."

"What do you need me to do?" Henry inquired.

"Have Hall call the Washington office. Have them send whatever proto-types they have, anything they can get us."

"Okay. I'll see what we can do."

4:55 PM: NIB HEADQUARTERS: MANHATTAN:

Stephanie escorted Jeanne Leroux through the atrium with a hand gripped tightly under her arm.

Agents came pouring in before them, carrying their wounded towards the infirmary with haste, but most bearing only scrapes. Hall and Henry came to meet the two in the center of the main communications room. Hall wore a childishly gleeful grin as he looked down at the short, silvery terror leader. "About time we caught you," he jeered.

"Detainment room six," said Henry, an arm extended to point the way.

When she reached the room, Stephanie planted Leroux into a metal chair. Two agents followed them in and chained Leroux's arms through a loop in the table in front of her. Before the door shut Leroux peered into the room across from hers. She saw two other agents guiding Kenneth Parsons out into the hallway.

For a short moment, Parsons looked back, but the sight was cut off by the detainment room door slamming shut. "Where's the bomb?" Stephanie asked tersely.

Leroux's eyes finally veered away from the closed door, as if her train of thought had been broken. "I don't know."

"Let's not play this game, Leroux. Tell me where it is and I'll see what I can do for you."

"Oh, please," scoffed Leroux.

"You don't think I can help improve your conditions? There are a *lot* of people here that want to see you rot in a hole. Not me. I'm not *Counter ACT Division,* or whatever they call it. I'm just a cop."

"I don't need to be kept comfortable," Leroux replied. "We both know how this ends. For all of us."

"So that's it?" said Stephanie. "This is how you wanna go out? The end of the ACT? All that history. The promise of an equal future for western society... the legacy of your father... *evaporated? Poof?*" Leroux's dark frown became softened. Stephanie was reaching her by emotion somehow. "Come on, Jeanne. You don't want millions to die. You might not be afraid to die, but I can't believe that you *want to.* Where's the honor in that? Where's the glory? Snuffed out before you can make a real difference. Tell me where it is, Jeanne."

Leroux saw herself as a blurred reflection in the glossy silver of the table. Stephanie studied her internalization, her gears spinning. The woman whispered, "I don't know."

"You don't know? Or you don't want to tell me?"

"I gave it back to him. *I don't know* where the bomb is."

Stephanie refused to believe it, her expression turning sour. "You'd better think hard. Because if we can't stop this bomb, I'll make sure you're the first to feel the heat."

Leroux's smug grin returned, her pearly white teeth stained with dried blood from her cut lip. Stephanie left the room, her face tired and defeated. When the door was shut, Leroux slammed the table angrily with tightened fists.

CHAPTER EIGHTEEN:

5:00 PM: MANHATTAN:

John's phone was clipped to the dash, a red dot pinging on the screen only a few streets away from his blue arrow. Henry spoke through the speaker, "NIB's sending the prototype, John. It'll be escorted by a military convoy. They should be at the meeting point before nine o'clock."

"Cutting it close," said John.

"They're moving as quickly as they can," replied Director Hall.

"Before you hang up," continued Henry, *"there's someone the other line."*

"John, this is Doctor Eugene Bresci," Hall introduced. *"A nuclear physicist. Graduated from the University of Florence, but since has been teaching at Columbia. Doctor,"* he directed his speech, *"sorry for taking time out of your busy schedule."*

"It's no trouble at all," said the physicist in a sinuous Italian accent that seemed to embellish every syllable. *"But... how did you come to contact me?"*

"As you know, we're based in New York as well. You were recommended to us by our research experts." Get to it already, Hall, thought John, tapping the wheel with angst. *"I assume you've been watching the news."*

"Oh, yes."

"We wondered if there was anything you can tell us about the bomb," said Hall. *"Our analyst, Henry, has sent you a screenshot of the news feed."*

"Just by the picture alone, not much, surely. But, eh...." The doctor was studying the image, his voice suggesting an elderly gentleman, perhaps just under seventy years of age. *"Have we any idea of the size of the device?"*

John interjected, "I only saw the storage container they smuggled it in. Couldn't be more than five or six feet in diameter."

"Doctor Bresci, that was our special agent in charge of the investigation," explained Hall. *"John Spears."*

"Well, eh, Agent Spears, if what you say is true, There are a number of possibilities. One, this highly efficient miniaturization suggests a thermonuclear fusion device— not a pure fission bomb. Don't let that fool you. Fusion devices can and are often vastly more powerful than the latter. To get one down to that size is an exceptional task that only a handful of engineers and physicists in the world are capable of doing."

"What else?" prompted John.

"The casing material is likely titanium, designed to withstand the immense pressure and heat generated by what I can only assume is a uranium-two-thirty-five core. Or plutonium-two-thirty-nine. It's quite impossible to tell."

"What about the yield? What kind of damage could we expect God-forbid this thing goes off?" asked Hall.

"Five-feet diameter.... Eh... historical scaling laws would assume two-to-three megatons of TNT. That can mean anywhere up to an eleven kilometer blast radius."

"Manhattan is only twenty-one kilometers long," Henry put into perspective.

"Yes," Doctor Bresci replied. *"Yes, it would do a considerable amount of damage."*

"What about weaknesses?" said John. "What do you see?"

"The exposed wiring suggests multiple shockwave detectors carefully con-nected to the core for a multi-point detonation. But the way the wires are wound—"

John remembered now. "There's a port. The picture didn't show it but in the schematics it was there. The wiring is fed into a hole that leads to the core."

"Perhaps, but this does not mean it can be simply disarmed—"

"This might be the key. We'll just have to wait for the military to get here with the prototype to find out," said John.

"I don't understand," the Doctor lilted.

"We have a plan, Doctor Bresci," said Hall, *"that we can't really discuss over the phone for security reasons. But we thank you for your invaluable insight. If you can, get out of the city as soon as possible."*

"Will do, Director."

"We'll let you go, John," said Hall, *"in the meantime, we're still looking out for any suspicious behavior among the employees here. Not much else we can do to find the traitor besides confiscating every phone and running a lengthy analysis."*

"You just might want to get started on that." John watched the blip on his GPS stop and disappear. "What the... Henry, Meyers is gone."

"What do you mean?"

"The ping was just there, now it's gone." said John, putting the car in park in the middle of the usually busy but nearly deserted third avenue (centered in the four-block neighborhood of Gramercy Park).

"He must've started jamming our signal again...." Henry's voice trailed off as John saw a gleaming red laser sparkle and singe his irises, then land with a dot above his heart. His eyes stretched; he plucked the phone out of its clip and dove shoulder-first into the driver door, landing on the street as a zipping bullet exploded the leather seat cushioning.

John raced to the back of the truck and knelt, shaking, a split second from having been gored. He looked across the street and saw, in the reflection of an apartment window, a bright glare twinkling a mere second before another shot shattered the glass. He spotted the building it was coming from but missed the floor.

He felt the truck sink as several more shots deflated the tires and cracked the ground beside him.

At the intersection of third avenue and east nineteenth street was a short, blocky apartment building with beige herringbone bricks crisscrossed up the corner where the sniper, Bell, was knelt atop the fifth floor fire escape. His .308 rifle was vented and light, gripped comfortably in his hands. He let out a short exhalation between every shot, just the precise amount of time to land where he wanted to, though Bell's target was never where he needed him to be.

John was clinging to the right side of the street as the shots were coming from the left corner of the nearing intersection. He was still a half-dozen cars away, and each vehicle was getting smaller and more exposed so that his crouch became a crawl. He took out his cellphone and swiped to the camera. He held it slowly out and over the roof of a short sedan trying to see a reflection.

Instantly the phone was pierced and sparked, went flying out his hand, which vibrated with such force that it went numb and hot. John cradled his hand with gratitude that his fingers had not been inches higher, trying to shake feeling back into it.

He kept his breathing steady until it was time to move again. That time he held his breath and sprang out to the next car. Bullets grazed the hood and splashed its windows into hundreds of shards that poured over him like stinging rain, obliterating the concrete ground and ricocheting off the metal grates where hot air was blowing from.

One risky peek and John saw finally where the shots were coming from, but how could he get across the street without becoming a beet-red sponge?

As if a divine stroke, the distraction came *whooping* up the road; a pair of police cruisers was speeding towards the building with sirens blaring. As the bullets attacked another target, John made it his chance. He rolled out from behind the car and zigzagged across the intersection.

When Bell's attention turned back, John was out of his line of sight. Grumbling, the sniper folded his rifle and retreated into the apartment. Inside the body of the tenant was sprawled lifelessly on the ground. Bell stepped over it pinching his nose from the fetid stench. He went out the door, into the hall, and around the staircase railing— where John was already a set of steps below.

Bell's weapon came down quicker and he pulled the trigger, but the rifle clicked empty. John brought up his pistol and fired— Bell dove out of the way as debris from the peeling green walls scattered over him.

John snapped his aim into the fifth floor corridor but Bell kicked his gun away. The sniper unsheathed a tiny military knife out of his black boot and started slashing. John dodged and ducked with bravura, catching a thrust and twisting Bell's wrist so he would drop the blade.

Bell forced weight on his arm, bringing John low whilst also raising his knee. John knelt, ears ringing as he took the brunt of the strike with the side of his head. Bell clinched John and drove him into the wooden railing, but John clung tight. Both men went careening through the railing and tumbled down the steps.

Bell rose first, punching down at John still with his back flat. He reached for the pistol which had fallen beside them. John gripped the pistol with one hand and Bell's wrist with the other, trying to pry it out of his hands or, at the very least, keep the barrel away from his face, but it was becoming more difficult the more pressure Bell applied to John's fractured side. "Would've danced with you in the first place had I known you were this weak," sneered Bell. "Ah... and you were so close," he faked lament as the barrel was inches from John's forehead.

"FREEZE!"

"DROP THE GUN!"

A squad of police officers stormed onto the floor aiming directly at Bell. He seethed, his crooked teeth biting the air. "Coppers saved you again, Spears. Guess we'll have to take out more precincts then." His fury turned quickly to pomposity as he was forced to his feet and dragged away in irons.

5:37 PM: MANHATTAN:

"His name is Kevin Bell, former SAS, just like Kenneth Parsons. Not an operator like Parsons, though, a marksman... a covert sharpshooter," Henry broke down over the loaned NYPD walkie talkie John was holding.

"Needless to say, John," started Hall, *"stay vigilant. We don't know how many more of them there are."*

"I'll be alright, Hall." He wanted to say the worst had passed but was far from sure. "Steph?"

"I'm here, John."

"Don't suppose you got anything out of Leroux?"

"I tried, really. NIB interrogators are working her now," said Stephanie.

"I'm on my way back with the cops who caught Bell. When I get there, I'll get all three of them in a room together."

"One minor complication there, John," Hall intoned. *"Parsons is being transferred."*

"What?"

"To be fair, it wasn't my idea. CIA only offered us more information on the Hierarchy if we agreed to hand him over. I know, it's a steaming pile."

"How long ago did he leave?" John said with tense inflection.

"Couldn't have been more than ten minutes... he was being prepped and held in the car for a half hour until now—"

"Tell me you know where he is," John cut his brother off. "Tell me you're tracking that transport."

"Well, yeah, but it's out of our hands now," said Henry. *"CIA is—"*

"Where, Henry?"

There was a slight hesitation but Henry asked, *"going south down Park Ave. Just passed fifty-ninth street."*

John wrenched the wheel of his truck and veered around the police car-avan. *Fifty-four,* John read the nearest street sign in his head as he sped past it. Swerving left, John came upon Lexington Ave, then pressed towards Park Ave, ignoring the chatter over the walkie.

John drifted right, tires screeching. He sped down the wrong side of the road, cutting past honking vehicles down fifty-fifth, down fifty-sixth.

The transport truck was in sight. John yanked the steering wheel and stopped directly in front of the van. He got out before the two agents could, gun aimed. *"Don't!"* he yelled at the first. The passenger came out shooting; John forced down the driver and peeked through the door at the passenger, out in the open. John fired off one shot that hit the agent low in the midsection, caught in his bulletproof vest.

John kicked away the driver's gun, aiming for him to follow to the left side of the van, then slid away the passenger's pistol. "You'll be alright," he said to the writhing agent. "You," he pointed at the driver on his feet, "the back."

"Why are you doing this?" the agent pled as his keys jingled.

"Open it," ordered John.

The doors swung open. John trained his gun, ready to fire if Parsons came out attacking— but no one was there. The van was empty. John pulled on the driver's collar and pointed his gun at the trembling man's forehead. *"Where is Parsons?"*

"Who?"

"The terrorist you were transporting! *Where is he?"*

"We already transported that Leroux woman to NIB! We're out on patrol! No Parsons!" the agent whimpered.

John weltered, horror across his face. *The wrong truck? How could Henry make that kind of mistake?* His unruly thoughts stirred, his heart pounding rapidly.

Elsewhere in the city, sitting in a car on his burner phone was Eric Meyers. "Did you do it?" he whispered.

"I've taken a lot of risks for you today but this was *too far.* It's only a matter of time until he realizes I hacked into his station!" The woman was in the shadow of a hall, cool blue light bouncing off of pink slip-ons as she anxiously rapped the floor. "I was able to feed Spears the wrong transport truck but Parsons, Bell, and Leroux are still in custody!"

"Jen, Jen," the Englishman calmly beckoned. "You needn't worry yourself so much. You've done extraordinarily well."

"What next?" she asked.

"Next... I think it's about time for a little reunion." Meyers's cold laugh was enough to send a shiver down Jen's back.

"Great," she muttered when Meyers hung up. She composed herself, taking in a deep breath and letting it out with a sigh. Jen blinked nervously, adjusted her square glasses, then slunk out of the hallway into the main communications hub of NIB headquarters.

5:58 PM: NIB HEADQUARTERS: MANHATTAN:

Jennifer Nolan maintained the pretense of odious computer work, paranoid eyes darting around.

"Jen?" The voice calling her name made the hairs on Jen's arm raise.

"Yeah, Henry," she drawled, clicking shut the application across her screen. "What's up?"

"What are you working on?"

Did he know? Was she about to be found out? A lump in her throat the size of her fist grew. "Just... the same as everyone else. Trying to track Meyers." Jen's face morphed as if the worry lifted with her pivoting speech, and she became confident in her new course. "Sorry if there's little result. That I'm just as useless as everyone else here. There's not much to work with—" To help with the act Jen started clacking against the keyboard extra heavily.

"No, Jen, I'm sorry," said Henry. "I know you've been through a lot today same as everyone else." Henry crossed his arms, rolling the sleeves of his tucked-in shirt higher above his elbows. "I've been doing my best to help John, but... it feels like everything we do fails. Sorry if Hall or I have been hard on you."

"I..." Jen merely nodded, showing Henry she understood.

Henry nodded and walked away.

Jen let out a breath of relief and reopened what she was working on. Her face went dull. She fumbled nervously to pick up her phone and dialed. A moment later she whispered, "Eric... remember you told me to warn you if and when he showed up?" On her screen was a blurry camera feed, an overhead screengrab of a man in a black suit. "Well... he's here. In New York."

6:00 PM: MANHATTAN:

The sun began to lower again. The effulgent, flaming orange was reaching below the visor in front of John, serving the annoying purpose of forcing his eyes open where they drowsed. All he wanted at the present was to sleep, but a moment's rest, John imagined, would continue to be elusive. It did not help that he had made a wrong turn and was now six cars behind the entrance of the backed-up Queensborough Bridge. Dozens of vehicles were fleeing this way towards Long Island. *They should be getting as far as possible... Long Island will still feel the effects if...* John fought away the thoughts of what would happen should the bomb go off. *It won't.* On one hand the desertion was welcome, on the other it proved an inconvenience, since John needed quick access around the city should something come up. Perhaps his phone starting to vibrate was the queue. "Henry," he answered.

"*I think I'm narrowing it down, John.*"

"What are we talking about?" John moved up, a breeze from the opened window nipping at his cheeks. "You found Parsons's actual location?"

"Nothing on Parsons yet. More about the bomb. CIA hasn't offered much," his brother began, *"but they revealed where the bomb's schematics might've come from."*

"Go on."

"Remember what Doctor Bresci said? Only a handful of engineers and physicists in the world are capable of creating a bomb that size. Turns out, it became a secret goal of the British government. But the production was held in abeyance."

"Temporarily scrapped... why?" John prodded. His voice carried an irritable edge, the bags under his eyes blackening under every fleeting sun-cast shadow of a building.

"It started more than a year ago. A terror attack in London killed a Turkish diplomat. To this day, the case has gone unresolved." Meyers, thought John. *"The Turkish government reportedly lashed out against Britain's, leading to a temporarily cancellation of their export of— you guessed it— uranium-two-thirty-five to England, under the threat that the foreign secretary and secretaries of state for business, trade and energy security all resigned."*

"But they wouldn't," John remembered. "He fired them all, didn't he?"

"Yes. That led to an unprecedented— and very public— sacking of half of Prime Minister Bain's Cabinet, only a year into his premiership."

"Lack of uranium," John pieced together, "must have threatened defense subsidies."

"Bingo," said Henry. *"The defense contractor White Rook has Britain's top nuclear researchers. Their subsidy threatened to dry up during this whole Turkish affair. That's why they were forced to put the new bomb plans on the back burner."*

"But doesn't the UK get like ten tons of enriched uranium from the States? Why did they need to import it from Turkey to keep with their new bomb?"

"I suspect to keep it a secret even from the US. But they must know the CIA monitors those exports every step of the way," Henry speculated.

"I'll bet anything Meyers is secretly pulling the strings at White Rook. If he's tied to the defense contractor, that'll explain how he got his hands on one of those bombs."

"That covers the 'how.' All that's left is the 'why?' What's his aim? What about the Hierarchy?"

John had little time to explore the questions before the air descended into gunfire and panic. He left the phone in the car, plucking himself out of the driver's seat with his weapon at his side. John kept his head low, side-stepping a vehicle that nearly crushed him and ended up colliding with another on the opposing lane. Other cars were bumping and crashing; the ones that weren't had their drivers and families racing away from the gunfire. John knelt in front of one civilian who was cowering behind her opened car door, covering her ears. John lightly squeezed her wrist and pointed away. Hesitant, she did as he bid and ran in the opposite direction of the gunfire.

Above the abutment were five ACT terrorists— John assumed by their paler complexion and civilian clothing and backpacks, unlike the tanner, tactical-geared Hierarchy members he'd clashed with before. Behind them the packed bridge had become overrun with fleeing civilians who could not hope to get far enough in their vehicles.

Directly in front of John were a pair of police officers firing back at them, taking cover behind their vehicle. John joined them and let off a couple of rounds, dropping one of the terrorists. They did not question him, only continued their return barrage, though pistols against automatic weapons was an unfair game.

When he heard magazines hitting the ground John popped up from behind a bullet-ridden car. His initial shot missed, but the second hit one of the terrorist's bags. An explosion chained between the terrorists' charges, a massive blast— the front end of the bridge crumbled in a blaze of fire and the shockwave rippled across the intersection, knocked over John and the two officers.

After John stood, ears ringing, he approached the massive breach in the road. The bridge— the way out— was severed.

He hurried back to his truck, to his cellphone. *"Henry!"*

"What's happening?" Henry sounded unnerved, and for good reason.

"It's the ACT. Or Hierarchy— doesn't matter!" John ran back to the bridge, where the police were looking after civilians that stayed behind and were quivering with shock. "They just blew up the entrance to the Queensborough Bridge! They're trying to prevent people leaving the city—"

A bright red blaze shot into the air from the south, a few miles away but still visible. *Midtown tunnel. "Henry?"* His brother was quiet. *"Henry?"*

"John…" Henry shuddered.

John's eyes widened with the realization. *It's happening everywhere.*

6:24 PM: NIB HEADQUARTERS: MANHATTAN:

Jennifer Nolan had slipped out of the main communications hub at the height of the crisis, so it would appear. Bridges and tunnels all across the city were being blown up. No way in, no way out. With everyone's attention scattered, she didn't even have to come up with an excuse to leave the building.

Jen bustled through the parking garage where, on the street, the orange sunset was slashed by the shadows of towers and patterned by the swaying of greenery. She looked over her shoulder. Even the guard at the swing gate was on his phone, red horror filling his eyes. He took no notice to Jen swiftly entering the backseat of a black SUV and roving off.

"Jen." Meyers's voice was the opposite of enigmatic. The way he merely said her name suggested he was pleased.

"Are we on our way to a helicopter? Or a ship or something?"

"Helicopter? Ship?" he repeated with condescension. "Whatever for?"

Jen's heart was coming up into her throat. "Well... you destroyed all the bridges. And the tunnels. There aren't any other ways out."

"And what will you be needing a way out for, Jen?"

"I did everything you asked! You said you'd let me and my family go!"

Meyers glacial gaze bore down upon her, piercing her every hidden emotion. "About that," he said. "No one's leaving this city... not now, anyways."

Tears started ribboning. *But you promised. If I did what you—*"

"I was never *actually* going to let you leave. You know that, don't you?" Now, now," said Meyers, the back of his hand coming to caress her cheek. "Our work isn't done here. I've still got things left to do."

Jen slapped his hand away, which only seemed to please him more. "What more do you want, you psychopath?"

"I want you to *find him.*"

"Who?" she quavered.

"You *know* who."

"Why don't I tell them where the bomb is instead?" A newfound confidence snuck through her disconnected, weepy chatter. Meyers's eyes tightened, his fist closing then opening, control being infused into his mannerisms. "Didn't think I knew that, huh? I'm the one whose been jamming their satellites which means I see *everything!* So what's stopping me from telling them?"

Meyers look unfazed, rather smiled. "I still have your family."

"And what? You'll kill them? You're going to do that anyway!"

"Yes, they will die. But in a flash, like the rest of you. However, if you do not do what I ask, I will see to it that your family experiences a certain agony so beyond your comprehension that they'll beg for relief." Jen saw a horrible fire in Meyers's eyes, reflected in his tortoise shell glasses. Her face went pale, her own fuchsia-framed glasses fogging. "Is that clear?"

"Yes," she whispered.

"What was that?" he replied arrogantly.

"Yes... yes, Sir," she said slightly louder.

This time Jen did not slap away Meyers's hand as he slid a tear off of Jen's cheek. With an unmistakable look of disgust he scraped the wetness away from his finger. "Good," he said, the truck coming to a stop in front of the NIB parking garage again. "Now find my *brother*."

6:43 PM: MANHATTAN:

John was patrolling the same two block radius around headquarters for the past half hour, he and at least four other NIB trucks. He was on the phone with Henry, who said, *"Parsons's transport was intercepted. He's gone."*

"It was only a matter of time." John tasted a bitterness, though that could have been dust and gunpowder, the same air that filled his nose.

"Why did it take them so long to report back to us?" There was frustration in Henry's voice.

"Three agents are dead, Henry. Getting them out of there was their first priority," John heard Stephanie's saccharine voice say.

"Yeah... yeah, you're right." Henry's words altered into a more understanding tone.

"Something did come out of it though," said John. "If you were fed the wrong information from your own station... not just any agent could do that."

"An analyst!" Henry whispered, a lightbulb going off.

"There are more analysts than agents here." Stephanie shut down hopes of narrowing it further. "How do we find out who it is?"

"Hall's ordered phones confiscated already but it'll take hours," said Henry.

"Hours we don't have," muttered John.

"What if," Stephanie furtively brought her inquisitiveness to a lesser volume, *"we set a* trap?"

"What kind of trap?" said Henry.

"Now that you know somebody here is hacking into your station, we get them to do it again. Only this time, you'll be ready."

"How exactly do we do that?"

John felt out of place in the conversation, driving without aim and circling the building…. Suddenly one of the vehicles he passed by on the road seemed a little different. The men inside… they were not NIB. The vehicle swerved onto the sidewalk, drove on a patch of grass in the southwest edge of the glossy black building. *"Henry! They're here!"*

John made an abrupt U-turn and veered onto the sidewalk, heavy wheels trampling the grass. Bullets began flying his way, forcing him to stop the vehicle and duck behind the dash. He caught a glimpse at the terrorists exiting their truck, one of them with a long black cylinder— a *rocket launcher. "GET DOWN!"* John yelled into the phone.

A torrent of flame sped towards the side of the building and obliterated a chunk of glass and concrete support. Two of the terrorists stayed behind to keep John pinned down, whilst the other two entered the building, opening fire.

Inside, Henry and Stephanie hid beneath Henry's desk as NIB agents were belting towards the hallway branching from the main communications hub. That was where the explosion emanated from. A cloud of smoke traveled into the atrium, obscuring the terrorist duo as they broke open one of the detainment rooms.

"They're going after Bell and Leroux!" yelled Stephanie. She crawled out from under Henry's desk and raced towards the hall, gun drawn.

As the smoke cleared, she saw Kevin Bell being hurried across the hall to the left by one of the terrorists, towards a hole in the wall. The agents were too late to catch him, but Jeanne Leroux was next. Stephanie made little hesitation to open fire, but the terrorist whose arm was wrapped around Leroux's shoulders shot back, forcing Stephanie into cover. Before he could get her to the other side, however, another agent fired the fatal shot. Stephanie lurched towards Leroux, her handcuffed wrists trying to shove her away.

"Let's go!" John heard the terrorists clambering into the truck with Kevin Bell behind them.

When the automatic fire ceased John stomped the gas. The chase was on. John's front bumper collided so powerfully with the rear of the terrorists' truck that it was launched onto the street, even helping it to a moderate speed for which they were pursued.

Bullets came through the shattered rear window making John yaw and skid, his deflating tires at risk of *popping* any second now.

"They got away, John! They got Bell, but our agents killed one of them, stopped them from getting Leroux," he heard Henry saying, his phone still on speaker.

"They haven't gotten away! I'm on them!" John gave the steering wheel a powerful wrest, right on the truck's tail as it took its turn.

The buildings were grey and black checkerboards darting past, little flecks of gold pelting his smoking hood. *"No, no!"* John's foot was to the floor; he could go no faster. Bullets were whizzing past his face; he made no effort now to duck and move his head. He used his own pistol and started firing through a hole forming in the windshield, but none hit their target.

The hood burst open, hot smoke billowing out. John had to stop the vehicle, his vision impaired. John slammed on the steering wheel steaming mad. He lost them.

CHAPTER TWENTY:

7:05 PM: NIB HEADQUARTERS: MANHATTAN:

The red-painted Hierarchy symbol on the floor of the one-walled detainment room was partially obscured by fragments of glass and concrete. "Damn fools," said Hall. "Could've probably got Leroux too if they didn't stop to make modern art." It was a lame attempt at a jest, one John was profoundly in no mood for. "How did they know Bell would be in this room?"

A good question, thought John, *one we know the answer to already.* There was a leak, an informer. Someone was feeding Meyers with intel, but who?

Stephanie entered, Henry trailing close by, and said, "I have an idea."

John, Henry, and Hall followed Stephanie to the conference room, leaving their phones on Henry's desk to make sure their ears were the only ones in attendance. No time was to be lost; neither of the four even bothered to sit. "What's this idea you're proposing, Detective?" said Hall.

"A trap." John remembered her mentioning something about a trap over the phone, before gunfire and explosions rang out. "Whoever is leaking information to Meyers gave us the wrong location of the truck holding Ken Parsons, right? This time, we give *them* the wrong location."

"Elaborate," suggested John.

"We say that we're afraid the terrorists will come back for Leroux, so we'll drive her around and keep her location a secret. So when the mole hacks into Henry's station he'll be waiting, and they'll have sent Meyers's goons bad info."

"What if the leak finds out the real transport truck? Or sends terrorists to intercept them all? It's not like the ACT and Hierarchy are lacking in manpower," said Hall.

"We don't need to fake the info. We'll give them the real location of the truck. But before they come to intercept it, I'll have already broken her out," Stephanie explained, her last words causing the men to look at each other with uncertainty.

"What do you mean, you'll *break her out?*" said John.

"This is an opportunity," Stephanie insisted, "not only to trick the traitor, but to trick Leroux as well."

"By making her believe you're the mole. You think she'll actually buy it?" said Henry, he, John and Hall sharing a similarly skeptical look.

"I don't know. If it's convincing enough, maybe."

"What if Leroux already knows who the leak is?" questioned Hall.

"And what if she asks you to confirm your relation to Meyers?" added Henry.

Stephanie waved her hands defensively. "Look, there are gonna be a lot of what ifs, okay? And a helluva lot of risk. But if this works, we find the traitor and get Leroux to lead us to Meyers. We kill two birds with one stone." She looked to John, who was quiet between Hall and Henry. "What do you think?" she asked him.

John knew he'd rather she stay out of danger, but it was too late for that. "It seems... like the only option right now."

Stephanie grinned. Hall and Henry, despite the unsurety, nodded along. "Alright, then," Hall agreed, "I'll get the transfer set."

"The escort agents can't know the plan. They have to be shocked that I'd betray them and set Leroux free," Stephanie expanded.

"Understood," said Hall. "Henry, you start logging the transfer window so the leak gets it from your station. Don't make it *too* easy. Gotta make sure they take the bait. John, Stephanie, you two start building a cover. You can bet Leroux will ask you a host of questions. You'd better have answers to them."

John and Stephanie nodded and each took a seat across from one another while Henry and Hall left the conference room. John looked at her, the worry in his eyes reciprocated. "You ready?"

7:25 PM: MANHATTAN:

The apartment was one of many such adjacent dwellings. The night was quiet in Greenwich Village, the streets— seldom forsaken— shared only an uncanny whisper. The smell of smoke drifted down the deserted lane. Bullet casings spilled out from behind the sliding door of the van. A band of ACT terrorists stepped onto the street lacking the usual subtlety. With them was Kevin Bell, his sloppy hair and black eyes barely illuminated by the yellow coach lights that flickered like candles.

The men entered the apartment, whispering and yammering as they shoved Bell sideways into the living room. The chamber was lit by fire, a narrow yet grand arrangement of bookshelves, paintings and velvet furnishings. Above the mantel was a golden candelabra. Eric Meyers detachedly ran his fingers through the twinkling flame. "Mr. Bell," he said, his lenses flitting with fire, "good to have you back."

Sitting in one of the chairs against the green floral wallpaper was Kenneth Parsons, polishing a knife on his lap. He shot an indifferent look at Bell, which he met with a slight nod.

"Good to be back," replied Bell. He keeked askance over his shoulder where the ACT members were chattering. "Sent the Frenchmen to come get me, did ya?"

Meyers did not answer at first. He turned, his eyes glinting firelight. He stepped towards Bell, his leather oxfords tapping lightly along the carpet. Much to Bell's surprise, Meyers put a hand on Bell's cheek, gave him a lenient shake. "You did well," he said. "You said nothing."

Bell smirked. "Yeah, well... nothing I really *could've* said, init?"

Meyers turned towards Parsons, whose head was hung with what Bell construed to be shame. "Kenneth thinks me *upset* with him. I'll admit, initially I was. How could I not be?" He started pacing for the other end of the room, bearing down upon Parsons. "NIB at my front door. I was sure I was going to be caught. It was only due to our new friend, Madame Leroux, that I escaped. A shame we couldn't free her as well. In due time.

"But no, Kenneth," he continued, standing over Parsons's red chair, "I'm not angry with you. After all, I can't blame you for being a hired gun. I pay you to kill, not to keep my secrets. And after all... neither of you two signed up to *die.*"

Bell was not quite sure what he meant, his brow twitching. "Sir?"

Meyers merely jerked his head upwards and the apartment was cleared of ACT men. "You see, this bomb will go off in less than five hours. Now only a select few will be allowed to leave with me. Leroux, her freakish advisor, Alec, and the two of you. I have no intention of staying, needlessly sacrificing myself any more than the two of you do."

"Suppose it's good to get clarity on that," said Bell. "But this Leroux woman…." Bell came closer to Meyers and lowered his tone to say, "Do you really need her?"

"Perhaps not," mused Meyers, "perhaps so. Her men grow restless without her. We cannot wait much longer. We risk them turning against us."

"Let them," challenged Parsons.

Meyers ignored. Bell proposed, "Well come on, then. Let me and 'im set back out to their headquarters."

"No," said Meyers. "They'll have taken extra precautions this time. We must wait to see what my woman on the inside tells us."

"Ah," Bell crowed admiringly. "An ace up your sleeve, I see."

"She's to thank for you being here." Meyers turned again to the fire, his hands cupped behind his back. "She will not fail us. I've made sure of it."

7:34 PM: MANHATTAN:

John trailed an entire block away from the prisoner transport vehicle. When it turned, John turned several moments later, rolling slowly down the tower-lit road.

Stephanie sat across from Leroux in the back truck, the two locked in an unblinking staring contest. The carriage was a pale grey with a single strip of green-white light overhead. Brief, quiet chatter could be heard through a slit in the barrier separating the driver and passenger seats and the rear.

Stephanie peered out of the scant grated windows in one of the rear doors. They passed a certain building she recognized as the truck ambled beneath a canopy of trees that obscured the road with leafy shadows. It was time.

She returned her gaze to Leroux and let out a controlled breath. Stephanie scooted to the end of the bench and knocked on the partition. One of the agents slid it open. Immediately Stephanie unholstered her pistol and aimed it at the driver. "Any sudden move and I will pull the trigger, you understand?" The passenger crept as far back in his seat as he could, aghast. Leroux was not quite sure what to make of it. "Stop the truck." The driver did as she requested. "Open the door. You first." She aimed at the driver.

When the driver came around back and opened the door, Stephanie stepped out. "Come on," she told Leroux. "Now you," she said to the passenger. Both agents had swapped places with Stephanie and Leroux. Stephanie held out a hand and the driver reluctantly handed over his keys. "Goodnight, Gentlemen." Stephanie shut the door, hooked Leroux's arm and guided her onto the sidewalk. "I should've shot them," muttered Stephanie.

"What is this? What are you playing at?" spluttered Leroux.

"What does it look like?" Stephanie threw her cellphone on the ground and stomped it to ensure.

"*You?* No, it can't be you."

Stephanie turned the corner of the street and came upon an apartment that was boarded up, under renovation. On the corner, lights off, was John, keeping a close eye from his car, hearing every word in an earpiece.

"Believe it, Sister." Stephanie opened the door, craning over her shoulder with a tenable level of paranoia.

The two entered the apartment. It was completely dark save for the orange streetlamp outside. Stephanie peered through the blinds and whispered, "We're clear. For now."

Leroux kept a reasonable distance. "This is a trick," she claimed. "Why else would you do that?"

"I'd've thought Meyers would've told you. He does like to keep things close to the chest." It was something she remembered Ken Parsons saying to John during his interrogation; it felt sensible, and Leroux seemed to bite.

"You're the one who arrested me!"

"Gave you every chance to escape, didn't I?" Stephanie was firm, completely different in her demeanor than normal. "I had to make it look realistic. Sorry about that by the way." She pointed at cut on Leroux's forehead. "For the record, I could have done way worse."

"Lies," said Leroux. "Prove you're Eric's. Call him."

"Didn't you see me crush my phone just now? NIB is rounding agents up, confiscating and monitoring their phones. They'll know where I am and hear every word."

Leroux bit her nail, still maintaining a distance. "Then what? They'll know you've betrayed them soon enough."

"Obvious isn't it? We go see Meyers."

"Fine. Lead the way."

"If I knew where he was, I would have stopped *there*. Why would he trust me with his location when I could've been captured at any minute?" Stephanie argued.

"The same could be said for me," said Leroux, her silver locks bronze in the streetlight. "What makes you think I know where he'd be? We fled from the same place. Only *he* made it out."

"I know how the Hierarchy operates," countered Stephanie, "*and* the ACT. Always a contingency. Always another hideout. He must've given you a place to meet him should this situation arise. He told me so himself."

"Did he now?" Leroux was still doubtful. *Who could blame her?* John thought. His heart was racing arguably faster than Stephanie's. "I asked you to prove your allegiance. You haven't yet."

"And how should I do that?"

"Give me your gun."

Stephanie twitched, a diamond smile cutting the tension. "Why would I do that? I said I'm on your side, I'm not a fool."

"If you're on my side, you have no reason to fear me holding your weapon for you."

John gnawed on his fingernails, a habit he might've once broken but has now since returned. *"What does that prove?"* said Stephanie.

Leroux held out her hand, her emerald eyes shimmering. Stephanie had no recourse, no other options. She knew the risks involved. It would take another risk to gain her trust. Stephanie unholstered her pistol and slowly, hesitantly, placed it in Leroux's palm.

Leroux was the one smiling now. She gripped the pommel of the pistol. *Please... please,* thought John. Leroux made to strike— John heard Stephanie yelp and was prepared to ram through the front of the apartment. "That was for earlier," said Leroux. Stephanie wiped a bit of blood from above her brow where Leroux hit her with the gun's pommel. "Fair?"

Stephanie gritted her teeth but managed to calm herself. "Fair." Leroux flipped the pistol and gave it back to Stephanie, handle-first.

She's done it, thought John, finally able to breathe. *Thank God.*

"Now," remarked Stephanie, "shall we?"

Leroux nodded. "There is a place. Like you said, in case of this very moment. But we don't have a way of getting there, do we?"

"I know how to hot-wire a car," Stephanie said in braggadocious manner.

Leroux smirked again. "Perhaps we'll grow to like each other after all."

7:57 PM: MANHATTAN:

Heavy traffic up Amsterdam avenue led them to Washington Heights, where citizens in droves were bottlenecked by the collapsed Henry Hudson and Broadway bridges to the north. Stephanie and Leroux stepped out of the stolen car in front of a warehouse on a vacant street. It was exceedingly dark, enough for Stephanie to ask, "You sure there's anyone home?"

"There's nobody," said Leroux. "We must call them from inside."

John watched from afar, his car one of many wedged onto the side of the road. Once the two women went in, the signal jammed, turning into a static so loud John threw out his earpiece. Not a moment later, there were *gunshots*.

John opened the driver door and raced onto the street with his pistol at the ready. Leroux was running out of the warehouse and in the opposite direction. *"STOP!"* John called, but it was no use. It was either pursue Leroux or help Stephanie... *if* she was still alive, that was.

John did not linger. He beelined for the warehouse where flashes of yellow and loud *pops* were being discharged. Stephanie was inside, crouched behind a row of blue metal barrels, clutching her bleeding shoulder.

John let loose three bullets towards the darkness and slid beside Stephanie, a barrage narrowly zipping past him. She was in panic. John brushed the almond waves out of her face to see tears streaming down her cheeks. "It's okay, I'm here. Let me see." She let go of her arm so John could inspect the red gash, not too deep but seeping blood. "It only grazed you. You're gonna be fine."

"'Fine?'" she repeated, ducking from the loud panging that rung their ears.

John popped out and shot another couple of bullets. When he lowered himself again he took out his phone and dialed. *"Henry!"* he yelled. *"We need help!"*

CHAPTER TWENTY-ONE:

8:00 PM: MANHATTAN:

Leroux was chuffing on the side of the road with her hands over her bent knees. The sounds of gunfire were still loud around the corner. An SUV black as midnight rolled in front of her and out stepped three men. "Madame Leroux!" called Alec, the lanky, spiky-haired second-in-command. "Are you alright?"

"I'm fine, Alec," she panted. "Let's get out of here."

After Leroux, Alec went into the backseat. She sat between him and another man— not a Frenchman, but a South American member of the Hierarchy— who held out a phone in front of her. Leroux took the phone and put it to her ear. "Meyers."

"I'm happy to hear you're okay, Dear Jeanne."

"Sure you are," she jibed. "How did you know where to find me? Did Alec tell you?" Leroux frowned at Alec, who evaded contact.

"Your protégé is ever loyal, Madame. There are others in your organization who worry for your safety. But that leads me to question... why did you not trust me with the knowledge of your contingency?"

"The warehouse backup was a plan put in place before we met," said Leroux. "You had no reason to know."

"Ah, but if I didn't, your men would not have been allowed to patrol the area, would they?"

"No one gave you leave to command my men." Leroux's elfin face was scrunched and stern.

Meyers let out a frigid laugh that made Leroux want to pull away from the phone. *"Of course. But perhaps their behavior in your absence might provoke some reflection. The way they flocked to a new leader. Perhaps it is a good thing they'll all be dead in a few hours."*

"Indeed," Leroux agreed. "Speaking of. Are we set to leave?"

"Almost, Madame, almost. We can't leave until we know for certain my bomb is protected. I must wait 'til only minutes remain."

"We must wait," Leroux corrected. "How do I know you haven't left already?"

"What little trust you have...." Meyers took in a sharp breath and exhaled into the microphone, a windy rippling filling Leroux's ears that made her cringe. *"I have a small matter to handle. In an hour or so, you will see me."*

"So you say."

"If you don't hear from me, the driver will bring you directly to the heli-copter. You can leave without me." Leroux went silent, perhaps flirting with the inclination to do just that. *"Dear, Leroux. I told you. We are partners."*

John knelt behind a row of blue canisters *pinging* and drumming with every bullet that bombarded them. Stephanie clutched her shoulder, her breathing calmer than before with the realization it was just a graze wound. "What are we gonna do?" she stressed, looking at the entrance to the warehouse that they had drifted away from, fleeing across the warehouse from the terrorists. "I'm running low!"

"How many mags do you have?" said John.

"Including this one, just two."

John weighed his options. He only had one clip, the one presently in his pistol. The warehouse was a small space, but many rows of shelves lined with crates and barrels offered cover between him and the terrorists. "Give me the extra mag." Stephanie handed it to him without question. "I'm gonna give you cover. When I do, you need to run there," he pointed to a stack of metal that was tucked against the back wall of the warehouse and forming a small L-shaped gap, "hide. Once I clear the way, if you can, make for the entrance and get out of here."

"What— no—"

"We can't hold out long enough for backup," declared John. "All I care about right now is keeping you safe! Don't worry about me!"

"That's not gonna happen!"

John put a hand on Stephanie's cheek. Words were not needed. She understood the assignment, nodded. "Ready?" John sprang upwards and emptied his magazine. He saw silhouettes scurrying into deeper shadows, the yellow gun flashes pausing for John's single strobing spark. Stephanie dove for the heap of scrap metal and stacked canisters, tucking her body behind it and becoming near invisible.

John knelt again and started crouching between a set of shelves to the right side of the warehouse. It was pitch black. He wished for a moment he still had the TXPS glasses his brother gave him, that way he might see, at the very least, how many terrorists pursued him.

He was walking backwards, his pistol aimed at the spot he and Stephaine just were, waiting for one of the terrorists to show. He glanced quickly to his right, where he could hear footsteps coming around and splitting between the aisles. Very suddenly, he was stopped, bumping backs with one of the terrorists he had not realized was behind him. Both men reacted at the same time, but John was the first to make a move, wrapping his hand around the terrorist's neck. The man jutted back his hips and flipped John over his shoulder. From the ground, John redirected the rifle that was coming his way, and with his feet twisted and kicked the terrorist's knee to bring him down. When John finished the terrorist with a punch to the face, the loud grunt alerted two men in the next aisle over.

John saw their feet rushing past. He aimed, shoulder to the ground, and shot the shins out from under two terrorists. His last bullets ended their lives.

French intermingled with Portuguese, the screams of the combatants giving John some slight reassurance. *They're disorganized, arguing,* he observed. John picked up the rifle of the ACT terrorist at his feet. He tried to pick apart the voices as he rounded the eastern wall of the warehouse. *At least three distinct.* Three men, two ACT, one Hierarchy.

The terrorists came upon the place where John had knocked out one and killed two others. John snuck into the adjacent aisle, seeing one in the next, and two in the row after that. John drove his body into the shelf and tipped it on its side. Like a domino effect the first fell overtop the nearest terrorist, then the next into the final two. The two ACT members weren't crushed like the first, though. They got up and immediately started firing in John's direction.

John sprinted westward back to the center lane of the warehouse, where the two met him. With a quick draw, John shot first and killed one. The other came charging two rows down to John and swung a knife round the corner. John blocked his forearm with the rifle, drove him back and struck with the gun's stock. The terrorist lurched forward, thrusting with the knife but John swatted it away with the rifle. It was the kind of training he had never put into practice, especially since John was never a good shot. Yet months with the Israeli army gave him a set of instincts with a rifle that did not allow an enemy to pierce his guard. John struck upwards, swiped downwards, then finished the combination with a powerful thrust of the rifle's barrel into the terrorist's chest. With the man knocked down, John lunged with the gunstock and sent him into a deep sleep.

John spun, his neck cranking. The only sound was that of his heavy breathing. The coast was clear. "Steph?" he called, praying she was okay.

"John!" he heard her yell.

John followed the voice to the front of the warehouse. *She made it out,* he thought, relief allowing captured breath to escape his chest. John wrapped his arms around Stephanie and hugged her. She winced, her lacerated shoulder rubbing against John's army jacket. John wanted to split, to apologize, but she held him tighter.

When she released, John's heart was still. He saw the blood above her eye where Leroux hit her, the gash on her shoulder. *What have I done? I should have never called her.* She seemed to know exactly what he was thinking and lifted his hung head with a finger under his chin. "We're okay now," she said.

John's pocket vibrated. He took out his phone and answered, "Henry. How far is the ambulance?"

"The traffic is worst to the north, John. It's still gonna be another ten minutes or so."

"Alright, we'll stay put. Thanks, Hen—"

"That's not all. It's the military, John."

"They're here?"

"They'll be at the meeting point in less than thirty minutes," Henry replied. *"Since the bridges and tunnels are wiped out, they're coming by boat from West New York."*

"Where's the meet?"

"Upper West Side," said Henry. *"I'll send you the location."*

John looked at Stephanie sitting on the curb. "I can't leave Stephanie here alone. Tell them to hold off—"

"John," she said, "I'm fine. You go. I'll wait for the ambulance."

"Absolutely not." There was no argument to be had.

She stood and faced him, her dark eyes twinkling in the smoke-occluded moonlight. "This thing you have to do. It's far more important than sticking around here with me."

"No, I can't—"

"Thank you. For saving me. But think for a second. There are a lot more people yet to save. *Go*. I'll be fine."

John gave her a lasting glance, hoping desperately it would not be the last. Without another word, he walked towards his car and did not look back.

8:40 PM: MANHATTAN:

John sat in his car at the end of a short dock. Three spotlights were shining across the water from long Coast Guard cutters like red arrows slashing towards the island. "They're here, Hall," John said into his phone.

He got out of the car when one of the three boats was anchoring. Overhead were tall white lights illuminating the concrete path where a suited agent was approaching, holding a briefcase with two camo-clad soldiers on his left and right. "Agent Spears?" the man said.

John nodded. *"Alright, John,"* he heard Hall in his ear. *"No time for lollygagging, just make the drop, get the device, then get out—"* A giant spark flew from John's phone and stung the side of his cheek. He slapped the screen but it wouldn't turn on. In that same moment, the lights overhead went off, as did the lights from John's truck, and the beams protruding from the Coast Guard vessels anchored just beyond the dock.

"What's going on?" the agent hissed.

"Did you activate the device?" scolded John.

"Why would I—" the agent's protest was cut short by his chest bursting, the *snap* of a bullet coming a millisecond after.

Meyers has an EMP? The thought made John petrified, so much so that he almost failed to make a run at the briefcase while the soldiers opened fire into the darkness. John seized the case and took cover behind his NIB standard.

The two soldiers dropped and were quickly replaced by others pouring out of the boats. John opened the metal case. Inside was a cylinder with a hexagonal top and bottom. There were slits between the hexagons where lights would be but they were deactivated. *Please come back on,* thought John. John stuffed the device into his inner jacket pocket.

Unarmed, John held the metal briefcase to the side of his head and neck and started running across the strip of nothingness separating him from the street. Bullets landed at his feet and plinked off the case. John sidestepped the bar gate and cut right behind the fence, where the bullets were clinking, metal on metal. *"IT'S SPEARS! GET AFTER 'IM!"*

The voices were not entirely unrecognizable. That is, they were *English,* in accent and in language. *More of Meyers's assassins?* John had nothing to make of it and made no attempt to. He sped across the road to where he could see streetlights. The radius of whatever caused the blackout must have been a hundred yards, he figured.

When he slid into an alleyway still cut off from the light, there were two terrorists chasing after him. John knelt behind an acrid green dumpster, waiting for them. *"Split off! Go around!"* one of them yelled.

The terrorist slowly stepped, a feint buzzing coming from around his head that John found peculiar. "In one of these buildings, are ya? Come out, Spears!"

Definitely not the Hierarchy or ACT, John thought. *If they're like Parsons or Bell, I ought to be careful.*

The terrorist's gun was first, making for an easy target. John jumped out from behind the dumpster and locked grip around the weapon's body. His elbow slashed backwards and caught the terrorist on the nose. John used the butt of the rifle to double down, knocking the terrorist to the ground. He aimed for the back of the alley and realized what was especially peculiar about these men— the rifle had a thermal sight, showing him hues of cold blue and green, and the warm yellows and reds of the man turning the corner. He pulled the trigger twice and laid the man down. The one on the ground had sprung up and wrapped arms around John. He wrenched free with a swing, tossing him down again, then finished with a kick to the face.

John walked towards the dead body curiously. He exchanged weapons. This one's was the same. Thermal scope, capable of seeing through the blackout. John rushed to the sidewalk where streetlights were glowing a dismal orange. He kept on a swivel, making sure he wasn't being followed. He reached into his pocket and took out his cellphone. It came back on.

As he dialed, he reached into his glowing jacket pocket. The EMP device was now powered on, blue neon lights cascading down its six sharp sides. "Henry, Hall. We were ambushed. I got away but I don't know what happened to the soldiers."

"Did you get the device?" said Hall.

John twirled the blue shining object in his hand. "I got it."

"Report back to headquarters immediately, John," Hall ordered.

"I'll need help with that. Had to leave my vehicle behind. You're not gonna believe this... I think Meyers has access to these types of electromagnetic pulse devices."

"What? How?" worried Henry.

"I don't know. One minute the lights were on, next second all electronics shot out. They also had these weapons. Thermal scope. Kind of like those prototype glasses from earlier," explained John. "And they were English. Not like any other Hierarchy members, more like Parsons and Bell, only way less trained. They had me pinned down in an alley but I managed to take them."

"We're running out of time, John," his brother said. *"You have the thing you need, that's what matters right now. The last step is finding the bomb."*

Something itched at John. He would have a hard time ignoring his concerns. *Who were they? How did they...?* He set it aside then said, "Let's get started."

8:55 PM: MANHATTAN:

There was a modest corner shop in Chinatown, steam billowing from its exposed pipes. Along the misty entryway, where a red light shone, two armed guards stood out front.

Eric Meyers approached, two of his own men escorting him. One of the guards merely gestured to allow entry but held up a hand to halt the other two. Meyers turned, nodded, and bid them to stay outside.

Like a common deli there was the counter on the left, glass display cases empty and darkened. Along the right were tables and booths pressed against the wall of windows. There, sitting with his back to the door, was a figured bathed in neon crimson.

Before Meyers saw his face, he asked, "What the hell are you doing in my city?"

"Your city?" He was an Englishman as well and boasted a similarly pompous laugh that sounded like a series of short, disconnected hums.

"That's right." Meyers sat across from him.

The man was a mirror to Meyers in every way, from the all-black suit, silver watch, to the black eyes that needed not be hidden behind a pair of glasses. He had a similar field of freckles upon his cheeks and nose, and the same prince-like jawline, but with more loose, aged skin under his eyes. "Just wanted to check in on you, make sure you weren't mucking things up."

"Always have to be the one to pick up after my mess, huh?" said Meyers. His brother was scratching the brown melamine tabletop with short fingernails, smiling. "Our father gave us our tasks back in London. So I ask again, why are you here?"

"Our father was clear. If it seemed you were losing a handle on things... I should be on standby, ready to step in—"

"And what makes you think I've lost the handle on things?" Meyers was steaming, his usual calmness broken for the first time. His brother, on the other hand, was entirely relaxed.

"That little message you gave on live television. I could've guessed you'd try to make it all about you. Were you *trying* to expose us all? Or did you actually, *naively* think that it wouldn't be seen outside this city?"

"No one can challenge me. Why shouldn't they hear my name? See my face?" said Eric. "They'll never be able to connect me back to Father—"

"But when they're no longer distracted, they'll connect you to *me!*" His brother showed his teeth, crooked and unsightly. It seemed his calm was evaporating as well as Meyers's. "Or do you not care?" He did not need an answer.

Meyers's eyes evaded him. "What do you want?" he said.

"I have access to a military grade electro-pulse weapon that can target specific objects and leave others immune to its blast."

"*So?*"

"So... I have reason to believe Spears has one of his own."

"How?"

"Your military contractor isn't the only one I sold the patent to," said Meyers's brother. "Anyway, it doesn't matter. His EMP is more likely to *detonate* the bomb rather than disable it. Another way I can be of assistance."

"No." Meyers shut him down without a thought. "I don't need you interfering. And in the off chance your little device *does* disarm my bomb...."

Meyers's brother put his hands up beside his head in a surrendering pose, saying, "Message read, Brother. You don't want me stealing your spotlight, I can understand that. You won't see me getting in the way... that is, unless Spears *does* get the better of you."

Meyers did not bother to entertain the notion. "He won't."

"I hope you're right." His brother snapped his fingers and one of the guards entered. "Take care, Eric."

The guard was motioning for Meyers to get to his feet. When he did, the guard was slowly nudging him out without being forceful. The look of disgust on Meyers's face suggested this would be the last time he looked upon his brother's face, or so he hoped. "And you," he said, "*Aaron.*"

CHAPTER TWENTY-TWO:

Jen's auburn hair shone in the light of her computer monitor. Her fingers trounced the keyboard, a rapid clacking that filled the noise around her. Glimmers of numbers, coordinates, and maps reflected in her pink glasses and her magnified eyes, when they weren't wandering about the atrium with paranoia.

Henry was whispering something to Director Hall. Something about *them covering their tracks well. It was worth a try.* Jen hoped they weren't talking about her— she covered her tracks better the last time she hacked into Henry's station. The way Henry glanced left at her made her flinch and evade. They hadn't found her, not yet.

Jen got up, neatly slid her chair under her desk, and retreated somewhere where there would be less eyes, though Henry's followed her. She strolled towards the hall across the bullpen. On either side were the detainment rooms, the first on the left sealed away from the hole in the wall, which she could see through a window in the door. She had her cell phone in hand. Jen pressed herself around the corner between the restrooms on either end.

Henry peered down the hall from the atrium suspiciously. He slowly tread, hearing susurrations from around the corner.

"I found him," she whispered.

"Rather late for that, Jen," said Meyers. *"I just spoke to him. At his own invitation."* Henry became close enough to hear a masculine voice, but no semblance or words to identify.

"What did he say?"

"I'm afraid that's none of your concern," replied Meyers.

"Not my concern? *You* asked me to—"

"I don't owe you any explanations, Jen," he said coldly. *"Do you remember what we agreed? About your family?"*

"I remember." The words were hot coals in her windpipe.

"So tell me you'll continue to do what I ask."

"I will."

Meyers's tongue clicked thrice. *"I need to hear you say it, Jen."*

"I'll do what you ask," Jen stuttered.

"Good.... Now if you'll excuse me, I have a message to relay. It starts in an hour time."

"'An hour time?'" she repeated. "What starts in an hour?"

"War." That word Henry could hear as clear as a whisper in his own ear. His eyes widened. *It starts in and hour time... war.* His heart started to race, Jen's final words muffling before she hung up and rounded the corner. Henry walked forward as if he was only just coming and collided with Jen.

"Oh! Henry!" she said, feigning pleasant surprise.

"Sorry," said Henry coolly. "I was just on my way to the restroom."

"I see," Jen murmured, something off in her eye. "I was on the way *from* the restroom." She smiled, hoping that could ward off Henry's suspicion.

"Well, uh, I'll see you." He cleared his throat. Jen nodded. The two awkwardly parted, Henry walking past her and pushing open the door to the men's restroom. The second the door closed, Jen had spun on her heels and, instead of making her way back to her station, was rushing past the restrooms the opposite way. Henry pushed back open the door and spotted her veering left where one of the stairwell exits was. He pulled out his phone. "Hall," he said to the answerer, "it's Jen. Jennifer Nolan, it's *her.*"

"How do you know?"

"Never mind that now! She's fleeing! Lock down the building!"

Hall immediately hung up. From the glass office overlooking the atrium— James Michaels's former office— he clicked a button on the phone base on the corner of the desk. "This is Director Steven Hall. Lock down all exits and entrances in the building. We're looking for a rouge analyst named Jennifer Nolan! Red hair and pink glasses! Find her!" Hall grabbed a walkie talkie from the desk and clipped it to his side, leaving the office and hurrying down the catwalk.

Jen was approaching the north exit down in the parking garage, far from the high-foot-traffic ones west towards Central Park and south at the main entrance. She flashed her identification badge to the guard stationed at the gate. Behind him, silhouetted by streetlights, were three more agents. Jen knew she would have to get past all of them. "I repeat the target has red hair and glasses!" Before the guard beside her could grab ahold of her, Jen reached for his belt and unclipped a long taser baton from his side. She pressed the spark under his neck. While he seized and fell, Jen snatched the guard's ID badge. Just then she heard yelling from up the ramp and on the street. The agents were after her.

Jen raced back to the door. Down the stairwell she scrambled, almost losing her footing. She found a maintenance area she'd never been in, yet she seemed to know the layout. There was another exit in the far back. Jen ran, was stopped by an electrician with a raised hand. "What are you doing here?" Jen tased him, watched his body drop and convulse. No time to linger.

She made for the door and pressed the guard's badge against the panel. The light overtop the panel flicked from blue to red. In that instant all the lights overhead flipped to red, and an alarm siren was going off.

On the floor she found a toolbox and started digging through it. She picked up a crowbar and brought it to the panel. Jen popped off the front and exposed its wires, beginning work on getting the door open.

"There she is!" said Henry, pointing at one of the security camera feeds on his monitor.

Hall called it in over the radio then ordered, "Shut down power to that room!"

Just after Jen got the door open and she launched herself into the vestibule, the lights shut off, including the panel beside the next door, the exit. Jen groaned with frustration. She wedged the crowbar into the first door handle right before agents started slamming it trying to gain entry.

She scanned around but there was no way past the exit door. She wedged the taser baton in the door, barring herself in.

After a moment of banging, a voice from outside called for her, "Jen, come on out!"

"It's too late now, Henry!" she cried, backing away from the door.

"You know we don't have to blow this door open, we can *cut* it open! You have nowhere to go, you're stuck!"

"Then I'll be stuck!" Jen slunk to the ground, wrapping her arms around her knees, trembling.

"The man you were on the phone with.... It was Meyers, wasn't it?"

Jen's eyes were filled with tears as she swayed back and forth. She took a jagged-but-sharp car key out of her pocket and held it over her wrist. "If you try to open that door... I'll kill myself. I can't help you! He'll *hurt them!*"

"Hurt who, Jen? I can help you! *Tell me!*"

9:25 PM: NIB HEADQUARTERS: MANHATTAN:

Stephanie came with short steps to the maintenance room, where Henry, Hall, and a group of agents were huddled around the first of two exit doors. "You haven't gotten the door open yet?" she asked.

"She's threatened to take her own life if we do," lamented Hall.

"Let me talk to her!" demanded Stephanie, but Henry raised a hand in her path.

"There's someone else that wants to talk to her," he said, holding up his cellphone.

"Alright, let's clear out," ordered Hall. The agents followed him to the stairs and it was only Stephanie and Henry on this side of the door.

"Jen? The agents are gone," said Henry.

"Like I'm gonna buy that!"

"My brother would like a word. I have him on speakerphone."

Jen stayed a safe distance away from the door, but when she heard the voice say, *"Hi, Jen,"* her ear perked.

"Agent Spears," she greeted with a lilting voice.

John was in the back of an NIB vehicle, blood on his knuckles, above his eye, and on his clothes. Multicolor city lights were flashing over his face through the rear window. "It's me," he confirmed.

"Why are you calling? I'm not coming out! Not like *you* could convince me anyway!"

"Jen, people are going to die if you don't help us. *A lot* of people, including yourself—"

"They'll die anyway!" she yelled loudly. "The bomb *can't* be stopped."

"I have a way to disarm it. But I can't unless I get close enough to the bomb."

Jen's tears continued to pour down her face as she sat in the corner of the room. "You don't understand!"

"What don't I understand, Jen? Everything's been turned upside down for me the same as you. I've had more men try to kill me today than at any point in my life." Jen was silent, so John continued, "It was you, wasn't it? All day, blocking our satellite signals? Sending me to Mason Tower to fall for a trap—"

"I didn't want you to get hurt—"

"Doesn't matter what you want, does it? Meyers is blackmailing you, isn't he? You fed him information, like when Parsons was brought into NIB. Before that he thought I killed him. You even told him when I'd be alone in the conference room so he could call me that first time. Am I right?"

Jen was silent, shaking.

"I give you my word. If you help me find this bomb and put a stop to him... you'll face no charges, no consequences for—"

"You *should* put me in prison!" she wailed. "I've done terrible things to-day! But I *have to!*"

John realized his way as getting him nowhere. He decided for another approach. "Four years ago... I was in France, uprooting ACT terror cells. You never think you're gonna make a fatal mistake until the moment it happens. I should've known, I should've been prepared. There were men after me, you see. I boarded a train, had final say over security, and I *let* them onboard. By time I realized my mistake it was too late. No time to evacuate, to stop the train being derailed. The amount of people afterwards who told me things like, 'It could've been worse.' 'Only twelve dead.'" John sniffed, his eyes reddening. "It was all my fault. Not only did I get those people killed, I brought shame to our agency. After that our relations with France were at an all-time low. They denied consent to secret US operations on their soil... and within months, the ACT had infiltrated their government."

"Why are you telling me this?"

"You're at your lowest point right now," said John. "It's only right that you hear about mine.... After that, I resigned as director of CAD. I tried to quit entirely but Hall forced me to stay on. Said I was overreacting. Maybe I was, but... four years later and I still feel the weight of that. I still feel *guilty.* I never got close to anyone again after that. There was one, but... no matter how hard I tried, things felt... different. I couldn't remain in the moment, I couldn't enjoy or see beyond my doubt.... I drove her away. *That* was my greatest mistake of them all."

Stephanie and Henry shared a look; a tear streamed down Stephanie's cheek. John continued, "You might feel like you've gone too far, Jen. But I promise you, there's always a way back. Please... tell me how to find the bomb."

Jen's head lifted from the damp fabric atop her knees. "I- I don't know where the bomb is. They've been moving it every few hours and Meyers has blocked me out."

"You must know something," said John.

"I'll give you all the intel I've gathered on Meyers and his family—"

"Great, great—"

"But *only* if you do something for me first."

John sighed, almost of relief but now out of frustration. "What is it?"

"*My* family," she revealed, "they're being held hostage! He threatened to torture them if I told you anything."

"*We don't have time for this!*" whispered Henry.

"I'll get them back," John declared. "Do you know where they're being held, Jen?"

"I- I think so .... You'll get them back? *You promise?*"

John did not hesitate. "I promise."

John and two NIB agents stormed the lobby of a hotel skyscraper, fanning out with pistols in hand. The lobby was empty. One of the agents clicked the elevator button and the three entered.

"How's Stephanie?" John spoke through an earpiece as they ascended.

"She's alright, John," his brother replied. *"She was with us, you know. When you were talking to Jen."*

"Good. I should've told her those things myself." He inspected his gun. The metal was cool in his hands as he slid the full magazine back into the handle and pulled back the top.

Ding! They reached the thirtieth floor. Before he could step out, gunfire came at them. The agents in front of him both fell. John rolled across the hallway and shouldered through the door of an empty suite.

A terrorist followed him, pointing his rifle through the doorway. John diverted it downwards then smashed the terrorist's nose with his pistol. He reeled him in and tripped the terrorist, mounted him, then made his nose smear red with his pommel.

John reached the door joining this luxury room with the next and shot the handle. When he opened it, two more terrorists were waiting for him. He sent one crumbling with two bullets to the chest, but the other was still standing. John retreated to the door of the suite again, but two more terrorists were down the hall firing sporadic bursts. John remembered the success of laying on his side so did so, tucked behind the unconscious terrorist as a shield. He peeked over the body, which was jutting out into the hallway, and shot. He dropped one of the terrorists, but the other persisted and pushed forth.

From his side, the terrorist in the adjoining room came rushing in, but did not expect John on the floor. John killed him and emptied his clip. He picked up the rifle from the grounded terrorist beside him and wrapped around the doorway again. Two short bursts, and the terrorist was dead.

The floor was quiet. John rose, his gun still trained down the end of the hall. The wallpaper was a deco gold over black, where it wasn't stained with red. He entered an opened door at the end of the hall where moans and cries came from. Inside were three people, two men, young and old, and a woman, Jen's mother. They were tied back-to-back-to-back with gags in their mouths. "Anybody else here?" said John. The younger man shook his head, tears running down his and his parents' faces.

John knelt beside the family and pulled the cloth gags from their mouths, hearing their thanks and praises as he cut away their zip ties.

There was little time to waste. John took out his phone and dialed. The family held each other tight following him to the elevator.

"Did you get them?" quavered Jen.

"I got them," John said, wiping sweat from his brow. "Say hi to your daughter," he told the older gentleman.

"Sweetheart? Is that you?"

"Dad!" she cried. *"It's really you! Oh my God, oh my God, thank you, John, thank you!"*

"I made a promise. I can't take them to NIB myself, that'll eat too much time. But Henry already sent a car after me. You'll have your parents back soon." John could hear Jen crying on the other line as he sent her parents down the elevator, while he stayed put, pacing in one of the open hotel suites. "Now. Your end of the bargain. Intel on Meyers. What do you have?"

Jen cleared her throat, sniffled. *"Where do I even start? Meyers is a commodity speculator. He stands to make millions depending on how the market moves. When he stages terror attacks it's usually strategically done to disrupt supply chains. That way he can accurately predict how certain goods and prod-*

ucts change in value." Panama Canal, John remembered the Hierarchy's recent work. *"The capital he's earned allowed him secret ownership of shell companies in different export industries like metal, weapons, gold, cars, petroleum, medicine... who in turn weasel their way onto the boards of government contractors."*

"White Rook," mentioned Henry. *"We've pieced together some of it already."*

"I guess you should know how and why he became the head of the Hierarchy," said Jen.

"The Brazilian arm is a proxy group, isn't it?" Henry probed.

"Yes, but their motivation goes far beyond money. They're not like Parsons and Bell. Not mercenaries."

"Your nation will burn... for what it did to us." John remembered Gabriel's words but hadn't wondered what they truly meant until now.

"They're too proud to admit this. Getting them to break, as you saw, is near impossible. As far as I've been able to gather, the Hierarchy's vendetta is against wealthy Americans. Billionaires who came into their homeland under the guise of humanitarian aid, providing vaccines and supplies. But what they actually did was experiment and kill, treating them like lab rats. The vaccines implemented there were recalled only months later, but the damage was done. Nobody was tried or went to jail."

"What about Meyers? The way you explained it, he's already wealthy. What does he want besides money?" said John.

"What any terrorist wants, I assume," replied Jen. *"To destabilize the West. Create a vacuum, a need for global conflict... for military contraction. He's a millionaire now, but if New York is decimated, within weeks he'll be a* billionaire. *Him and his brother."*

"His *brother?"* John's ears pricked.

CHAPTER TWENTY-TWO

"Him I know even less *about. Eric is sloppy, you see. But his brother, Aar-on, he's more careful."*

"I overheard something when you were on the phone earlier," Henry mentioned. "Meyers said... *'war.'* What was that about."

"Oh my... that was almost an hour ago!"

"What?" asked John, confusion running amok within him.

"In an hour's time... Time's Square! That's where the final showdown will be!"

"Time's Square?" *Final showdown?* John thought.

In that instant, great pillars of fire rose in the distance. John saw it from a window on the thirtieth floor. Yellow flares zipped through the air, the *cracks* and *whips* of gunfire, emanating from the glowing beacon in the center of the city, from Times Square. *War.*

CHAPTER TWENTY-THREE:

10:00 PM: TIMES SQUARE: MANHATTAN:

Dark vans like looming storm clouds screeched to a halt, meeting the previous group that had formed the roadblock on either side of One Times Square, whose wall of bright, shifting advertisements illuminated the scene of battle. What awaited the ACT members who exited their vehicles was not battle, though. It was a massacre. They looked at one another, sharing unease, yet were pushed forth by the Hierarchy terrorists ahead of them to begin opening fire.

What civilians were still wandering this part of the city were scattered, running from bullets and blazes of flames erupting from grenades both thrown and rocket-propelled. Concrete cracked, cars flipped and exploded, storefronts shattered.... From the thirtieth floor of a nearby skyscraper, John was witnessing it all. He rushed out of the hotel room and rapidly pressed the elevator button.

From the other side of the long stretch came a trio of police cruisers. Their cars came to a sideways halt, creating a wall of cover a football field across from the terrorists, in between which civilians were fleeing for their lives.

The officers emerged holding their fire. Too many civilians, dozens, were running towards them. The most they could do was wave them closer and hope they made it. Some officers were cowering behind the police cruisers, others were putting themselves between the civilians and machine gun-armed terrorists.

Two of the six officers had already fallen. When the wide street and flood-lit sidewalks were clear, the remaining hid behind their vehicles. Popping out to let off a few shots from their pistols proved an unreliable method, as a third was killed. *"CALL FOR BACKUP!"* one of them yelled, just as a propelled rocket hit its mark near the gas tank of the police cruiser. The officer was engulfed by the raging heat.

The remaining two officers shared a look of pure horror. One of them opened the door to his cruiser, bullets *pinging* around him, deflating his tires, smashing his windows. He reached in for the radio and yelled, *"TEN-THIR-TEEN! TEN-ONE-THREE! NEED ESU BACKUP AT TIME'S SQUARE!"* Over a dozen terrorists— and counting— lined the two streets across from them.

The officer beside him began firing over the car hood and was grazed by a bullet to the cheek. He went for his stinging face and looked back at his partner, his fingers covered in blood, his eyes wide and filled with fear.

"SEND EVERY UNIT WE HAVE!"

NIB headquarters had turned into a small city, bustling with agents and analysts racing back and forth across the bullpen. Analysts were crowding the stations, chattering with no control over their volume. Agents, both suited and in tactical gear, were handing each other weapons and filing collectedly towards the park-ing garage.

"Every available agent is on the way!" Hall was yelling into a cellphone, darting from one end of the atrium to the next, stopping to blare orders at agents as he passed. *"I want you running point!"* he told one agent in full riot gear. *"Co-ordinate with FBI and ESU when you get there, you'll have full command!"* He continued with the person he was on the phone with, *"You heard that? My man*

will organize the barricade! I want your agents to come together to help pull back those brave officers and get them out of the line of fire!"

While Hall was running around the building, Henry was in the conference room with Jen and Stephanie. He was typing on his computer, Stephanie facing the screen mounted on the curved wall anxiously. *"Got it!"* he said, his raised voice low compared to the rampant conversation beyond the glass box.

On the television, live camera feeds appeared, showing the firefight, the terror that awaited these agents. Stephanie put a hand over her mouth and Jen whispered, "Oh my God...."

Jen's eyes went swiftly to the door, where a suited agent had opened it for her family. *"Mom! Dad!"* The agent turned quickly to join the others, jogging towards the west exit. *"Thank God you're okay!"* Jen wrapped her arms around her parents and her brother. Jen was the spitting image of her mother, red hair, freckles, and glasses. Her brother and father were more similar, with strong chins and curly black hair. They held each other in a tight bundle, tears flowing.

Henry tried to force a smile but his eyes were inexorably linked to the fire and destruction on screen. Then, an idea hit him. "Jen," he said. She turned, wiped the wetness from her cheek and sniffed. "You can help them."

"Help them? How?"

Stephanie turned to hear Henry's plan, "The same way you helped *him.* Signal jamming! Meyers may have locked you out, but together we can *hack back in!"*

Jen's eyes brightened. There was hope. "You're right! Meyers is probably overlooking the attack, giving orders to his forces! But I can block their communications!" Jen sat down at the glass table, her family hiding themselves in the corner of the room, a proud glimmer in her father's eye.

"Might not amount to much," Henry conceded, "but it's something."

An ineffectual feeling plighted Stephanie, overwhelming her. She grabbed her blue blazer wrapped around one of the chairs. "I have to go there."

"*What?*" Henry stood and walked to the door, blocking Stephanie's way. "What are you talking about? You can't go there!"

"Everyone here is doing their part, I can't sit back and *watch* this go down!" shuddered Stephanie, her tan cheeks going pale, the red in her eyes matching the scarlet of Henry's disheveled tie.

"Stephanie. You've done enough. You're in no condition to—"

"I'm a police detective!" she hissed. "Those are my colleagues, my *friends* out there!"

"And *John* is about to be one of them. Do you think he could focus if he thought you were in danger too?"

"Wh—" Stephanie was at a loss. She rubbed away a tear.

"He got you here safely. Don't let that be for nothing," Henry appealed.

Stephanie dropped her jacket and planted herself into the seat next to Jen. Jen put a hand on her shoulder, looked at Henry, and the two started typing on small laptops.

At Times Square, the two unexploded police cruisers had become five. There was still no sign of ESU, NIB or FBI, but one black truck came to a stop at the intersection.

John leapt out of the vehicle with is head low, bullets already piercing behind him. He slid to one of the police cars and leaned against it, flinching from shots pelting just above him. *"Backup on the way?"* he asked the nearest officer. She nodded, firing over the hood of the car. *Good,* John thought, poking the corner of his face over the back of the car so that he could see through the growing smoke cloud. He saw at least twenty men, ACT and Hierarchy terrorists alike, crowding a bumper-to-bumper row of black vans.

He watched a grenade being chucked towards him, land with a *clang* on a metal grate, and roll just beside him under the cruiser. *"Get away!"* He and the officer jumped in opposite directions, just barely escaping the rippling burst. A hail of shrapnel from the explosion dissected one of the officers next to John and the torrent of flame singed another's right side.

John's chest felt like it housed a grenade of its own and the pin had been pulled. *We're gonna need all the firepower we can get.*

10:24 PM: MANHATTAN:

There was nowhere left to run to. Rows of smoke and whizzing rockets were cascading over them, crashing glass from overhead, laying waste to the police barricade. Only two cars were left, separated by blackened, fiery wreckages. A half-dozen officers and John were shoulder-to-shoulder, some praying, some finding the courage to ascend and fire back at the terrorists, who seemed not to lose any of their numbers.

Then, the intersection behind the cruisers went alight. Four armored trucks and four more SUVs halted, creating another barrier behind the police line. Out of them came SWAT officers with rifles, suited agents and tactical teams from NIB and FBI... they pressed forward unafraid, bombarding the terrorist blockade across Times Square.

"OFFICERS! RETREAT! BACK BEHIND THE LINE!" One of the full-geared agents ordered. John helped the female officer beside him, put an arm over his shoulder and guided her back to the intersection. The firefight intensified, more bullets coming from either end, so loud John could hardly form thoughts. It was a warzone in every aspect.

John and the six surviving officers made it behind the armored trucks, where they could take a breather and were treated by agents. One of them approached John, but he waved him off to check on the officer next to him.

Now the SWAT, FBI, and NIB counterforce was walking back after getting the officers to safety— *relative safety,* John thought. Grenades came flying towards them but they were far enough that they were wildly inaccurate and unlikely to hit their targets.

The center of Times Square became no man's land. The terrorists started scattering from the street blockades and swarmed the buildings, the restaurants and stores on either side.

One of the agents, the one in charge of the NIB tac teams, approached John and said, *"We're going to breach one of these buildings! Try to cut them off before they can get an advantageous angle on us!"* Surely the same strategy as the terrorists, John figured. He nodded and followed the agent-in-charge and a small unit to the street corner.

John ducked a few shots coming not from across the way, but from the invisible enemies situated in the storefronts and ground floors of buildings on their right.

The agent in the rear passed a black bag to the person in front of him. The bag made its way to the front of the line, where two men were knelt in front of a concrete building base. They opened the bag and pulled out a pair of silver discs and stuck them to the building's side. *"CLEAR AWAY!"*

Within seconds a hole was blown through. The agents filed through the cloud of smoke and debris with weapons trained, very quickly facing opposition from across the department store. Bullets bloomed rows of clothing racks and platforms into multicolor bursts. Terrorists screaming, *"MORE LEFT!"* in French were being yelled at by their Portuguese-speaking counterparts among them.

John rushed forth with the agents, taking a terrorist down with three surprisingly accurate shots to the chest. He took inadequate cover behind a mannequin then dove out of the way of a falling light sign that was swinging from the ceiling.

The tac team took fire from inside the building and out, from the first floors of buildings across the street. Agents returned fire, dropping one after the other.

"GO AROUND!" the agent-in-charge ordered, leading a group of his own to the right of the store's ground level, away from the hole the terrorists had blown through the other side. Leading the way a bullet hit him square in the chest. He fell, was dragged from the gunfight, moaning, *"Don't worry about me! Go!"* The bullet only hit his vest, but the wind was knocked out of him. Still, the agent grabbed a pistol from his side and continued firing at the opposition, while his unit pressed on to the enemy's breach.

The terrorists were retreating from the right side of buildings, but their numbers far from dwindled. Four more vans appeared along the forty-third street blockade and unleashed a relief force of a dozen more from the ACT and Hierarchy.

Meyers was forty-seven stories up in Times Square Tower, overlooking the battle from an aerial view behind the ACT and Hierarchy line. He strode back and forth in front of a window wall, surrounded by four terrorist guards patrolling the large, dim office, where diamond patterns in different shades of blue carpeted the floor. "Still?" he beckoned to a man sitting in front of a computer and wearing headphones. The man shook his head. "It has to be Jen." Meyers punched the window, gritting his teeth.

"You're a military general now, are you?" he heard the silky tease come from Jeanne Leroux's lips. She sat at a cubicle facing the window wall, facing Meyers. He ignored her derision and pulled out his cellphone. "Who are you calling?"

"Our friend at NIB," said Meyers.

"For what?"

"To tell her I know what she's done, and that it won't mean a thing when this bomb is detonated!" he seethed.

"Such arrogance."

At NIB, Jen's phone shook the glass table with a clattering rumble. Henry's eyes widened. Jen looked at the number and muttered, "It's *him.*"

Henry paced, biting his nail. "Answer it. I'll run a trace." Henry sat down and started clacking the keys on his laptop.

"I don't know," said Jen. "I'm nervous."

"You have to try!" Henry handed her the phone vibrating in his hand. "Try to keep him talking."

Jen took in a sharp breath, looked at her family, then answered the phone. "Eric," she said calmly.

"Jen," Meyers replied. "What took you so long to answer?"

"Well, you know, I had to get in a good position, make sure nobody noticed I left," her voice raised slightly, trying to find the right nonchalant tone.

"Let us stop pretending, Jen, shall we?"

"I- I don't know what you mean," said Jen.

"You think I wouldn't know that Spears freed your family? You think I don't know it's you that's jamming my signal to my men. *Bravo.* I must congratulate you." Meyers's obvious disingenuity made Jen shiver.

"Someone's tracking our call," the hacker next to Meyers said.

"Ah." Meyers was calm. "Tracking me, are you?"

"Hang up then!" yelled Leroux.

Stephanie recognized the voice and shared a knowing glance with Henry. "We're gonna stop you, you son of a—"

CHAPTER TWENTY-THREE

"Take care, Jen," said Meyers. "I hope you like the *heat.*"

The call clicked. Jen lowered the phone, her lip quivering. "Did you?"

"We got it!" Henry cheered

Meyers dropped the burner and stomped on it for good measure. "You fool," Leroux leered. "What now?"

"Now... I'm going to relocate the bomb."

"I'm coming with you," she declared.

"No. One of us must be here lest our troops think we abandoned them—"

"We *are* abandoning them! You'll not leave this island without me, Meyers!" Leroux's right-hand man, Alec, stood tall, pale, and revolting. He held a pistol in his hand.

"I hadn't planned to," said Meyers. "Pier forty, Hudson River Park. That's where I'll be. Meet me ten minutes before midnight. But don't leave *yet.* If our men see us both leaving now they might get the wrong idea."

"I don't believe you. My man Alec will go with you. To make sure you can't leave without me."

Meyers took in a controlled breath through his nostrils, smiled, and said, "Fine. Come along, Alec. We have work to do. The day isn't done."

10:53 PM: TIMES SQUARE: MANHATTAN:

John and a unit of NIB agents had taken the long route far to the right, the next street over (eighth avenue), and one street down (forty-second street), which would get them behind the terrorists' blockade spread across forty-third street, Broadway and seventh avenue. They were nearly there. Across the way, a parallel tac team was flanking from the opposite end.

When they met near the center, they had the terrorists pinched under fire from the front across Times Square and from both sides of the rear. *This is it,* John thought. He shot a couple of bullets but they missed, his pistol not adequate at this range. The dozen counterforce of NIB, FBI and SWAT was digging into the blockade, taking heavy fire and grenades in return.

John's phone vibrated in his pocket. If it was ringing he surely could not have heard it over the barrages of rapid gunfire. It was Henry. *"Hey!"*

"John, we found him! He's right above you! Times Square Tower!"

John peered right. The tower was indeed right above him across the street. John tapped the shoulders of two agents and had them follow.

John kept his sights aimed. Suddenly one of the agents beside him dropped. The bullet had come so close to his face that he felt the wind snap under his ear. *Sniper... Bell! Coming from the building!*

The second agent fell from another shot. John rushed to the base of the tower. He entered, the lobby dark and uninhabited, grey and blue, with marble floors and a white concierge's desk.

John made for the elevators, but a powerful *thud* hit him in the back of the head. He turned from the ground, his gun sliding towards the elevators. Silhouetted by the multicolor lights and the glow of fire behind the doorway was a man. "On your feet, Spears."

John did as he wished. The man came towards him carrying a short knife. He stepped into the cool blue dimness of the lobby, flanked by white chairs, a glass coffee table, and potted plants. His features became visible. It was Kenneth Parsons. *Here for round two?*

CHAPTER TWENTY-FOUR:

11:00 PM: TIMES SQUARE: MANHATTAN:

John looked at his digital watch as it beeped. *One hour left.* His eyes returned to his opponent, the black-clad SAS operative spinning a knife between his fingers. "Let's make this quick, shall we?" said the Englishman. "I've got a flight to catch."

Instead of charging headfirst into the fight, John reached for one of the white-cushioned chairs to his right and threw it at Parsons. During the momentary distraction John dove for his pistol, raised it, aimed— Parsons threw his knife and it hit the gun's pommel just above John's thumb. Now both men were unarmed.

John lurched forth and drove his shoulder into Parsons's gut, recklessly omitting any thought of a second blade. In fact, there was one, but it was in a sheathe at Parsons's boot. Parsons reached down for it but John seized his forearm and wrestled, using his head as a ram to re-rearrange Parsons's face.

Outside, the agents on either end of the street who had performed a successful flank on the ACT and Hierarchy terrorists were being picked off one-by-one. It did not take long for their sights to be set higher, to the center-story of Times Square Tower, where Kevin Bell lay in a nest of cloth and carpet.

John stuffed a knee strike to his injured side with an elbow, driving away the knee but leaving himself open for Parsons's fist. Now Parsons shoved him back with a headbutt of his own, then he slid the knife out of its small scabbard and *thrust*. John stepped around the Englishman's long reach, palmed away the return strike, then lunged sideways with an elbow.

Parsons reeled, nose leaking. *Clang,* his knife hit the ground. He and John stared at one another. The corner of John's lip curled into a slight smile. Parsons's brows upturned. He spun around to the screams of agents in tactical gear and suits flooding the building lobby with guns pointed at him.

"Have fun!" John picked up Parsons's knife and his pistol and made for the elevator. He hit the elevator button but realized, *which floor?* He took out his phone, instead opting for the staircase. He looked up forty-seven stories, already struggling to draw prolonged breaths, then started the ascent.

"John! Are you in the building?" said Henry.

"I'm here! Parsons was in the lobby but I got around him," rasped John. "Listen to me. Bell must be here in the building. Reach out to someone on the ground. I need to find out what floor the sniper fire is coming from."

"On it! What about Meyers?"

John panted, heat building in his quads. "I'll figure out where he's hiding."

11:20 PM: TIMES SQUARE: MANHATTAN:

Thirty-nine floors up, John was waning, breathing heavily, sweat trickling down his neck and face and mixing with soot, dirt, and blood. John opened the door from the staircase, gun aimed. The volleys of gunfire, the rumble of explosions sounded like they were underwater. The office level was completely dark except for the orange glow of fire from the street below, shining through a wall of windows.

John waded through a sea of scattered papers and office equipment, toppled cubicle walls and chairs, shards of glass from conference rooms that were smashed. *Terrorists have been here alright,* he thought, imagining Meyers could have been here and decided to retreat higher up when he saw John coming... *he should be afraid.*

He felt a cold breeze and heard the whistle of wind rolling into the office. One thing struck him, perhaps a little too late... where were the sounds of sniper rounds being fired into the counterforce below? John's breath became less frequent, more controlled, as he approached the sniper's nest. He saw the long metallic body, the bipod spread beneath the barrel, but no Bell.

In that moment, *footsteps,* racing for his back. John sidestepped, making sure whatever hit him didn't launch him out of the removed windowpane. It was Bell, forcing John against the window wall, swatting away his pistol, and forcing his forearm against John's throat.

Bell's knuckles met John's side. "You think I ain't know you'd come?" he barked.

"I was counting on it," said John, pulling one of Parsons's knives from his back pocket and plunging it into Bell's gut. He pushed Bell hard and sent the Englishman back-first into a table. Bell, gasping heavily, gaped at John with wide eyes. He turned tail and ran away towards the elevator hall. *Coward.*

John checked his watch. Time was ticking fast. He leaned over, his ribs prickling, grabbed his gun from the carpet and kept moving.

At the top floor, Leroux was pacing, gnawing on her fingernail. "It's almost time," she said with palpable angst. "Why hasn't Alec called?"

There was not an answer from either of the three terrorists that remained with her, small specks in the large, empty floor, silhouetted by booming firelight.

Leroux had had enough. "That's it," she announced. "I'm going. *Don't you try to stop me!*" None of the Hierarchy terrorists made a move against her, nor appeared to have any interest in doing so. She wore an appearance of paranoia, her pale cheeks becoming flushed and furious.

As she stomped over the blue diamonds patterning the floor and made for the end of the office, John was coming up to the final landing. Leroux came past all the desks, entered a hall where there were elevators on either side— just then, John barged through the staircase door out of breath. Leroux's eyes were wide enough for them to fall out, like she had seen a ghost, her mouth agape. John aimed his pistol. *"DON'T MOVE LEROUX!"*

She dropped her purse and coat and sprinted back past the desks. John fired a few pursuing shots but they landed at her feet. He chased her around the corner and onto the office floor — bullets came pelting the ground in front of him. He fired the rest of his clip, killed one of the terrorists, at the same time leaping aside behind a wooden desk bordered by a cubicle wall.

The grey felt blew apart and came over John's head like falling feathers. John peeked around but the terrorists' guns were waiting for him. He could not make them chase. It was easier to stand their ground. They acted as shields for Leroux, who was breathing so quickly there was little room for her lungs to expand.

John kept crouched, shifting between desks and sneaking from row to row. He popped out at an advantageous point to the far left and fired. The window shattered and powerful gusts were blowing into the office from the hole in the wall.

In the lobby downstairs, Parsons was wiping blood from his face then cleaning his blade. There were dead agents at his feet, half a dozen of them. He heard the *ding* of the elevator and aimed a pistol. *Bell* came stumbling out, blood leaking down his side. "The bloody hell happened to you?" said Parsons.

"I'm getting as far away as I can— Meyers didn't tell you where he was leaving, did he?"

Parsons hung his head. The answer was a clear no.

"Well then... what are waiting for? You coming?" stuttered Bell weakly.

"I'm no coward."

Bell gave a conceited laugh, waved him off without a second's hesitation. "Fall on your own blade then, Parsons."

Parsons watched Bell limp and groan towards the exit. Reluctantly, Parsons let out a sigh and followed him out.

On the top floor, only one terrorist remained. Leroux picked up the pistol of one of the fallen and fired blindly into the sea of dark tables. *"COME OUT! DIE WITH DIGNITY!"*

John used their diverted attention to roll between the aisles of desks to the right side. He weaved between a few cubicles with silent feet. Now he was behind the two. John sprang out towards the window wall and pistol whipped the terrorist. Leroux turned, alarmed, and shot her own man in the chest. John shoved the body towards her and she crumbled under the dead man's weight.

He knelt and picked Leroux up by the collar and by a handful of her hair, rough enough to rip out a few silver strands. She shrieked in pain, clawing and fighting back, but John only wrenched harder and pulled her to the edge of the shattered window. *"WHERE IS HE?"* John darted around to make sure another wasn't creeping up behind him. It was only Leroux. *"You tell me where Meyers is!"*

"Or what?" she challenged.

John pulled on her hair and forced Leroux to her tippy toes at the edge of the floor, a forty-seven story drop awaiting her below, a black battlefield of smoke and fire. Terror filled her eyes at once. *"MEYERS! NOW!"*

"Okay! Okay! But you have to take me with you!"

John did not respond, merely grunted and pushed her further to one toe, her other foot dangling over the ledge. *"NO, PLEASE! Please!"* she sobbed. "I can take you to Meyers! He's with the bomb! He's going to escape without me! I don't want to die! I can't d— I can't! Please! *Please, I'll tell you!"*

John's face was scrunched with unrelenting savagery. He looked upon her tear-filled face. *Pathetic.* "Tell me. *Now,* Leroux."

"You promise you'll—" John nudged her ever-more slightly past the edge— *"Okay! Okay! Pier forty! Hudson River Park!"*

"If you're lying to me—"

"Lying? You fool! I need to get there to get out of this hellscape! The bomb is going off! At this point all you can hope for is a spot on that helicopter with me!"

John could see she was telling the truth. He felt a certain pity for her. She was muttering things under her breath. *A prayer? This monster?* John thought.

Then he pictured Stephanie. He saw her on the ground, crying, bleeding, afraid she was going to die. A rage overtook him. He let go of the handful of Leroux's hair and she *fell.*

The hideous shriek echoed in his head. There would be no grand thud or noise. Leroux's death was silent, shrouded by the deaths and warring of her followers.

John squeezed his bloodied knuckles into a trembling fist. *Hudson River Park.* Strong winds brushed back his choppy patch of dark brown hair, his eyes alight by the glow of multicolor advertisements and scattered flames. *Meyers... I'm coming for you.*

11:54 PM: HUDSON RIVER PARK: MANHATTAN:

John unzipped a duffel bag under the passenger seat of his SUV. The glowing blue light was the first thing he saw. He took out the EMP device and stuffed it into his inside jacket pocket.

Afterwards, John got out of the truck and made his way towards the bright stadium-style lights. Underneath the PIER 40 banner was a tunnel. John approached the light at the end with his gun aimed.

There was a patch of green, a turf soccer field behind a tall black fence. John swung open the gate. In the center of the field was a small black helicopter. In front of it was the bomb.

John examined the five-foot-tall silver sphere, its red and blue circuitry sticking out and looping around between its grooves and slits. There was a timer. Four minutes remained.

John wasted no time reaching into his jacket. He circled the bomb searching for the port that reached its core, the weak point in its schematics.

Before he could get around the device, he heard a gun clicking behind him. John turned, aiming his own. Standing before him with an air of hesitance was Eric Meyers. The suited Englishman flicked his tortoise shell glasses upwards on the bridge of his noise. "Well here we are," he said. John hid half of his body behind the bomb. *He won't risk shooting it. He doesn't want to die either.* "I always liked it here. This was one of the first places I visited when I arrived in New York. It's a shame it'll have to be the first place to burn."

"I don't think so."

"No, of course not," Meyers teased. "Why don't we make a deal, John?"

"We don't negotiate with terrorists," John declared.

"Now, now. If there's no way out for me then I might as well wait out the next three-and-a-half minutes, don't you think?" Meyers's pistol was shaking in his hand. *He's desperate. Afraid,* John observed. "So, what do you say I hop in that helicopter, fly off... and you get to be the hero who prevented this bomb from going off."

"Or I set it off. You know how this device works, don't you?"

"Vaguely. The way I see it, it's a fifty-fifty chance."

"And a hundred percent chance you walk free if I let you off this field," John struck back.

Meyers forced a smile. "Stalemate."

"Not quite," said John. "I'm not afraid to use my gun."

John fired a single bullet, that hit Meyers in the wrist. The Englishman howled and fell to retrieve the pistol, but John was there, his foot stomping the bleeding hand. He knelt, picked up the pistol. Meyers clutched John's arms but he pushed him off and punched him in the face.

John turned to the bomb, found the port in its side. He held his breath, twirling the neon-glowing, hexagonal cylinder in his hands. *It should fit. This needs to work.* *"Stop! Don't!"* he heard Meyers screaming. *"YOU FOOL!"*

Two minutes.

John twisted the top of the EMP device, where there were markers for distance. One click was all that was needed. John dropped it into the sphere's port. He backed away as the timer ticked down. John shut his eyes.

It was the sound of a jet engine firing up, infused with a metallic screeching, and the sparking of electricity. He opened his eyes again. The timer had gone dark. The bomb was deactivated.

He was able to breathe again.

John heard Meyers crying from the ground beneath him, squeezing tufts of faux grass between his fingers. His glasses were shattered where John hit him, so that his tears looked like hundreds. *"NO! NO! You've ruined everything! DAMN YOU!"*

John stood over him, the same look of disgust mixed with pity that he saw Leroux with. "If you think I'm the only one, you're sorely mistaken, Spears. You have no idea what comes next. Death is too easy! But everyone you care for? They will know true *agony!*"

John pointed his pistol at Meyers's chest and said, "Not today." He pulled the trigger twice.

Meyers was no more.

John's hand was bloody, shaking. He managed to holster his pistol and take out his cellphone. He dialed his brother's number slowly, as if he suddenly had all the time in the world. He put the phone to his ear as it was picked up. "Henry."

"It's me, John." John's eyes shut with an unheard-of mix of relief, dread, and joy. It was Stephanie's voice, a soft near-whisper. He could picture her as if right in front of him. All it would take to be with her is to reach out.

"Stephanie," he sighed, walking out of the tunnel back towards the street. "Where's Henry?"

"He's on the phone with his fiancé. Just in case this is the end. Is this... the end, John?"

John smiled. "Afraid not."

He heard a release of breath and crying, likely of happiness and relief. *"You did it! I can't believe it! And Meyers?"*

"Dead. Same with Leroux."

"Thank God," said Stephanie. *"It's over."*

The corner of John's eyes were filled with shadow. He was fully surrounded. Another man stood in front of him, aiming a rifle directly at John's head, glittering shades of red and blue and green. *Thermal scopes.*

"Not yet," said John cryptically. It was better that Stephanie not worry. He dropped his phone on the ground without hanging up, then he unclipped his digital watch from around his wrist and allowed it to fall.

The next second, a *thwack* to the head. John hit the ground, unconscious. The surrounding men picked him up and heaved him into the back of a black van parked in front of his SUV.

John's phone lay cracked on the concrete. *"John?"* Stephanie's voice shuddered. *"John!"*

The time on John's scuffed watch blinked and began beeping:

12:00 A.M.

Acknowledgements

The most important people in my life are also the ones who have supported my quest since day one. Never once have my parents tried to deter me from following my dream. It is they I thank. It is to them that I dedicate this work.

About the Author

Jacob R. Colon is a writer, filmmaker, music producer, performer, and comic book creator raised in the suburbs of Linden, New Jersey. His writing career began in the third grade, at the tender age of eight. He would write short stories and post them on the bulletin board of his classroom, where students lined up to read them. Soon after he moved on to heavier themes, and the tougher task of writing a novel.

His first book, *Manhattan 24*, was written over two years, from ages twelve to fourteen, and was followed the next year by its forthcoming sequel, *Manhattan 48.*

Flash forward a decade: after having written a plethora of unpublished screenplays, comic books, and a few other novels—as well as attending two years of film school with the support of his parents—Colon returns to revise his earliest works. What better way to begin his publishing career than with the stories that started it all?

He currently lives in New Jersey, spending every waking moment creating.